His
Hand-Me-Down
Countess

Lustful Lords, Book One

SORCHA MOWBRAY

Published by Amour Press 2020, Second Edition

Copyright © 2017 by Sorcha Mowbray

ISBN eBook: 978-1-955615-02-0

ISBN Print: 978-1-955615-19-8

Cover design from Fiona Jayde Media

Chapter Images from Illustration 13209099 / Victorian Vines © Freeskyblue | Dreamstime.com

Chapter One

London, May 1859

"**O**n your knees." Achilles Denton, the Earl of Stonemere, towered over the trembling female with hands bound at her back, eyes downcast, and cheeks flushed. He stepped closer, allowing the toes of his boots to nudge her foot. His size alone often intimidated. When paired with a cold, implacable tone toward the target huddled on their knees? He was, in a word, masterful.

Utterly in control.

"Yes, sir." She lowered her body, an awkward proceeding without the use of her hands.

Stone's cock twitched in his trousers.

All around him, the carnal delights of his friends could be heard. To his right, his best friend, Robert Cooper, the Earl of Brougham, had two sumptuous wenches occupied. One serviced his rod as he licked the cunny of the other. Another grouping consisted of Matthew Derby, Marquess of Flintshire, and Grayson Powell, Viscount of Wolfington, who shared a lovely piece. Hands bound to the bench she knelt on, her mouth stretched wide to accommodate Flint's member while Wolf fucked her from behind. To his left, Stone spied Marion Thomas, Baron Lincolnshire, taking a cock up his arse from a masked man while he filled another of the girls they had selected for the evening.

Any and all debauchery was accepted among the five friends, dubbed the Lustful Lords by Society. And The Market offered the requisite services in a luxuriant environment draped in velvets and silks, all dusted with gold gilt. His attention returned to his current pet. Lush, full lips

1

framed a generous mouth, one sure to look superb wrapped around his cock. Her frame shuddered, either from desire or the remnants of her orgasm. Possibly a bit of both. The musky flavor of her desire lingered on his tongue and lips to tease the flames of his lust higher.

He opened his trousers and freed his straining erection. The girl's gaze darted up to his manly endowment as her little pink tongue crept out to swipe over her lips. She would, no doubt, enjoy the next few minutes. "Suck my cock, pet. Show me how grateful you are for your orgasm." He stroked his throbbing prick as she leaned over and swallowed him whole.

The warm wet heat of her greedy mouth engulfed him. All of him. And that was quite a talent considering his cock's proportions. He sighed and sank his fingers into her sable curls. Without missing a beat, she adjusted for the thrust of his hips, allowing him to push deeper into her mouth and down into her throat.

Her moans told him she was, in fact, enjoying the rough handling. Fist locked in her hair, he thrust deeper on every stroke until the noises she made grew louder and more earnest. "That's it, pet. Take every inch of my prick. That hot little mouth feels bloody good."

In a sudden move, he jerked his length from her mouth, unwilling to spend between her lips. A cry of dismay escaped her even as she surged toward his crotch.

"Silence." His command shut down her mewling. "I own your pleasure for the evening. You came because I permitted it. You will come again if and when I decide you will. Are we clear?"

"Yes, my lord," she replied in a husky tone indicative of how close to the edge she was again.

It would not be a surprise if she climaxed when he thrust into her quim. Tight was, without a doubt, too much to hope for despite his thickness, but he had pushed her boundaries all evening. He'd taken care to ensure she enjoyed herself, had helped her along. Helped her as he couldn't help the other women...

The Market faded away, replaced by reeds slapping at his face as he slithered through the marshes along the banks of the Ganges in the dark of night. All the while avoiding the sepoys, even as the screams of the women and children rent the air, and his very soul.

Pushing the morbid—though persistent—thoughts aside, he circled behind his current pet and pushed her forward onto the cushions on the floor. Control. *He* was in control. Deep breath in, deep breath out. Her arms remained bound by his necktie, his will. He was *not* helpless. Kneeling behind her, he notched his cock against her slippery opening. She pressed backward a bit as though she might be in charge somehow.

Slap.

The crack on her left rear cheek caused her to jerk up and forward. Then she stilled and awaited his pleasure. In one swift plunge, he sank balls-deep into her sopping pussy. She moaned, and her body shook with his invasion. Heated, feminine flesh gripped and released him as she exploded.

He'd been right.

As the spasms continued, he reversed direction and withdrew. Then he shoved in again. She shifted forward, unable to stop the momentum. Stone took a firm grip on the bindings at her wrists and proceeded to piston in and out of her body. "Once more, pet. Come for me again."

"Nay, sir. I can't." A wild gaze clashed with his over her shoulder.

"You can and you will." He smacked her other buttock, then reached down to tweak her pearl. She groaned and met him thrust for thrust. Fingers drenched in her juices, he brought them to the tightly puckered muscle on display between the tempting mounds of her bum. He stroked and circled the taut opening with ruthless determination.

She whispered as he dipped the tip of one digit in. "Oh. Oh, sir."

He pressed deeper as he continued to fuck her. Once he wedged a finger past that tight little muscle, he wiggled deeper, then worked it in and out of her. Her head thrashed as she wailed incoherent words. Stone pumped harder into both holes as she spasmed around him. His cock shuttled in and out of her with a ferocious rhythm matched by his digit in her anal passage.

Then the first fiery sparks fired from deep in his balls to shoot up his spine. Jolt after jolt of pleasure ripped through him as he emptied his lust deep inside her. A surge of feeling—something akin to happiness—overwhelmed him, pulsing with a life he worked hard to smother.

His ragged breath slowed until his gasps softened in conjunction with his member. He withdrew from her, released her hands, and rolled onto his back with his eyes closed tight.

One breath. Two breaths. He imagined the walls he'd erected two years ago to protect his sanity being reinforced. Without those sturdy walls, all hell would break loose. It wouldn't do for a decorated war hero to round the bend to Bedlam.

Particularly one recently named earl.

Earl of Stonemere. He still couldn't believe Odysseus—his brother and the elder son—had been declared dead. While Stone relished his experience in the military, he regretted the time lost with his brother. Time he'd never get back. A brother he'd never see again, never laugh with, never hug. After Odey's death, he'd expected the House of Lords to take years to make a declaration, not a few months. But for some reason, they'd made a swift decision and called him to take his seat.

Perhaps it had simply seemed fast to him because by the time he'd gotten word of his brother's fate in India, made travel arrangements, and then made the trip, two months had passed, as well as his father. Another reminder of time lost and weakened bonds.

And now, a year later, he was faced with a decision he could no longer put off, according to his distraught mother. Despite the fact that he had yet to figure out *how* to be an earl, slept in two-to-three-hour bursts, and detested Society, he apparently still had to do his duty to the earldom by presenting an heir. All of which meant he needed a countess.

A career soldier, he'd never imagined himself married. After Cawnpore, it seemed even less likely. And yet he found himself considering not only taking a wife, but one he had only recently met. Lady Theodora Lawton, daughter of the Marquess of Coleridge, had been his brother's fiancée through an arrangement made between their fathers many years ago, when that sort of thing was still fashionable.

Did he take the hand-me-down bride or go find his own? A shudder rippled through his limbs. Knowing her to be fair of face and pleasant in her bearing, he deemed her to be as good an option as any other socially acceptable chit. With a shrug, he rose from the floor of The Market along with his chums, who seemed to have recovered themselves. They pulled on trousers and shirts as their recent partners departed the room, likely headed to freshen up before returning to the common rooms below.

Stone slapped Cooper—the group's Adonis; the ladies flocked to him like bees to honey—on the back and plopped into a chair at the table they'd been gambling at for most of the night. "Well, boys. A fine evening of sport, wouldn't you say?"

"Passable entertainment." Wolf sprawled in a chair, poured a fresh drink, and fell silent. The man was handsome, with golden-brown hair and light-blue eyes that drew his fair share of interest from the ladies, but there was something afoot with his friend. The man spent more time brooding sullenly than he once had, but Stone had his hands too full at the moment to push Wolf into spilling his guts.

Flint, as dark in appearance as he was inside at times, cracked his knuckles and grinned. "I feel ready for a bit of a brawl. Anyone want to go a few rounds?"

Linc, their resident jokester with laughing green eyes, chuckled. "Didn't Langston take you enough rounds this afternoon at the boxing club?"

"He did, but there is nothing like a fine bit o' tail to rejuvenate a man." Flint winked and tossed back what was left in his glass. Though a bit dark, the man was as good-natured as a sport could be.

Stone laughed along with the others, but then decided it was time to come clean with them all. "Gents, I have a bit of sour news to share. It seems there is nothing for it. I must tie on the old ball and chain."

The foursome gasped as a collective unit. Linc plopped a glass on the table and dumped the last of the scotch into it. "What tripe is this, you say? Our fearless leader cannot desert us! Who will lead us into the best kinds of debauchery if not you?"

"Bollocks! That's a real clanger, Stone. Who would be desperate enough to marry one of us?" Flint asked.

"The dowager is after me to do my duty to the title and all that. Barely slighted the black and she is on me about marriage. Since my brother won't be using the fiancée he left behind, I figure I'll snap the chit up and make Mother happy."

Cooper snorted and slumped in his seat. "Sounds ghastly, but I suppose a little bird like Odey's won't keep us from our fun."

Stone scratched his stubble-lined jaw. "Well, I may have to limit some of my activities. Can't go giving the girl the Foul. That wouldn't be right."

They all groaned. A brick to the man, they knew he had the right of it. It was a damned shame, but true nonetheless.

The next afternoon, Stone's carriage sat across Bond Street as he stopped for his final fitting of his new waistcoats. Eager to be on his way, he opted to cross over as opposed to making his driver circle around, and stepped off the curb. The crunch of wagon wheels and the clopping of hooves on the cobblestones made it impossible to yell out to his driver to wait. Unfortunately, his driver spotted him and moved to circle around to pick him up on the side of the street where he now stood.

Dismayed as his driver pulled away, Stone checked his watch. Damn, he would be late meeting Cooper and Linc. With a shrug, he moved to step back from the curb when he stumbled over something. With his balance overturned, his weight tipped backward until a helping hand righted him, and then shifted his momentum until he was utterly tipped the other way.

Stone looked up to see a dray cart bearing down the street as he flailed about in an attempt to right himself.

"Look out!" The warning was pointless. There was nothing he could do as he tumbled into the street.

His shoulder hit the stones with a bone-rattling thud as he curled into a ball and tried to roll out of the way of the large horse and cart.

As he rolled, feminine screams rang out all around him. But, for once, with a sense of energy and purpose thrumming through his veins, he was able to block out the waking nightmares.

Breath held, he watched Achilles—he refused to call him Stonemere or any other derivative of the title he didn't deserve—take a header between the wheels of the wagon. With any luck, the man would get caught on the other side. Hope bloomed in his chest.

He would prove them all wrong. Show them who was meant to be Earl of Stonemere. Not some barely civilized soldier who spent most of his life harassing or killing people. It just wasn't done.

He peered closer from his hidey-hole between two buildings. Had Achilles come out the other side? Did he lie broken in the street, crushed by the wagon wheel? The cart stopped, and the driver leaped from his perch. A moment later, a coughing and wheezing Achilles leaned against the wagon.

"Damn and blast." Achilles was harder to kill than a cat with nine lives. Of course, hiring incompetent fools to kill the current earl certainly was not helpful. He'd told the fool to give Achilles a shove into traffic, but the useless buffoon had barely nudged him! A single-handed push wasn't enough to move that mountain of muscle. He should know; he'd pushed more than one bully down in his life.

But this one... This one had always been the bane of his existence. The one his father had looked at and wished he'd be more like. A Corinthian. He sneered at the thought of the word. Well, he'd prove them all wrong. *He* should be the earl. He was the type of man ruthless enough to ensure his family's lineage would continue for generations to come, both financially and politically. With one last curse, he turned and retreated down the alley and away from the debacle. Another time, he would see the fruits of his labors.

Chapter Two

S tone heard the butler intone his name and title loudly enough for all of London to hear, let alone the population of the Devonses' ballroom. Had anyone suggested three years ago he would bear the family title, Earl of Stonemere, never mind be contemplating his future nuptials, he would certainly have laughed. True, he never actually laughed anymore, but he certainly would have found such a claim incredulous.

It was no longer an amusing matter.

Having survived the receiving line, he eased through the crowded ballroom. Every few feet, he stopped to speak with one acquaintance or another. Not so long ago, these same people would have been running for the hills and hiding their daughters. But fate, a fickle mistress to say the least, had other plans.

Moving with a quickness born of desperation, he barely acknowledged the next three men as the heat from the crowd paired with the stench of perfumes and body odor to choke him. After his service in India, crowded entertainments such as a ball had grown difficult to endure. The press of bodies and the loud murmur of conversation punctuated by the occasional shrill laugh smothered him, too similar to the roar of battle and the cries of the dying.

Moving past a swarm of silk skirts, he spotted a dark, hidden alcove, an oasis from the overwhelming onslaught, both real and imagined. If he could shut it down quickly enough, he wouldn't embarrass himself. If he failed, all of London would learn just how broken he was.

He was an earl. Not a soldier. Never again a soldier.

Once the cool darkness enveloped him, he opened his mouth and drew a breath. His pounding pulse eased as the vise around his chest released and his damp skin dried. After another quarter hour spent tucked away, he believed he could manage the crowd long enough to find his betrothed.

As any good officer would, he had a strategy. Find her, claim his dances, and then await each one either on the balcony or on the dance floor, if required. Even the cardrooms at these soirees bordered on disabling.

He reached for the drapes to his hideaway, but hesitated as two women tittered in the immediate vicinity.

"Why, Gladys, I heard his name announced earlier. I'm certain Matilda invited Stonemere despite all the gossip."

"I simply cannot imagine what she was thinking," the one called Gladys said.

"Can't you? Having one of *the* Lustful Lords in attendance at your ball? I daresay everyone who is anyone will wish to be able to say they were here. It's all so deliciously scandalous and yet possible now the unmitigated rake is off the market." Gladys's friend sighed with a bit more drama than anyone in their right mind or otherwise would deem necessary.

"Well, one should hope that man can contain himself what with all these poor young virgins parading around. It would serve Matilda right if he debauched each and every one of them while here under her auspices."

"Oh, do be sensible, Gladys. He could perhaps ruin four or five in one night, but all of them?"

Past ready to find his fiancée and escape his hidey-hole, he stepped out next to the ladies in question, turned to them, and bowed over each of their hands. The shock on their faces far outweighed any notion of good manners on his part. "Why, ladies, you both give me far more credit than I deserve. Even in my heyday of debauchery, I could only service three ladies in a single evening."

As the two ladies sputtered, he departed their corner. The temptation to turn and wink at the gossipers won out, which caused another round of tittering and sputtering from behind him. Of course, he was well aware of what proper Society called himself and his friends. But the Marquess of Flintshire, Earl of Brougham, Baron Lincolnshire, and Viscount Wolfington—as well as himself—held little regard for polite society. Each of them had learned the hard way that they had no place amongst their peers.

All of a similar disposition with regard to marriage and the business of pleasure, they opted to establish their own society and engage in their entertainments at their private homes or establishments such as The Market.

Of course, his engagement had changed everything.

Skirting the edges of the crowd, he worked his way around the room until a flash of particularly golden hair caught his eye. He pressed forward into the mass of people to greet one Lady Theodora Lawton, his fiancée.

Her blonde hair lay tight to her head, tucked beneath a pearl-studded monstrosity that covered its fine golden luster. The wide set of her mouth kept her from being a classical beauty, particularly when her lips spent much of their time compressed as though guarding her words. Her blue-eyed gaze failed to rise above his kneecaps, let alone clash with his own. It had been at least a month since he'd last seen her, last attempted attending a ball. He acknowledged—at least to himself—that her propensity to hide from him contributed to his lack of attendance. "Lady Theodora, you look lovely this evening, as do you, Ladies Coleridge, Carlisle."

She glanced up at him and dropped her gaze back to his shoes. "Thank you, my lord. You also look quite fine." Her soft tones were all but drowned in the cacophony of voices around them.

"My lord, it is so good of you to join us this evening," Lady Coleridge intoned.

"My pleasure." He restrained his frustration and the urge to sigh. "Have you collected your dance card, Lady Theodora?"

"Of course, my lord." She curtsied and extended her program for the evening.

He took the stiff paper from her and marked his dances.

He chose two of the three dances he would claim, the opening promenade and the final waltz of the evening. The third, by unspoken custom, was a dance of her choosing.

She selected an early waltz.

In the past, she had always chosen the second set of quadrilles. The early waltz was a distinct change in her behavior. Odd.

"I shall return shortly to collect you for the opening dance." With a smart bow, he escaped the crush and found the nearest balcony. There, he drew in the sweet relief of the cool night air and relished the welcome space.

A short while later, he led Theodora onto the dance floor for the opening procession. They refrained from dialogue as the dance made it difficult to sustain a conversation with its intricate weaving patterns. At the end of the set, Stone escorted Theodora to her mother and took his leave to go in search of his own mother, who would no doubt be in attendance.

Slowly, he worked his way through the morass of bodies—far too many for his liking—as he considered his fiancée. Everything seemed normal on the surface. She barely made eye contact and mumbled a few polite words, but something else bubbled beneath the façade. For the first time, there was something there that actually intrigued him about her. Then again, perhaps the crush was getting to him, pushing him closer to the edge of insanity he'd been fighting for so long.

A light sheen of sweat broke out on his forehead, and he stopped moving. A quick glance ahead revealed his mother, but another glance to the left revealed an exit. Space. Safety. He closed his eyes and willed his hands to cease trembling as he dabbed the recalcitrant moisture from his forehead. Stolidly, he shoved all the panic right back into the box he kept it in. There would be no spectacle tonight, so he strode forward, into the lioness's den.

As he suspected, he found the Dowager Countess of Stonemere lording over her circle of friends. He approached with caution, since one could never be certain what mood she might be in. With this gathering being the first event since coming out of full mourning, her mood promised to be even more unpredictable. "Mother." He stopped before her and bent over the hand she presented to him. "You are in fine fettle this evening."

"Stonemere." She nodded and eyed him critically. "Quite dapper, I am pleased to see. And your fiancée is also looking lovely. Do be sure to bring her over at some point this evening."

"Of course, Mother." With the pleasantries over, he bade the ladies farewell and faded into the crowd to find his next partner.

By the time his second dance with Theodora arrived, it seemed certain he appeared as frayed as he felt. No fewer than three partners had trod upon his toes, and the poor girls had been tongue-tied at best when addressed. At least his fiancée was a proficient dancer and he could dispense with the charade of polite conversation.

"Elizabeth, do stop fidgeting. You are a marchioness now. You must act the part." Theo cringed as her mother once again browbeat her sister. It was all done out of love, she truly believed that, but poor Lizzy struggled under such a heavy burden.

"Mother, I do believe I see Lady Morton waving to you." Theo sent her mother off on a wild goose chase, if only to give herself and her sister a moment of peace. "Lizzy, you look unwell. Do you need a moment in the retiring room?"

"I'm well, but this corset is laced rather tight." Her sister fidgeted again.

"Please tell me you do not still adhere to Mother's philosophy on tight laces? You are a marchioness. You run your own household. If you wish a looser corset, then, by all means, loosen it." Theo tried to hide her exasperation with her sweet younger sister, but she knew she failed as Lizzy looked at her with big gray watery eyes.

Dash it. Her head ran away with her mouth again.

Theo dug deep for more patience. "Go to the ladies' retiring room and have one of the maids help you adjust your laces. I am sure Lord Carlisle would be most displeased to hear you were so miserable in such lovely finery. The man fairly dotes on you, you know."

Lizzy blushed a pretty soft pink across the tops of her cheeks. "I believe I shall."

Her sister Lizzy was a slightly shorter, darker version of herself, with her dark blonde hair and big gray eyes. Not to mention her sister had naturally abundant curves, where Theo tended toward more gentle slopes. And then there was the distinct difference of personality. Whereas Theo was headstrong and determined, Lizzy was much more amenable. Theo wished, every once in a great while, that she could be so sweet and demure, as her mother had taught them. But then reality would come crashing back, this time in the form of her fiancé.

Stonemere appeared for their next dance. A waltz.

"Ladies, are you enjoying your evening thus far?"

Despite the dread that weakened her resolve to complete the first of two such dances, she needed to speak to him, hence the choice of the second waltz. The usual country dance she chose would not serve her purpose. She ignored the butterflies flitting in her belly as the stoic but handsome man greeted her sister. His dark mahogany locks were shorn near his ears and left a bit long on top, allowing one stubborn lock to flop into his mesmerizing green eyes, as though it possessed a rebellious streak. His large, imposing body, wide at the shoulders and tapered at the waist, allowed him to loom over her despite her statuesque condition. And the man seemed to enjoy looking down the length of his classically Greek nose as though assessing her. But she could never decide if he found her wanting.

"Indeed, we are," Theo said, all the while feeling as though her thoughts of the man had conjured him from thin air.

Which was a silly notion since his name was scrawled on her dance card.

"May I have the honor of this next dance?" He bent over Theo's hand in observance of all the proprieties.

"Of course, my lord." She curtsied and allowed him to lead her onto the floor. With a quick glance back, she noted with satisfaction that Lizzy had headed toward the retiring rooms. Now she needed to focus her efforts on her own behalf with her fiancé.

As the first strains of the waltz sounded around them, she held her breath. The improper thoughts she'd harbored for this man since the first time she'd spied him all but bubbled over after nearly two years. Notions of his lips on her skin—and not just her wrist or hand; no, her thoughts strayed far more scandalous places, such as her neck and her breasts—titillated and caused an uncomfortable throbbing dampness between her legs. In fact, she found it difficult to meet his gaze for fear he might see the truth in her eyes.

And it was truth, an inconvenient one, but truth nonetheless. She found him attractive, more so than his brother, whom she was originally to marry. She wondered how two brothers could be so different. Where Odysseus had been kind and gentle, a friend even, his brother was quiet, brooding, and rather overbearing. At one point, not long after Odey's death, she found herself lamenting his loss for wholly selfish reasons. Now? Well, now she'd resigned herself to her fate. Or she was trying to.

His big, firm hands tightened on her waist and her hand as he stepped closer. The improper proximity of the waltz disconcerted her as he all but pressed her breasts to his chest. It was not the time to discuss their future, considering how addled her thoughts were, yet it had proven to be her only opportunity thus far. The dratted man had failed to linger near her after their first dance, and she expected no less at the end of this set.

"My lord," she ventured as he spun her around. "I wish to speak with you about our future."

He looked down at her, surprise evident in those glittering green eyes. "By all means. What do you wish to speak of?"

She swallowed her fear, met his gaze, and pressed ahead. "I believe this marriage contract is as foreign a concept to you as it was to me when my father informed me of its existence."

"Indeed, quite foreign." He looked impassive as they continued whirling around.

She took a deep breath and attempted to let her sincerity shine through. "While I'd hoped a solution might present itself to save us from this arrangement, I lament the hopelessness of praying for divine intervention that shall never appear." She bit her lip. *Blast it*, she was mucking this up as badly as she had feared.

"It would appear we lack any hope for such divine intervention." Not a single eyelash flickered on his chiseled countenance.

He humored her, and the arrogance, the sheer indifference, made her blood surge and her cheeks warm. It certainly could not be from some unladylike attraction to the man. No, she refused to believe it could be anything other than annoyance. "I propose that we use these last few weeks to acquaint ourselves with each other. After all, it would seem there is no other recourse for either of us. I realize that you may well have had another choice of bride in mind since you were not meant to be the original heir. However, under the circumstances, I dread the idea of marrying a complete stranger."

"And so you propose, having no other recourse, that we should acquaint ourselves?" The faintest hint of a smile danced around the edges of his lips before it flitted away.

Really, does the man need to be so maddening? Continually parroting my words back? "That is what I suggested, my lord." She resisted the urge to cease dancing and stomp her foot. It would make little noise in her flimsy dancing slippers, and only serve to hurt her appendage, as well as her pride.

"How do you see us going about such an endeavor?" His warm baritone, so at odds with his stony exterior, hummed between them, adding a richness to the music.

Her heart beat in her chest like a caged hawk moth seeking escape. "I suppose the usual way would suffice. We could take tea together, along with the odd outing to allow us a chance to discover our interests and intellectual pursuits." She hesitated, suddenly unsure of her plan. "You do have intellectual pursuits, do you not?"

He stared at her.

"I-I mean to convey—" *Oh, now I've done it.* "What I intended to ask was, do you have more interests beyond the physical?"

Both eyebrows shot up to his dark hairline, and he smiled. At her. Though sheltered, she had no trouble understanding how wretched her turn of phrase had sounded. Her face burned with mortification, but she forced herself to meet his gaze.

"I assume you have interests other than riding horses." She fought for her former cool façade. The one she had employed since she'd realized how dangerous her handsome husband-to-be would be to her business pursuits. Crushing the initial impulse to simper and fawn had proven a most onerous effort. After that, she managed to contain such odd, debutant-like behavior under her rigid discipline, and by not meeting his gaze. And it had worked, at least until he'd smiled.

After her clarification, their gazes locked, and the heat in her cheeks migrated somewhere significantly lower indeed. His lids hung at half-mast, giving him a slumberous appearance as he contemplated her with an intensity she had not previously experienced from him or any other man. The music continued to fill the air all around, as well as the silence between them.

"I have interests other than horseflesh." His gaze traveled down over her bosom and lower still, to her waist, before returning to her face. Then he appeared to consider her suggestion. "You know, Lady Theodora, you may be on to something here. It is true you are left with little more than the second-choice heir as a husband. As dismaying as that may be, we should certainly consider aligning ourselves so we may better endure our preordained future."

"Precisely my thought, my lord." She offered a stilted nod of agreement.

"Splendid. Do you have a moment in your dance card to visit the Dowager Countess Stonemere? She wishes to see you."

While she liked the dowager countess, at the moment she wished to retreat from her fiancé with her victory in hand. To her consternation, the music ceased and a quick perusal of her card showed her next set open for a short break. "I'd be happy to accompany you, my lord."

"Excellent." With a bow, he presented his arm, and with a deep steadying breath, she placed her hand in the crook and followed where he led. With a few deft maneuvers, he navigated their way through the crowd and before his mother, the rather intimidating Dowager Countess of Stonemere.

Gray hair was piled high upon her head in a regal display adorned with a simple lavender band, which matched her gown. The woman was still beautiful, in that way of older women who age gracefully and are well aware of it. The dowager presented a picture of serenity that Theo envied in that moment. Stonemere bowed as she curtsied, and then they both straightened.

"Mother, Lady Theodora Lawton."

"Oh, do cease such overdone formality. The chit is your fiancée, and I have met her on several occasions." She waved her fan in a never-ending motion designed to beat back the heat of the gathering, and possibly the smell. The older woman's bold stare drilled into Theo as she asked, "Child, is my son treating you well?"

Theo truly wished someone's wig would catch fire, or perhaps a dancer would faint to distract both the dowager and her son. Instead, the woman waited with barely feigned patience, as though even having to ask the question was a nuisance. Theo swallowed and offered a smile. There was only one possible answer in this setting. "Of course, Lady Stonemere."

The sharp-eyed woman glanced at her son, then back to Theo. "If he fails to uphold the Stonemere honor, you will inform me immediately. Your marriage may not be a love match, but I expect him to treat the future of the family line with care."

Theo nodded her assent and prayed for dismissal so the awkward interview could end. But, to her dismay, another man joined them.

"Lady Stonemere, I heard you had emerged." The smiling man bent over the dowager's hand as she presented it.

"Denton, do not be coy, young man. Have you met Lady Theodora Lawton?"

He turned his attention to Theo and again bowed over her hand. "I have not made her acquaintance as of yet."

"She is Stonemere's fiancée." The dowager smiled with a smugness that suggested she might be responsible for this situation, when in fact it had been her husband and Theo's father who had saddled her so. "Lady Theodora, this is Mister Hugh Denton, Stonemere's cousin and my nephew."

The man turned to Stone. "My felicitations to you both, 'Chilles."

Stone nodded and offered a kind smile. "Thank you, cousin. It is good to see you are back in town. How was your tour of the Continent?"

"An excellent adventure, though I would hate to bore the ladies with my tales," Stone's cousin demurred.

"That will do. Return her to her mother, Stonemere. Denton, off with you, too. It is high time you found a wife as well." She dismissed them with a wave of her fan and turned to the gray-haired lady beside her to resume their conversation.

Stonemere escorted Theodora back to her mother. And while she had secured his general agreement during their dance, there had been no time to lay out her specific plans. How fortunate that they had another waltz later during which to plan their future outings on a more detailed basis. Despite her father's belief that she sought trouble, in truth she attempted to avoid such scrapes. But the best-laid plans—particularly hers—often went awry.

"Thank you for the dance, Lady Theodora. I look forward to supper, and our final dance later." And then, with a bow, he departed.

Theo watched his retreating back as she stood beside her peacocking mother and wondered where her plan had once again gone awry. She repressed the unladylike sigh that simmered inside, fueled by her frustration. Granted, her foray had been, by and large, a success. But somehow she was certain she had not established herself as his equal in the relationship. While not an ardent follower of Wollstonecraft, she did share similar notions of equality. These were ideas she needed to introduce to her future husband before it was too late. The hoped-for path to extricate herself from an unwanted marriage had yet to reveal itself, rendering her behindhand from the start.

The arrangement of her own ruination flitted through her head as she considered all possibilities. Were it not for the shame it would level upon her entire family, she might have considered it. But she discarded the scandalous possibility.

As supper neared, she resolved to return to her plan, though she would have to be more discreet while they sat in company. As expected after her last pre-supper dance, she was returned to her mother, where Stonemere waited to act as her escort.

"Have you been enjoying your evening?" He led her into the dining room, where their assigned seats awaited.

"Indeed. I have had a lovely time of dancing. It is one of the few parts of the Season I find bearable."

"And what types of entertainment do you prefer?" He pulled her chair out and waited for her to sit.

Following his lead, she lowered herself to the cushioned seat. "I much prefer a spirited salon or lecture. Particularly when discussing current social and political issues. The current debate on the validity of a married woman having the right to own property independent of her husband is of great interest to me."

Stonemere groaned as he took his seat. "And how does it interest you precisely?"

"Why, as a soon-to-be-married woman, the law would recognize me as a person despite our marriage and grant me control of any property held in my name."

He chuckled. "And what property might you hold that is not part of your dowry?"

Theo reminded herself to breathe. Many men were struggling with this concept. "Why, I happen to own two pieces of land purchased with pin money that I wisely invested. One property is the site of a china factory. They fire various types of dishware. The factory owners have been excellent tenants, though I shall say I was at first concerned with the volatility of the kilns they use. Once it was all explained, I was much more at ease with their business. Then there is the home for orphans that I maintain here in London. I often run various fundraisers to support the effort, but the house and land they occupy are mine and shall continue to be at their disposal for as long as such services are required."

Her partner's look of incredulity did not surprise her, however much it still smarted to know men could so underestimate a woman.

"And is your father aware of these properties and the business conducted in association?"

"Well, why would he be? I used my pin money and made arrangements through my solicitor. As an unmarried woman, well over the age of twenty-one, I am perfectly within my rights to own and manage my own property."

"I should like to have a look at your ledgers at your earliest convenience to ensure your man of affairs is on the up-and-up." He made his pronouncement and then turned to greet the woman who sat to his left.

Theo turned and did the same with the gentleman on her right. As everyone around her fell into their own conversations, she boiled inside over the high-handed nature of her future husband. Mayhap she had waited too long to attempt to know her fiancé? Drastic measures would be required if things did not improve as they became better acquainted. The appeal of ruination had grown by leaps and bounds since last she'd considered it.

Chapter Three

B y the time the first strains of the final waltz sounded, Theo was certain her heart would explode. Caught between her earlier indignation and an inexplicable fear, she had to force her slippered feet to remain rooted to the parquet floor of the ballroom as Stonemere approached.

"I believe the final waltz belongs to me, Lady Theodora." He offered a stiff bow over her gloved hand and then tucked it into his arm as he escorted her to the dance floor.

"Yes, my lord." She hated the uncertain breathiness of her response. He turned her into his arms so his hand rested against her upper back, searing her flesh through the interminable layers of fabric. Without conscious thought, her spine stiffened and her nipples pebbled as they pressed against the confinement of her corset. Heat suffused her face, leaving her to wonder if her cheeks would be in a perpetual state of pinkness.

Her partner studied her with an uncomfortable intensity. "Is anything amiss, my lady?"

"No, not at all." She uttered the shameless fib as she attempted to regain control of her physical and emotional reaction. Everything was wrong. She was betrothed to a man who was all but indifferent to whether or not she took her next breath, he had a scandalous reputation for being a Lustful Lord, had proved to be overbearing to an oppressive degree—and they had yet to even wed—and her body reacted to him in the most confounding fashion.

"Well, then. As you indicated earlier this evening that you had some interest in an outing or two so that we may have an opportunity to become better acquainted, I took the liberty of gaining your father's permission to take you driving Sunday at five."

Why she should have been shocked was hard to say, but Theo ceased dancing in order to comprehend how utterly totalitarian her future husband appeared to be. Anchored in place by her sudden stop, he cursed as another couple crashed into them. "I beg your pardon. The lady seems to be feeling faint."

He then turned and dragged her from the dance floor. "My lord," she hissed as he towed her to the closest balcony. "Stonemere!" she tried again, louder.

The cool night air swept over her sweltering flesh, causing goose pimples to ripple over her skin. He hauled her around, putting his back to the open doorway, and pressed her crinoline-draped bottom against the balustrade. "Explain yourself."

Heavy hands rested on her upper arms, a most effective means of dashing any hope that she might escape. Inner turmoil wreaked havoc with the frayed threads of her ability to reason, which in turn made forming a response impossible. "I-I..."

When had she developed a stutter? This man infuriated her. He ran roughshod over her and all her plans. He made her pulse race and her body flash hot and cold, with little rhyme or reason. How could she ever marry him?

"Please, explain whatever the issue is that drove you to a complete stop in the middle of a ballroom." His eyes were lost in the shadows, even as the lights of the soiree illuminated him from behind.

Her anger surged to the fore. Very well, if he wanted to know, she would be happy to oblige. "You, sir, are intolerable."

His eyebrows shot up. Could his lip have quivered?

"Please elaborate." His neutral tone slashed at the frazzled edges of her temper.

She drew herself up to her full five-foot-seven-inch stature. She had never considered herself a shrewish woman, but this man pushed her beyond all bounds of reason. Social niceties be damned! "You are an insufferable, pompous, overbearing lout. I shall not be bullied into showing you my ledgers, nor into taking a drive with you at your whim. I may be female, but I have both the intelligence to manage my investments and a schedule to keep." In a huff, she pushed his shoulder and attempted to break his hold to make good her escape.

Stone was so stunned by the previously shy and remote woman's sudden and thorough about-face that he bloody near let her slip away. Instead, he reached out and clasped her wrist in his hand. All momentum lost, she came to a halt but refused to turn and face him. Was this brazenness what he had sensed earlier beneath her typical bland façade? Her defiance sparked his interest as nothing else could have. "We are not quite finished, Lady Theodora. Do stay a moment more."

Rebellion was familiar territory for him, a known quantity. And hers was easily controlled. Without relinquishing his hold on her, he circled around to further block her escape. His gaze snared hers as surprise—or perhaps wariness—caused her eyes to widen and her breath to grow choppy. As her breasts heaved against her bodice in protest, he took a step toward her. She countered his advance and retreated to maintain the space between them.

With each step, the shadows slowly swallowed them until they were as good as alone. Pressed once again to the balustrade, she had nowhere else to go. He stopped with little more than a sliver of air between them. In some places, her gown eliminated the space altogether.

"My lord, what are you about?" Her voice trembled, betraying her uncertainty.

"I have done nothing but seek to ensure you are well cared for, and to accede to your wishes." The soft puffs of her mint-laced breath teased his skin and caused his nostrils to flare, as though seeking more of her sweet scent. The reins of his control drew tight. Damn women and their fastidious ways. "I am curious about your business dealings—intrigued by the notion of a woman in business, particularly a lady—and wish to see how you've fared. If there is nothing amiss, I plan to let you continue as you see fit."

"Oh." The lack of trust evident in her stilted gaze cut him to the quick, though he knew the reaction to be outright ridiculous. When had he become such a nodcock?

"As for the outing, we have so little time, I assumed an expedient result was desired. I am, after all, a decisive man. It comes from long years of military training." There, a reminder for them both that he was the one in command.

Her gaze dipped. "My apologies, my lord."

Her acquiescence, simple and elegant as it was after such fiery defiance, ignited a conflagration of need deep within his loins that obliterated rational thought, along with the infinitesimal kernel of concern for propriety that he had heretofore retained. Without warning, the reins of his control slipped from his fingers like the fog wafting across a battlefield. Without hesitation, he hauled her into his arms and pressed his lips to hers.

The softness of her breasts pressed against his chest, the zing of citrus and roses teased his nose, and the sweetness of mint from her lips all conspired to inflame him. His cock hardened, though her skirts shielded his evident interest. His tongue drove past her lips to tangle with hers. He explored the warm recesses of her mouth as she clung to him. A soft whimper escaped her when he pulled back to nibble on her plump lower lip.

Without warning, something akin to interest rushed through him in a startling flood. An inexplicable need to sink into her body, command her responses, and have her at his mercy rocked him. He broke from her heat and stepped back even as his breath heaved.

Fresh air swept through his desire-induced haze and cleared his head. Another deep inhale allowed him to slow his heartbeat. And a third gulp restored some semblance of his discipline. He fisted the reins of his control once more as his heart pounded a steady tattoo in his chest. What might have come next had he continued to kiss her? This woman could only be described as a detriment to his well-being.

"Stonemere?" The sound of his name on her lips threatened his tenuous grip. She must think him a candidate for Bedlam with his wild swings in behavior.

"Lady Theodora, my most abject apologies for such uncouth behavior. I assure you there will not be a repeat of these actions." He bowed and reached for her arm.

The lady stepped back in a swish of skirts. "Whyever not?"

Shocked by her question, Stone stared at her, mesmerized as her eyes flashed in defiance, but then the spark fizzled out. He remained mute in the face of her curiosity. There was no good answer to her question. No clear way to return things to the cool civility from before their first waltz. "Consider our drive canceled. I believe I shall depart."

She swept him with a gaze dappled by confusion. "As you wish, my lord."

Stone led her through the ballroom back to her mother, collected his cloak, and called for his carriage. A smidge past midnight, according to his pocket watch, left him ample time to retreat to The Market for drinks and cards. With any luck, he would forget the last half hour on the Devonses' balcony. But, what of Theodora? Would she forget?

Stone relaxed, sans mask, in the main salon of The Market. The Lustful Lords had never bothered to wear the ubiquitous disguises most patrons donned. It hardly seemed worth it when, despite the many masks, it was easy enough to identify the likes of the Marquess of Swinton and the Earl of Thorpe, among many others. A flash of brilliant blue caught his eye as Madame Celeste de Pompadour, styled after the famous Madame de Pompadour, floated across the room to settle on the arm of the chair he currently sprawled upon.

"My lord, may we entice you to enjoy some of our offerings this evening?" Her big blue eyes studied his every flicker.

"Madame, you know very well I am merely here to escape the virtuousness of Society, sadly no longer to be enticed by your establishment's many charms." He swirled his scotch and then took a large draft of the liquor. "My fiancée and I are making a go of it." He raised his glass in a semblance of a salute. A go of it? He must be mad. He needed to stay far away from that troublesome baggage, but how could he do that once they were married?

"If I may be so bold, my lord... There are pleasures to be had within that would leave you with a clear enough conscience." Celeste leaned into him, her many charms on display.

The scent of roses wafted over him, teased him, but he was unwilling to relent. His honor demanded a higher standard than even Society expected. "I am afraid I am well and truly burdened by my conscience. I shall imbibe good spirits, enjoy the jovial company, and perhaps risk a bit of blunt. But I shall not disgrace my future bride with flagrant acts of infidelity."

"And yet you sit in my *notorious* establishment, unmasked." Celeste tipped her head with a gentle lift of her brows.

"I did say flagrant acts of infidelity. I did not say I would refrain from all entertainments to be had in Society, polite or otherwise." He forced all expression from his face as he met his hostess's pointed stare. Besides, he was having grave doubts about his marriage to Theodora being a friendly alliance, if for no other reason than he was not sure he could control the beast within.

"Very well, my lord. You know Phillipe is at your disposal should you decide to make any other arrangements." She rose and greeted a group of young randy bucks who sounded well into their cups, not to mention more likely to part with their blunt in the pursuit of fleshly pleasures.

"Stonemere, I see you once again tempt our enticing Madame de Pompadour."

Cooper slapped him on the shoulder.

"Is it not to be expected? I am the most enticing of us all." Stone tossed back the last of his drink and rose with a chuckle. "Where are we tonight?"

"Upstairs. We thought a private game was in order along with some...company."

"The cards sound good. You know my stance on the rest, Cooper." He quirked a brow at his longtime friend and confidant.

"I do, indeed. Eventually you will have to sort things out on that score. In the meantime, the rest of us can still have a bit of fun. We remain unshackled, and with few prospects of such a dire fate."

Upstairs, the five of them sat at a card table with one of the ladies acting as a dealer for a game of vingt-et-un. Stone soon found himself winning heavily, while each of his compatriots became more and more distracted by the delectable ladies in their laps. As the couples paired off around the room to indulge in more pleasurable pursuits, Stone collected his winnings, intending to make his escape.

He glanced back as Cooper hooked the necktie laced around a redhead's wrists over a hook in the wall. In the blink of an eye, Stone had replaced the sultry redhead with a certain starchy blonde with big blue eyes. Where the deuce had such an image come from?

Where the image originated didn't matter as his cock hardened and need swept over him like the rush of war. With a groan, he opened his trousers, pushed his shirt up, and pulled his aching length free. A fist wrapped around his cock, he watched as Cooper knelt between the woman's thighs and worked her clit until her first orgasm burst through her. Stone stroked, imagining doing the same thing to the woman who seemed to be dominating more of his thoughts than she should. But as Cooper pushed his cock into the strung-up redhead, it was far too easy to imagine slipping into Theodora, feeling her heat engulf him as he stretched her body to accommodate his. He stroked faster, working his shaft as he closed his eyes and let his imagination finish the job.

His heart pounded as his fantasy version of Theodora screamed her climax, and he pumped faster into his fist until he too came with a low groan. He surfaced from the fantasy to the sound of flesh slapping against flesh and his own seed covering his stomach. With a few jerks of his necktie, he was able to clean up and decided it was time to go. Dread of the long nighttime hours that remained drew his focus as he departed.

A short while later, he settled into his favorite chair with a generous portion of brandy and a roaring fire for company. He watched the flames dance about as they licked the dry wood, a hungry devouring force. He nursed his brandy, having learned long ago that too much alcohol left him incapacitated, and not enough alcohol allowed the dreams to filter in. As in life, maintaining a delicate balance would see him through the night.

The warmth of the brandy paired with the fire to lull him into a drowsy stupor that soon led him to sleep.

He traipsed through the blackness until the glow of a flame drew his gaze. His heart twisted as he suddenly found his shirt sucked to his chest, soaked from the chill water of the river while the eerie glow of burning boats lit up the dark, early-morning sky.

Bullets sailed into the water as women screamed and men cried out in agony. Then a hand reached out of the horror and latched onto him. An unfamiliar face, but a soldier as well, the stranger searched the bodies for survivors. It appeared he was the first survivor found by the soldier. Together they made their way into the deep grasses along the bank and hid.

Stone clung to the unknown soldier as the horror unfolded around them. Helpless. Beyond control. A coppery tang hung in the air and blended with the musky odor of rotting vegetation. The dawn sky dripped a hideous red as the wretched sounds of death echoed and magnified, even as blood flowed all around. With each hack of a sepoy blade, another scream rose into the cacophony until Stone wished he, too, was dead.

A cry rent the air and jerked him awake. With a sleep-fogged sweep of the room, he found the fire had burned to coals in the predawn dark and his brandy glass lay on its side on the rug. His shirt clung to him, a sweat-soaked second skin that sent a shiver through his form as the cool air skimmed over him.

After setting his toppled glass on the sideboard, he trudged up to his room. Most nights were bearable, but when he had a bad night, he found little in the way of comfort or rest. Tonight was obviously going to be a bad night. And the unrest seemed directly related to his bride-to-be. Could he marry someone who stirred his personal demons so thoroughly? Someone who tempted him so mercilessly? Made him want things no sane man should want from his wife?

Chapter Four

O ver two weeks past her quarterly review with her man of affairs, Mr. Harrington, Theo sent him an early-morning missive to arrange a meeting. The need to escape her mother's unrelenting campaign to finalize the wedding details had become an imperative. While Theo was content to marry Stonemere, she had little interest in the infinite details that made such an event possible. That was her mother's area of expertise.

Young William, a groom, escorted her to the tidy but small office of her solicitor. Once ensconced, she reviewed each investment's progress and the appropriate balance sheets. Only then would she consider the topic of any new business opportunities.

As they wrapped up the day's business, Mr. Harrington scooted around his desk to escort her out of his office, as he always did.

She tugged on her gloves. "Thank you again for a job well done, Mr. Harrington."

He nodded. "You're very welcome, my lady. I certainly hope you and Lord Stonemere continue to be pleased with my efforts on your behalf."

Theo stopped and turned to look at her man of affairs. She drew in a slow, deep breath and strove for a calmness she no longer felt. "I'm sorry, have you met my intended, the Earl of Stonemere?"

The little man hesitated and sighed, defeat writ plain across his face. "I'm afraid I have met him, my lady. I fear now that you will be quite cross with either him or myself."

"Please explain, Mr. Harrington." She focused on a spot just past the man's shoulder on the wall. It would not do to cause him distress at what she was certain was Stonemere's gall.

"The Earl of Stonemere visited me last week. He reviewed your portfolio and gave his nod of approval." He shifted from one foot to the other, popping in and out of her peripheral vision.

"I see. Well, thank you for accommodating my future husband." She damn near choked on the words as she turned on her heel and departed.

As she climbed into her father's cabriolet and nodded at her driver, she fumed. Stonemere's interference was not to be borne. It was too much to ask. She had told him as much at the Devonses' ball, but he seemed to be unconcerned for her feelings on the matter.

Now to find the meddling man. "William, to White's please."

The man stared at her. "Excuse me, my lady, but I am certain were I to take you to a gentleman's club, your father would dismiss me out of hand and with no references."

"If you do not take me there this instant, *I* shall dismiss you out of hand and with no references," she snapped at the poor man, but her fury had surged past all bounds of politeness.

"Yes, my lady." He all but hung his head and directed the horses toward St. James's Street.

As her vehicle pulled to a stop in front of White's, Theo hopped down from her perch without waiting for assistance, no easy feat with all her skirts, and proceeded to knock on the front door. Had she thought Stonemere stodgy? The old man who answered her summons gave all new definition to the word. He made her fiancé seem footloose and fancy-free. "Yes?"

Theo wanted to huff and push past the ancient artifact, but instinct told her that would not be wise. Instead, she summoned her haughtiest tone, one she had only ever used in mimicking her mother's overbearing nature. "Please inform the Earl of Stonemere that Lady Theodora wishes a word with him immediately."

Without a peep, the man shut the door in her face and—she hoped—went in search of Stonemere. If not at his club, where else might she find him at this time of day? His home would have to be her next stop. But after she'd paced a few minutes on the sidewalk, the great door of White's opened again and spit out a rather annoyed Stonemere before being shut with a resounding thump. "What the devil is the meaning of this, Theodora? And how in the world did you find me?"

She flinched. When had she given him leave to address her so informally? "Finding you was no mean feat. You are a peer of the realm, and it is the middle of the day. If not here, you would most likely be home." She waved a hand in the air in annoyance at such a silly question. She needed to get to her reason for hunting him down. "What the devil is the meaning of you sneaking around to snoop in my affairs?"

Stone sighed, then glanced at the overly curious men traipsing past on the way to their various clubs. "If you will wait one moment." He disappeared back inside before she could object, and then, after a minute or two, reappeared with his coat and hat in tow.

He took hold of her arm and escorted her to the vehicle. He then lifted her up and sat her on the seat like a child before circling the rig. The nerve of the man was infuriating. She caught bits of a whispered conversation between her driver and Stonemere. *Dismissed, insisted,* and *home* were all she caught, but it was enough to know that her driver told him she'd threatened dismissal. Then Stonemere sent him home.

He climbed up next to her and picked up the reins. With a snap, they were moving down St. James's Street and away from White's. Before long, they arrived in front of her parents' townhome.

"Why have we come here?" Theo fisted the skirts of her dress. With her fiancé's rather notorious reputation, entering her home alone with him—she was fairly certain her parents were not in—could be a damning mistake. Granted, they were already engaged, but fantasizing about the man and actually acting on those fantasies were two different things altogether.

"If you wish to minimize any scandal beyond that of you pounding on White's front door like a madwoman, I suggest you hop down and enter the building forthwith."

The moment pulsed with words and thoughts unspoken. Fear and desire warred, until pride came to her rescue—or perhaps it merely helped her along to her doom. Time would tell. As soon as she stood, he swung her down and helped her up the steps of the front stoop. The butler took his coat and her cloak. "Jenkins, please have a groom take the horses around back and give them a rest. I shall call for a cab when I require it. Are Lord and Lady Coleridge at home?"

"No, my lord, they are out this afternoon. Will that be all, my lord?" The man bowed and disappeared, leaving her alone with a too-quiet Stonemere.

"The front parlor. Now." He marched toward the specified room without looking back to see if she followed.

By the time she arrived, he had settled himself on a couch with no room for her to join him. "My lord, I—"

"No, not yet. Close the door behind you and just stand there. I need a moment more to collect my thoughts."

Theo stood silently, feeling more and more like a recalcitrant girl than an enraged woman. In the end, her temper exploded, and she disregarded his directions. "I went to see Mr. Harrington today and learned that not only had you sought him out, but you nosed into my affairs against my express wishes."

"As I told you at the ball, I needed assurances you were not being led astray." He resembled his name in more than a passing way as his jaw clenched.

For the first time, she noticed a throbbing vein that pulsed in his neck as he watched her. Well, she was angry, too. "And despite my assurances that I was no featherbrained girl, you went behind my back to do your own assessment."

"As I said, if I am to allow you to retain ownership of all your holdings, I needed some assurances that you were managing things adequately, and that your man was trustworthy. I'll not apologize for looking after your best interests."

"I do not need you to look after my well-being." She paced the length of the couch, her skirts brushing him on each pass.

She was forced to cease her movement when his hand snaked out and grabbed her wrist. "I shall always take care of what is mine."

The hard, implacable words annoyed her while also making her go all soft inside at the notion that he considered her his. How could she feel two such contradictory things at once?

Then he pulled her down into his lap and tipped her face up to his. Her heart beat frantically as her blood pounded through her body. Heat suffused her face and spread to her extremities. He leaned into her, their lips a breath apart. "Make no mistake, Theodora, you are mine."

Stone kissed her. Somewhere in the course of their argument, he decided to lay claim to her. Right, wrong, or indifferent, she was his. Granted, he had never intended to make such a declaration, but out it came, and he would not deny the truth of his words.

As her lips opened to him, he plundered her sweet, warm mouth. He tasted her essence and sought out more. His cock throbbed as her bottom squirmed in his lap, and he thrust his tongue deeper, exploring the recesses of her mouth. More. Dear God, he wanted so much more, but he knew it would disgust her, the things he wanted to do to her and have her do to him in return.

Her arms twined about his neck until her fingers played in the fringe of hair at his nape to devastating effect. Chills raced down his spine as the embers of his need to be inside her flared to life and damn near scorched him.

He reached out and found a trim, silken ankle, and traced a path beneath her skirts. When he encountered warm unguarded flesh, he groaned into her rapacious mouth and pushed higher up her leg. But then she clamped her thighs down on his hand and pulled back. Her eyes were glassy with desire, but fear lurked in their depths. "S-Stone?"

"I'll stop if you wish it. Say the word, Theodora. But I'd like to show you what pleasures lie ahead." He all but growled the words. Stopping was not high on his list of desires at the moment, but stop he would.

Instead, her thighs relaxed as she released a breath. "Show me."

And so his hand moved upward until he found the slit in her drawers, and then the warm, wet flesh of her cunny. And heavens above, was she wet.

He traced the abundant honey on her nether lips as he eased back on their kiss enough to allow her the opportunity to adjust to his presence. When she dove back into the kiss, he pressed into her sizzling heat, sinking one digit into her tight, virginal passage. His heart pounded, causing the blood to roar in his ears.

"Ouch"—she cried out in surprise when he added a second finger. Her channel clamped down on his invasion and her breath hitched. He waited a few moments as he shifted his lips to her jaw and kissed down to her neck. But then she arched up into his hand. "P-please."

"Yes, Theodora? Please what? Tell me." He groaned as he tasted the pale column of flesh along her pulsing jugular.

"That feels so...oh, don't stop." One of her legs had slipped off his lap, and she was spread out across him as he investigated her core, pumping his fingers in and out of her silken folds.

With a swoop, he circled her nub, and she nearly flew off his lap at the intense sensations he knew she experienced for the first time. Her innocent reactions left little doubt about her lack of sexual experience. But his future wife had a wanton streak that fed his own base desires.

Then she tensed in his arms, and he kissed her to swallow her cries of release as she shattered in his arms. The clench and release of her channel around his digits made his cock throb and his muscles go weak. Her pleasure stretched for what felt like an eternity but could only have been a few moments. As she returned to awareness, he pulled out of her heat—despite every nerve screaming to remain—and helped her sit up. What had he done? What had possessed him to do that to her? Mortification opened like a gaping maw and swallowed him whole.

"Stonemere?" She pushed her skirts down and shakily sought a seat on the couch next to him.

"Are you all right? I didn't hurt you?" *Shame you? Disgust you with my demands?*

"Hurt me?" She laughed, a low sexy sound. "I've never felt anything so good in my life." Then she glanced down at his lap and spied his rather noticeable erection straining the confines of his trousers. She bit her lush, kiss-swollen lower lip and appeared to come to some decision. "Wha-what of you?"

"Do not be concerned. I shall be fine as long as you are well," he assured her. If she tried to touch him, to help him, he might consummate their marriage early. It wouldn't do for the newly respectable Earl of Stonemere to ravish his bride before their wedding day.

"It looks painful." Her whispered words of concern threatened to barge right past all his barriers and lodge themselves in his heart, not to mention steal his tenuous control.

In the nick of time, he deflected such sentiments and stood. "I should go. However, you should know I shall not cease to meddle in your business as I see fit. But I shall always try to discuss such business with you before I do so."

The sheer mutiny that flashed across her prettily flushed visage warned him of rough patches ahead. How he had ever thought her cold or aloof and imagined they would have some polite, remote marriage, he couldn't imagine now as she put herself back to rights.

"This is not over, Stonemere. My business is just that. *Mine.*" She rose and marched into the main hall. By the time he was able to tame his desire, and the resultant cockstand, she had disappeared into the depths of the house. As he made to leave, Jenkins magically emerged with his hat and coat. Stone stepped outside and decided the best way to work off his pent-up energy was to walk a bit. With thoughts of Theodora plaguing him, he walked and searched for his control.

Chapter Five

Three weeks later — June 1860

S ince the recitation of their vows that morning, Stone had barely spoken to Theo. Nerves stirred again as he glanced at the brave face she had pasted on upon their arrival at the wedding breakfast her parents were hosting. Despite the tension around her eyes, he assumed most of their guests wouldn't notice it, or would chalk it up to bridal nerves as she smiled and welcomed all their well-wishers.

Concern filtered past his walls until he asked, "How are you holding up, Lady Stonemere?"

Her cheeks flushed an enticing shade of pink. "I am fine, Lord Stonemere."

"Good. I believe these are the last of our guests and we may take our seats soon." He nodded at the group of arrivals just entering her parents' foyer.

Stone watched his bride beam at each guest and wondered how much longer they would be required to indulge their company. The last group filed past until they stood alone in the dark-paneled entry hall. The impulse to take her there and then, feed off her vitality, soak up her liveliness, and mark her as his lanced through him. He burned to stretch her out across his bed, bind her to it, and make her scream her pleasure. Yet he knew to use her thusly would at best shock her and at worst send her screaming from their breakfast.

Without any indication of his filthy thoughts, he tucked her delicate hand into the crook of his arm and led her into the dining room to their table. What kind of man desired to use his wife in such a coarse manner? Did his need to command her body and soul stem from some cancerous mass that tainted his own soul?

"Regrets so soon, my lord?" She watched him warily as she sipped champagne from a delicately etched crystal flute.

"Regrets? No." He frowned, confused by her query.

"Then you may wish to consider schooling your features when you look at me, or our guests may be led to believe that you intend to whisk me away and thrash me as opposed to ravish me like a dutiful bridegroom." She set her glass down and smiled sweetly at him.

Chagrined at being caught out by his bride, he dug deep to smooth his features and shut down his lecherous line of thought. Casting his most devastating smile in her direction, he took her hand and carried it to his lips. Skin against...moleskin. A strong reminder that his wife was a lady, not a prostitute, or even a widow. And yet his desire refused to abate.

His gaze lingered on the swath of skin exposed above her neckline. It pleased him to see the gooseflesh his touch raised. And the soft sigh that escaped her kissable lips teased his inner beast, made him desperate to elicit more such sounds from her.

She softly cleared her throat and lifted one silky eyebrow. His lips curved up at her less-than-subtle reminder. "I suppose I should have gathered from our previous conversations that you have a tendency to say unexpected things in the most inappropriate of places."

"If by unexpected you mean true, then I suppose you should." The little minx agreed so effortlessly with his observation that he couldn't resist smiling.

"Quite so. I see you shall keep me on my toes. Be warned, madam. You will find me equal to your challenge." A strange sense of contentment chased away his consternation and left little room for his previous inner debate. As long as his wife continued to engage him in conversation, he had no time to worry about things he could not change.

Toward the end of the breakfast, Theo excused herself and headed upstairs to gather her things and ensure Mary had everything under control. If she were being honest, she simply needed a respite from all the commotion and congratulations.

Only that morning, Theo had rolled out of bed and swept the drapes open. Sunshine had drenched the world in a sparkling display that rivaled the Crystal Palace. Of course there had been sunshine. And birds. The birds had chirped merrily.

All she had wished for were gray skies and formidable clouds to match her mood. Instead, she had the glorious day every girl dreamed of for their wedding.

Theo found Mary upstairs, flame-red locks still tamed in a neatly braided coil, as if to demonstrate that the orderliness with which she governed was the natural order of things. Everything was well in hand, leaving Theo no excuse to remain above stairs. No more time to brood on her fate of marrying a man—particularly one of questionable reputation with decidedly overbearing tendencies—simply because she'd come part and parcel along with the title he'd inherited. Certainly not the storybook wedding day every young girl dreamed of.

Though, if she were honest with herself, her husband's lusty ways had led to a rather pleasurable interlude not so long ago. Would that be the way of their marriage? Or would her mother's rather impersonal version of marital relations be the norm? It was hard to reconcile the two versions. She shook her head as she left her bedchamber.

On her way to rejoin the breakfast, she remembered her favorite shawl was in her reading spot in the library, and dashed inside to grab it. Wrap in hand, she turned to leave when she discovered she was not alone. A man—her husband's cousin, if she remembered correctly—sat in a wingback chair cradling a scotch, and it was not yet noon!

"Oh, please excuse me. I did not see you there." She took a step toward the door. What was his name? Hugh. Mister Hugh Denton.

"Don't run off on my behalf, *Countess*."

The sparkling new title felt uncomfortable, especially considering it would have been hers regardless. She thought of Odysseus and his tragic end, and a new sense of guilt washed through her. How was it fair that she should stand there the new Countess of Stonemere, and he lay somewhere at the bottom of the ocean?

Hugh shifted in his chair, a drink in his hand, and drew her attention back to the moment.

She gripped the length of cloth in her hand. "I was just collecting my shawl. Stonemere will be expecting my return any moment."

"I'm sure he's counting the moments until you return to his side. I certainly would be, with a bride as lovely as you." He tipped his glass in salute and returned to brooding, or whatever it was he'd been doing alone.

She paused and considered him for a moment. "Forgive my intrusion, Mr. Denton, but is all well with you?"

He turned to look at her. "How kind of you to inquire." His lips tilted up in a sham of a smile. "I'm afraid I've had some bad news today. I had hoped to hide away a bit so as not to dampen the spirits of your guests."

She stepped close enough to lay a hand on his shoulder. "I do not pretend to know what weighs upon you, but perhaps joining the party will help dispel the gloom? Come, escort me back to my husband. I am sure they will be cutting the wedding cake soon."

Hugh set his drink aside and, being a gentleman, escorted her back to the festivities. But sadly, it did not chase away her earlier thoughts of her first fiancé. All through the cake cutting and boxing, she could not help but consider how the wedding might have been different with Odey by her side. But then she realized, as far as husbands went, she found

Stonemere far more attractive than his brother. There was a sense of danger about her husband that made her heart race and her blood thrum. As much as she had liked Odey, even missed him, she could not remember him stirring her passions in such a way.

The guests were preparing to leave when she spied her husband speaking to a man across the room. When he stepped away, Stonemere turned to her. "Are you well, my dear?"

Surprise that he had both noticed her discomfiture and inquired after her well-being caused her to hesitate. "I am quite well, Stonemere."

He stared at her for a long moment, causing her to fret as she imagined explaining her thoughts of his brother on this, their wedding day. Determined to set aside what she could only accept as regret that a man she had come to like and respect was gone too early, she tried to bolster her words with a sense of cheer.

"Very well. I believe it is time for us to depart." He motioned toward the crowd gathering in the foyer to wish them well.

"So it is." She nodded with more confidence than she possessed, but ever the intrepid woman, she refused to start off her marriage on less than a strong footing.

Theo ran the boar-bristle brush through her hair until the strands shone. Mary had laid out her nightgown—if one could call the diaphanous garment a nightgown—and departed. Grateful to be alone, she strove to gather her inner reserves against what lay ahead.

If her mother were to be believed, Stonemere would creep in under cover of darkness, push up her nightclothes, go about his business, and then leave her. Her job was to lie still and not impede the execution of his duty. If the experience became oversetting, she was to imagine something pleasant, such as gardening or shopping.

All guidance aside, Theo hoped she might find the entire undertaking more enjoyable than her mother had. If her response to his kisses and the way he'd touched her in her parents' salon were any indication, then she had much to look forward to. A shiver of anticipation chased down her spine, followed by a shock of cool air striking her skin as she discarded her chemise. Determined to be properly prepared to await her husband, she slipped the filmy negligee on and climbed beneath the covers. A single lamp sat by her bedside as she nervously waited for what would come next.

A single sharp rap on the door that connected their chambers was all the warning given before her husband emerged from the darkness of his room. Covered head to toe in black but for the slash of skin exposed by the gap of his robe and the pale gleam of toes poking from his trousers, he all but melded into the shadows of her room.

"Theodora?" He scrutinized the bed, where she attempted to appear calm despite her body's determination to twitch in an uncontrolled and unladylike manner.

Her pulse pounded against her temples, a dizzying throb of panic urging her to hide. Or did it command some other response? His gaze traced over her flesh with an intensity that felt like a physical caress. Her nipples hardened in a distressing display that had her clutching the covers to her chest. Dear God, what if he should see? When he'd touched her in her parents' house, she'd been fully clothed. With only a thin layer of silk for coverage, she felt exposed and unsure, even as she clutched the bed covers to her breast.

Silent and brooding, Stone turned from her, and her heart skipped a beat. Had he found her a disappointment? Somehow lacking? Her gaze dropped to her lap as mortification enflamed her cheeks and cracked her resolve.

Then the sound of metal scraping on stone alerted her to his continued presence. He stoked the fire to a roaring flame and added wood to the conflagration. As he worked, the muscles in his back slid under the silk robe and caused her breath to catch in her throat. The sound drew his attention as he set the poker down. Still mute, he turned and faced her, his back to the fire.

With a lift of his hand, he broke the silence at last. "Come here, wife."

Stone waited with bated breath to see his tantalizing wife naked. She hesitated.

"Stonemere, I believe you are supposed to come to me in the bed." Her confusion was evident by both her words and the little ridge that resided between her brows.

"Drop the covers and come here." He paused in hopes she would simply respond. Still, she remained rooted. "Do not make me repeat myself."

Finally, she moved. The covers sank to the bed, taking every ounce of his blood with them. The silken web of a snow-white nightgown skimmed her delectable figure.

The very one he had fantasized about every night for the last seven nights as he waited for *this* particular night to come. Despite his having tended to his own needs every day, and again that morning, his staff throbbed and his bollocks ached with the intensity of his desire. He shook with the need to shred the sheer material of her gown and bury himself deep in her cunny. As she approached him, he curled his hands into fists to control his basest instincts. This was his wife, not some prostitute or merry widow who might enjoy or be accustomed to being used roughly.

He subdued the beast—for now.

"Turn around." The words were difficult to form since his mouth had gone dry, as though packed with cotton.

Again, she hesitated, chewed her delectable lower lip in indecision, and then complied. As she revealed the plunging back of the night dress that exposed her creamy white skin through a wisp of lace, he groaned. When she faced him again, he reached out and cupped her jaw. The first brush of his lips on hers sent a jolt of electricity straight to his erection.

A small gasp escaped her.

He pulled back and smiled, pleased with her response. "You feel it as well?"

"I don't understand precisely what it is, but my heart is racing and my mouth is dry." Pink dusted her cheekbones as he looked his fill. He could see her pebbled nipples pressed against the fabric.

An image of her hands bound behind her with her breasts forced forward by the tension in her arms teased him. Taunted him. Tortured him.

He reached out and drew her back into his arms and kissed her, again. Another slow press of lips. The same energy arced between them and spurred him on. He traced the seam of her mouth with his tongue. She opened like a flower seeking the sun and allowed him entrance.

He swept over her teeth and then delved farther inside. With a groan, he slanted his head for easier access and used his hands to angle her appropriately. Her hands wandered up from his arms to explore his chest. The delicate, unsure touch sent shivers down his spine as her cool fingers found his heated flesh. He burned with a desire he had not experienced since he'd first discovered The Market.

As he continued to drive his tongue into her mouth, she whimpered and then ventured her own reciprocal exploration. The feel of her tasting him and caressing him made his heart pound. Honey and cinnamon flooded his taste buds as he repressed the urge to drag her to the floor and ravish her.

Once her seeking hands snaked their way around his neck, he found himself pressed against her full length. The softness of her belly cradled his cock as her legs became practically entwined with his. Meshed against him in the most intimate manner possible—short of him being inside her—his wife was quickly succumbing to their mutual passion.

Breaking the lock of their lips, he trailed kisses across her jaw and over to her earlobe. There, he nibbled and sucked her flesh until she writhed in his arms. His thigh became trapped between her legs and tangled in her nightgown.

As he swept his lips down her neck and over her collarbone, her hips shifted restlessly against his leg. He locked one arm around her back and used his free hand to nudge the dainty strap off one shoulder. The material dipped and hung on her thimble-like nipple in defiance of his need to take that sweet bud in his mouth.

He yanked the fabric aside and, with a ferocity he could hardly contain, sucked her flesh. She gasped, but instead of cringing in fear as he had expected, she arched into the heat of his mouth. The little wanton shoved her nipple deeper and moaned. Then, to his shock and great pleasure, she commenced rubbing herself against his leg.

"Yes, that's it, love. Find your pleasure." The raspy voice he heard sounded nothing like his. Like most men, his voice typically grew deeper with arousal, but never so rusty sounding. She did this to him. Drove him to the edge of sanity to tease and titillate like the most practiced courtesan. Yet he knew she was a virgin.

"Stone—" The rest of his name was cut off by her cry of satisfaction. She continued to grind against him as he uncovered and suckled her other breast.

The remnants of her climax shuddered through her and into him. He caught her behind the knees and around the shoulders to carry her to bed. Their bed. He let her feet touch the rug but helped her to stand long enough to push the lingerie to the floor.

Glorious in her nudity, she moaned as he rained kisses over her flesh, across her well-loved breasts, and down her stomach. He pressed her backward onto the mattress. "Lie back, pe—sweeting." *I shall not slip into those habits with her. It's unthinkable.*

"Stone?" The intimate form of his name on her lips had his blood at a simmer.

He wanted to thrust into her and impale her on his cock in one driving, claiming motion. Instead, he took a deep breath and knelt between her thighs. Tipping the velvet had always been a favorite for him, and he expected doing so to Theo would be sublime.

"Lie back, Theo. Trust me. Trust me to make this good for you."

She nodded and reclined upon the mattress.

Stone knelt on the floor and slid her forward until her feet dangled over the edge of the bed, spread her thighs, and then used his fingertips to fully open her up. The pink folds of her pussy glistened with her juices. The tissues were swollen and hot as he leaned in, and then his tongue swiped up one side and along her nub. Her breath caught as he followed suit on the other side. Then he traced around her tight entrance and plunged his tongue inside. Salted caramel burst over his tongue as he tasted her. She moaned when he swirled his tongue around and again when he drew it out and up over her pearl. Her hips bucked against his face, and he had to press them into the mattress or be pushed away from his treat.

While he feasted on her, fucking her with his tongue, she moaned and thrashed. "Oh God, Stone. Don't stop!"

Never. He drove deeper and then used the flat of his tongue to swipe across her engorged center. She was close, so very close. With hurried movements, he untied his dressing gown and fumbled with his trousers. He centered on her bundle of nerves and sucked it until she exploded for him. As she arched up, he pressed her hips into the softness of the bed and drank in her honey. He rode out the crest until she seemed to calm.

With a restrained curse, he rose up, letting his trousers sink to his ankles. His cock ached to be inside her, but he had to go slow or he would hurt her unnecessarily. "Theo, this is going to hurt, but I shall get you through it, and next time will be pure pleasure. I promise."

She looked at him, still muddled from her peak. But he couldn't wait any longer. Standing between her creamy thighs, he notched his prick at her opening and pressed in. The high bed placed her at the perfect height for his entry.

"This is the part I can't make any better. I'm so sorry." And then he thrust into her in a swift stabbing motion.

"Ouch!" Her gaze sought his and the worry, pain, and confusion froze him. The emotions that flitted across her countenance had him pulling out.

As he withdrew, she gasped again, but somehow the minx knew what to do to keep him with her. She locked her heels around his arse and refused to let him remove completely. "Are you sure?"

"Yes." She smiled shyly and nudged him with her heels.

And then he was lost as he plunged into her welcoming heat. *Mine,* his soul cried as he pumped into her in a pistoning motion that would see him to his end. He controlled the impulse to pound into her long enough to see himself over the abyss. As pleasure rushed up from his bollocks and through each of his muscles, his cock swelled and her cunny clasped tighter. And then all went hazy, lights battering against his closed eyes as he drowned in the pleasure of planting his seed in her womb.

Withdrawing from her heat sent shivers of delayed pleasure rippling through him. On his feet still, he hovered over her for a moment, absorbing the beauty of her satisfied sprawl as she stretched lazily. Heart thundering, a feeling he dared not name surged to the fore. But he'd come prepared for just such an occurrence, and so he ruthlessly crushed any wayward feelings under the power of his control.

Chapter Six

T heo lay on the bed, legs still dangling. She would have
moved more fully onto the mattress, but since she had
been reduced to a quivering pile of aspic, she had little hope
of such activity occurring. Simply basking in the glow of
such wonderful intimacy was enough for the moment.

Her husband stood over her, taking in her wanton sprawl
across the bed, and said nothing. Nervousness cinched her
stomach like the drawstring on a reticule. Had she been
too enthusiastic? He'd attempted to leave her at one point,
but she'd wanted more. Needed something she knew he
could provide, though she'd had no notion it would be so
wonderful. But now he loomed over her, brooding. Again.

Without a word, he turned and stalked away, and Theo's
cinched stomach flipped over a few times. Had it not been
drawn so tight, she would certainly have tossed up her
accounts. Positive she had ruined everything, she sat up to
watch the retreating form of her husband disappear into the
changing room.

Her frame shook with despair. Clearly, the man was
disgusted by her comportment. She knew her mother had
said she was to lie there and let him conduct his business,
but once he'd placed that intimate kiss—the very one that
had her cheeks heating in remembrance—she'd assumed
something more along the lines of their previous encounter
was amenable.

Now, he'd disappeared.

She moved to stand up, but the sounds of muffled
footsteps caused her head to jerk up. There in the doorway,

her husband had stopped. He held a basin in his hands. "Theo, lie back down, please."

The words were pleasant enough, but there was no ignoring the command in his tone. He expected her to obey, and by God, she wanted to. But her pride refused to allow her to meekly lie back down. "Stonemere"—he winced at his name; that couldn't be good—"I-I wanted to apologize for before. For my unseemly behavior." Despite her location at least twenty paces from the fireplace, her face heated as though she stood only an arm's length from the flames.

He grunted at her. What the devil was she to make of that?

Then he moved forward and closed the distance between them. He pushed her, a gentle nudge, really, back onto the mattress. "I haven't the faintest notion what you are apologizing for. Now lie back."

She did as he instructed and returned to the position of lying on the bed with her legs dangling. She huffed, "Must I spell it out?"

"I'm afraid you must." He set the basin on the bed and picked up a length of cloth that appeared to be soaked.

Did her eyes deceive her? Were his lips twitching? "I was trying to tell you that if my wanton display at all offended you, I shall endeavor to restrain myself in the future. My mother warned me that men appreciate being in control of such activities, and that my job was simply to allow you unfettered access." She crossed her arms over her breasts and turned her head to studiously examine the coverlet and sham.

The blasted man laughed openly.

Her hands clenched into fists as her mortification was made complete. He found her laughable. Bloody fantastic.

"Well, I'd say your mother has the half of it right."

Something wet dragged between her legs, which brought her head around to see what he was doing. When she spotted the wet rag between her thighs, she slammed them shut. Or she would have, had her husband not been strategically placed between them.

"Men do tend to like to be in control, or at least I certainly lean in that direction. But your level of participation was not at issue. Had you lain there like a dead fish, I would have been displeased at the very least."

"Truly?" She quit trying to close her legs and focused on her husband's face. He didn't often give away much, except when she focused on his eyes. His eyes seemed to tell the story more thoroughly than his face alone ever could.

At the moment, his green eyes sparkled with a sincerity she could not question. He was not appalled by her immodest behavior.

"Truly. Now, into the bed with you." He swatted her thigh in encouragement.

Theo sat up sharply and stared at him for a moment. Unease glittered in his gaze, as though he had relaxed too much and allowed himself to act in a way that was somehow wrong. Theo scooted to the top of the bed and tried to focus on her husband's odd reaction instead of the warm tingling that shot from her thigh to her molten core. She refused to connect her body's reignited desire with the swat her husband had given her. That would be unconscionable.

Still nude, Stone took the basin away and came back to the bed. As he crossed the room, she took in the play of muscles in his thighs and his torso as they rippled beneath his skin. He was a fine specimen of a man, though she had nothing but Greek statuary with which to compare him. To the delight of her curious mind, she noted his cock had grown significantly smaller than his previous display, and she wondered how that worked. But then he slipped in beside her and made no move to hold her. Instead, he lay on his back and stared at the ceiling.

Still unsure of herself, as well as the whole experience, Theo curled up on her side away from him and tried to shut down her flare of desire.

"Come here, Theo." He reached out and pulled her up against his chest. The heat that seeped from his body into hers was a comfort that she desperately needed at that moment. His hands slipped around her from behind, one curved over her belly and the other cupping one of her breasts. The intimate touch assured her that all was right and well between them.

"Good night, Stonemere."

"Good night, for now, Theo."

She puzzled over his odd comment as she drifted to sleep.

Mary woke her bearing a tray piled high with rolls and even scones, as well as a pot of chocolate. Looking at the bed next to her, she realized Stone—she liked calling him that, even if only in her head—had slipped out sometime in the night. Well, eventually she might convince him to stay with her until the morning. A yawn escaped, reminding her that she had not slept the night through. Sometime in the dark of night, or perhaps it had been early morning, her husband had rolled over and awoken her with his touch. Soon after, he slid deep inside her again, and as promised, there had been no initial pain. It was all pleasure.

An optimism born of the night's activities helped her typically sour morning disposition. Content, she sat up and allowed Mary to place the tray in her lap. That was when she noticed a note bearing a masculine scrawl. She snatched it up and read the note from her husband. He apologized for his absence, but he had an errand to run before they left for the country. He assured her he would be ready to depart by noon, as planned.

A glance at the clock showed Theo she only had a few hours to eat and then finish the last-minute details before they departed. She refused to be anything less than punctual. Setting his note aside, she addressed her breakfast.

Evening settled like a blanket over the landscape, obscuring the countryside from her view. He'd given her a choice—they could take the coach and spend a day and a half with stops to travel to his estate just outside of Southampton, or they could take the train to Southampton and have a coach pick them up for a two-hour ride to Stonemere Abbey.

The notion of riding on a train so enchanted her, she'd easily agreed to the shorter travel time. As their coach pulled up to the abbey, Theo was amazed by the beauty of the fully lit home. Through her sleepy-eyed wonder, the huge building glowed in the moonlight, a hodgepodge of architectural details that portrayed the building's history. The crenelated ramparts delighted her as their carriage rounded the drive and pulled to a stop.

"Are you ready to meet the staff?" Stone queried as they arrived.

"I think so." She yawned, then clapped her mouth shut in surprise. "Perhaps I am more fatigued than I realized."

"Travel will do that to you."

"As will a lack of sleep." She blinked away the treacle-like sluggishness, pinched her cheeks, and sat up straight. Stone alighted from the coach before he reached out to help her down. Then they ascended the front stairs of the abbey, where some of the staff waited to greet the new lady of the house. "I wrote ahead and delayed the formal household greeting until tomorrow morning. I limited tonight to the core staff members: the housekeeper, Mrs. Hedley, the butler, Mr. Bentley, and of course the stable master, Mr. Hedley."

Theo went down the line and greeted each of them, hoping to convey warmth and strength. She believed in being even-handed with servants—though not overly familiar—yet also not so remote that she would need to worry about theft or betrayal. She assumed her husband paid well, which in the end was the most important factor in claiming a servant's loyalty.

Stone stood by her side, his hand against the small of her back imbuing her with warmth and an extra boost of confidence to carry herself as the lady of the house. Upon greeting the servants, they were led upstairs by Mrs. Hedley to their suite of rooms.

The gray-haired housekeeper left her and Mary to get settled. Once organized, Mary called for two upstairs maids to assist with the unpacking that was required, while Theo wandered downstairs to find the library. She explored a bit until she spotted a light limning a cracked door. Perhaps her husband had a similar idea. She went to the door and knocked.

Stone bid the unknown person at the door to enter. It was likely Mrs. Hedley checking on him in the wake of their arrival. To his surprise, it was his wife who appeared.

"I'm sorry to interrupt, but I was looking for the library. I thought I might search out a book while Mary sees to the unpacking."

"Do come in. I was doing much the same. My valet, Evers, seems generally happier when I am out from underfoot."

Theo flashed him a seductive little smile, though it was an artless one. "Funny how we feel like recalcitrant children at times. Mary and Evers are far more capable of unpacking without our direction than if we stayed and attempted to supervise."

Stone smiled and swirled the brandy in his snifter. That hadn't been the only reason he'd slipped away. He grappled with his desire to bed his wife—again. Could he survive another encounter with her and not lose control of his tightly leashed urges? The swat on her thigh the night before had been an unconscious gesture that reminded him how close to the edge he danced.

The heat that blanketed his palm from the soft slap had him itching for more. He'd wanted to paddle her bottom until it was bright pink, and then fuck her until she acknowledged to whom she belonged. Who her master was.

He gulped the warm liquor down and set the empty glass on the desk. "It is a rather startling realization that one can be so superfluous. I am glad you found me. I wanted to speak with you, and while I had thought I might do so later, I am not sure you will be up to a visit from your husband so soon."

Theo flinched, a fleeting movement before her composure returned. "I am happy to speak to you now. However, you should not alter your plans for a visit later on my account."

A satisfied warmth curled in his belly as he nodded. She was so naturally submissive. So willing to please. "Very well, then. In the meantime, I wanted to give you this."

He set a long velvet jewelry box on the desk next to his brandy glass and slid it across to her. Her lips parted as she tracked the gliding motion. "A gift? For me?"

"Yes. Who else shall I bestow such things on if not my wife?" Satisfaction morphed into coals of desire carefully banked since he'd left her bed that morning.

"But I do not have a gift for you." Theo bit her lower lip while her brow creased. It made Stone wish he could nibble it for her.

"It was an impulse I chose not to quell. Open it."

She lifted the box and pried open the lid. Her eyes sparkled in a display that shamed the jewels nestled inside. She lifted the strand of perfectly matched sapphires and held them up to the light. "Stonemere. They're beautiful, but it's too much. Where would I wear them?"

Foolish girl that she was, she couldn't imagine where she'd wear them, while he couldn't imagine where she shouldn't. "I daresay you could wear them to any number of balls. They'd be stunning in the sunlight as you shop on Bond Street, and you'd look magnificent in nothing but those while you graced my bed."

The flush that tinted her cheeks pleased him as much as her delight in the necklace. If he had his way, she'd wear them everywhere as a kind of mark that she belonged to him. Nothing stated that a woman was unavailable as clearly as an expensive bauble encircling her neck.

It was a stamp of ownership that he desperately wanted on her body. If he could, he'd lock the thing in place so that she could never remove it.

This possessiveness, his need to have a symbol of his mastery on her person, echoed how he'd felt about each woman previously under his care. But he could not deny there was an intensity this time he'd not experienced before. Of course, his pet had never been his wife, either. Nor, technically, was she now. He hadn't claimed her as truly his, and he did not suspect he ever would in any way that satisfied his sexual hunger. He doubted his pretty wife would appreciate how he wanted to strap her to his bed and demand she acknowledge him as her lord and master in the most primeval of ways.

"Stone..." She flushed even brighter. "Stonemere, you shouldn't say such things."

"Stone. I like when you call me that." Perhaps because that is what he became in her presence? Hard as stone. Every time. Without fail. The trip to Stonemere Abbey had been devilishly uncomfortable.

"Have I called you that?" She looked up, and he could see the little furrow in her brow that appeared when she concentrated.

"At least half a dozen times last night." He grinned. Teasing her was almost as enjoyable as bedding her, but none of it would compare to owning her. *Double damn.* He had to stop this perilous train of thought.

She turned crimson as she sputtered. "I-I... Really! Stonemere, you must not torment me like that. It is unkind of you."

"If you promise to call me Stone, then I promise not to tease you so unabashedly."

"Very well. Thank you for the lovely gift." She walked over and placed a gentle kiss on the outer corner of his mouth. Before he could react, she pulled away and floated toward the door, clutching the necklace. "I should go see to Mary. I am sure all should be put away by now." She turned to leave, hesitated, and turned back. "I shall see you later?"

It was more a question than a statement, but Stone knew the answer. "Undoubtedly." He couldn't have her as he wanted, but it seemed he would take her any way he could.

She nodded and scampered away from his inner sanctum. His cock throbbed wildly below the desk, and he groaned with the knowledge that he would not stay away from her. Not that night. Perhaps the next.

Chapter Seven

S tone crept into his wife's room hours after their exchange in the library. His intent to come to her had been thwarted by the arrival of a messenger from London. The poor soul had ridden deep into the night to ensure the urgent message was delivered. He'd read the contents of the missive and swore the fates were against him. His solicitor had good news on his acquisition of the majority shares of the London and Southwestern Railway. It had positioned him to take over as the chairman of the board for the company, but now it seemed there was a labor dispute he needed to address. Since he was interested in seeing how this growing mode of transport could be leveraged and made profitable, he needed to attend to the matter immediately.

Theo's excitement about taking the train versus the coach all the way from London had pleased him no end. Many women in her position would have turned their nose up at such *common* travel and insisted on a coach with all the trappings. As he reviewed the missive and the resulting plans for his quick return to London, the hour had grown late. He had assumed his wife would be asleep, and he was not wrong. What had surprised him was finding her nude in her bed and clutching the sapphires, as though she had contemplated wearing them, but somehow couldn't decide to. Or, perhaps she had worn them but removed them in a fit of pique?

The simple idea that she had considered his naughty suggestion sparked new, more dangerous ideas. Again he reminded himself she was no trollop, or even a welcoming widow, to play out such depraved ideas with. She was a lady, an innocent. She deserved to be treated and bedded with respect. Not manhandled in her parents' drawing room or paraded around nude bearing the mark of his possession.

Disgusted with himself, he turned down the bedside lamp and retreated to his own cold, lonely bed. He would have to redirect his lustful nature to other pursuits. Exhaust himself so he could scarcely collapse next to her, let alone soil her with his filthy needs.

He stripped down to his skin and lay in bed trying to banish the image of Theo wearing his gift and naught else. An impossible task.

Theo awoke in the dark of night. The lamp by her bed had been doused. As she turned up the light, another low, agonized moan pierced the fog that still clung to her. She rose and donned her robe before carefully grabbing the handle of the lamp to head in the direction the horrible sound had emanated from.

She pushed the door open that connected her room to Stone's and held the light aloft. With a few steps inside, she found her husband sprawled on his bed, sheets twisted about his hips and legs like the twisting tendrils of a jungle vine. He moaned again, a sound full of such anguish, it brought tears to her eyes.

What had he endured to draw such a horrific sound from him? His legs flailed about as he attempted to escape the bonds of his bedding.

"No! The women," he sobbed, and as Theo neared his bed, she could see the tears that escaped from beneath his closed lids. "The children." His voice broke on the last word as he shook violently.

Distraught but afraid to wake him, Theo set her lamp down and eased onto the bed next to him. Tentatively, she reached out to stroke his sweat-damp brow. With a light touch of her fingertips, she smoothed his furrowed brow. He mumbled more words, but his thrashing seemed to calm. She continued to soothe him with her touch. As he settled back into a deeper sleep, she hovered in case the nightmares returned.

Half an hour later, she unwound the sheets from his legs and covered him against the chill of the night. He had remained peaceful while she fussed over him. Confident that he would sleep the rest of the night undisturbed, she retrieved her lamp and slipped back to her own bed.

However, sleep proved elusive. Unsure of what might have caused such anguish in a man she had come to know as staunch and, at times, stoic, she could not stop the cogs from turning. Could something have occurred during his military service? Perhaps some childhood trauma that followed him into adulthood? She had a cousin who could not abide small spaces due to an afternoon spent locked in a steamer trunk as a girl. Even in the dead of winter, she rode only in an open carriage.

At some point after the first pink rays of dawn chased away the night, Theo drifted off to a restless sleep.

Theo entered the breakfast room to find her husband awake and looking refreshed despite the ordeal she knew he'd suffered during the night. He read the local newspaper while drinking his morning coffee. The bitter aroma of the strong brew drifted from across the room, and to her surprise, she found it perked her up. Mayhap she would try it in lieu of tea this morning.

"Good morning, Stone." Had her voice warbled?

"Good morning, Theo. I trust you slept well?" He turned the page of the news.

"As well as could be expected." She refused to mention his absence from her bed or her discovery of his nocturnal torment. She settled down at the table and poured herself a cup of coffee, and then asked the footman to bring her a piece of ham and a coddled egg for breakfast.

In silence, she lifted her cup to her lips, inhaled the bracing scent of the coffee and sipped. Sputtered. Choked. And coughed. In that order. Her husband slapped the paper down and rose to aid her. He patted her back as she regained her capacity to breathe.

The humiliation of the moment overwhelmed her. Crawling under the table to hide seemed a perfectly rational solution at the moment.

"Are you well?" he asked as he hovered over her.

"Yes." Her voice came out raspy from the abuse of choking on a hot liquid.

"Have you ever had coffee before?" One brow lifted toward his hairline.

"No." She stared at her plate and willed the tears of mortification back. "It smelled so delicious when I came in, and Mother had banned the drink from the house, calling it uncivilized. I was curious to taste it, but the stuff is vile."

"Many find it to be upon first tasting it. You also might try it again after treating it much as you do tea. Perhaps a bit of cream and sugar might make it more palatable?" He nudged the sugar and creamer set in her direction and then returned to his seat and lifted the paper up to cover his face.

Suspicion crept past her embarrassment and bedeviled her until she rose and peeked over the paper her husband perused so intently. The hidden tableau sparked her outrage. The man was laughing at her.

"You odious man, I cannot believe you are laughing at my distress," she pouted, only slightly serious about her indignation.

"I watched the entire evolution, and with such a violent and unexpected outcome, I couldn't help but chuckle a little. You are adorable in your curiosity and your eagerness to try new things. It is also the reason you wind up in such predicaments. If you had simply asked for my guidance, I could have offered the cream and sugar from the start and spared you the experience."

She laughingly glared at him as she spooned sugar into her cup, followed by a dribble of cream. Her late-night foray into nursing her husband was quickly forgotten. "I have found most experiences are best had uncolored by anyone else's perceptions."

"While that can be true"—a shadow flitted across his beautiful eyes—"such an approach can also lead to foolish mistakes that might get a countess in trouble." His gaze narrowed meaningfully.

"I shall consider your advice in the future when appropriate, Stone." Then she addressed the breakfast plate a footman had fortuitously delivered. With food to consume, she could cease having a pointless conversation. He would not be allowed to control her experiences. That point was tantamount to the success of their arrangement.

"Very well. Since you are already put out with me, I am afraid I have some bad news."

"Oh?" She paused in cutting her ham.

"Yes, it seems I shall have to return to London tomorrow morning first thing."

Her heart pounded. Things between them had been progressing well, or so she thought. But then he'd not come to her that night as he'd said he would. Had she done something to displease him in bed? "What time shall we leave?"

"No, no. I wouldn't want to drag you back so soon after we arrived. Besides, I know you have much to do here to take the reins. I shall hurry back alone and hopefully be able to return in a few days' time."

"I see. Well then." She laid down her fork and knife and rose from the table. "I believe I should be about those very duties you mentioned." And with that, she departed the room lest he witness her utter dismay.

Later that evening, after reminding herself that they were in fact married and that he was simply returning to London for a few days, she determined to be naught but cheerful at dinner.

She appeared in the dining room dressed in a beautiful light-blue silk gown made by none other than the House of Worth. It was an elegant confection with simple lines and subtle detailing around the neckline. The perfect dress for an evening meal in the country with her new husband.

However, she sat alone for nearly an hour before she resigned herself to his disappearance. Once she'd eaten, she headed back to her chamber by way of the library. She spotted the light beneath the door, hesitated, and then decided to continue on to her room. There was little point in making an issue of his absence. At the bottom of the stairs, she stopped one of the maids.

"Please ask Mrs. Hedley to see that a dinner tray is sent to the library for Lord Stonemere."

"Yes, my lady." The girl bobbed a curtsy and headed toward the kitchens.

Content that she could be sure he at least would not starve, she retired to her room, where Mary helped her undress.

"Which nightgown will you wear tonight, my lady?"

"The regular cotton, please."

Mary looked at her queerly but provided the requested gown. Then her maid brushed out her hair until it shone like spun gold. "Thank you. That will be all, Mary."

Alone, she slipped into bed and picked up the book she had selected from the library earlier that evening. The copy of *Wuthering Heights* was as good as new. All evidence suggested it had never even been opened. She settled in to read one of her favorite stories of tormented love. It seemed apropos in light of her current situation. She found herself infatuated with her husband, despite the arranged union, and he seemed to be continuing on about his life as though nothing had changed.

Perhaps tomorrow morning she could rise early enough to see him off. Content with that plan, she settled in to read.

Just shy of midnight, Stone found himself once again lingering over his wife's sleeping form. This time, however, there were two notable differences. As opposed to her nude state the night before, tonight a cotton sack some women might call a nightgown covered her from neck to toes. The second difference was that instead of clutching his gift to her, she lay grasping a book. The sapphires were nowhere to be seen.

I am undoubtedly the biggest fool in England.

He leaned over to slip the book from her grasp, but she woke up. "Stone, what are you doing here?"

Her sleepy little question caught him up. "Where else would I be?"

"Your library, on the way back to London, and in your own bed are all places that come to mind." She sat up.

He lowered himself to the edge of the mattress. His wife sat with her hair peeking out of a lace monstrosity that he knew women were prone to wearing at night. But beneath that distracting frill, her blue eyes held a soft, sleepy quality that brushed too near the look of desire she'd worn on their wedding night as he thrust into her body. The need to taste her lips again crashed over him like a wave swamping a ship. "But you see, you are here. So how would any of those locations allow me the opportunity to do this?" Then he gave in and kissed her.

Despite the hideous nightgown she wore, her sleep-hazed response fired his blood. She kissed him sweetly and then, when he delved deeper, she opened to him with a little moan. Her arms slipped up over his linen-shrouded shoulders to tangle in the hair at his nape.

God, how he wanted to be in her arms. The idea of leaving for London was both horrific and a boon to his drowning soul. He'd tumbled arse over boots, unsure how to right himself in the maelstrom that one woman created with a simple kiss.

Lost in the storm, he pushed the ugly cap off her head, drew the covers down, and cupped her breast over the cotton barrier she wore. He kissed down her neck and sought out the buttons of her sleepwear, swearing in his head when he found the row of tiny buttons—thousands of tiny buttons. One by one, he released them. The task seemed endless until the material parted to expose the pink-flushed flesh of her chest and breasts.

He tongued one nipple and then the other as he left her arms trapped at her sides by all the material. "Stone, please. Take the thing off. I want to touch you."

He groaned. If she were allowed to touch him right now, this would be over before it began. "No," was all he could manage as he worked to unfasten his trousers. The need to bury himself in her heat rode him the way Aries charged into battle, with fierce determination and unstoppable power.

Freed from its entrapment, his cock rose up long and hard between his thighs. He shifted, shoved the covers down, and then found the hem of the ugly night dress. He pushed it up until the hem doubly entrapped Theo, leaving her lower half exposed. Then he loomed over her and notched his prick at her opening. "So beautiful."

A shiver of anticipation racked his body, and then he pushed inside her. She groaned and rose up to meet him as best she could, tangled in the yards of cotton fabric. "That's it, pe— Love. Take me." He groaned as he pumped into her heat and gave them what they both seemed to want.

Her head thrashed restlessly while she lay practically helpless beneath him. Her hips rose to take him over and over again as he thrust into her, and then she groaned. "More. Stone, I need... I need more."

And his restraint snapped. He pounded into her with a brutal rhythm that seemed to answer her demand while sating the raging beast within. He fucked her hard and long until she shattered around him, helpless to do anything but take what he gave. He stamped her with an indelible imprint of him, or so it seemed in his mind's eye. Even if she didn't wear the sapphires every day, her body would know who she belonged to and who its master was.

It would be enough. It must.

With a growl, he exploded as he emptied his seed into her quim. *Mine*, he roared in his head. *Mine*.

And then they fell asleep still joined together, while her arms remained tangled in the fabric at her sides.

Chapter Eight

T heo woke to the sun streaming through her window. *No!* She lunged from the bed and tripped over the fabric that slid from her waist to her ankles as she raced toward the window. Despite kicking free of the nightgown, her limbs seized up with muscles that ached as though she'd tumbled down the stairs sometime in the night.

She stood in limbo between the bed and the window, naked. She stared out at the glorious sunny day and let flashes of her night visit wash over her. Her husband looming over her. Arms trapped by her nightgown. His refusal to free her. And then the pressure as he surged into her, filled her with such passion. The way he plundered her body and her soul with an utter ruthlessness that melted both her heart and limbs.

The memory of begging him for more and how he'd delivered all she had requested, yet had no words to name. The roughness of his loving matched the ferocity of the turmoil that had surged deep in her soul. Her heart. And then at the end, as he planted his seed deep inside her, left a bit of himself for her to cherish and possibly create a child, he'd bellowed loud enough to bring the rafters down. *Mine!* He had yelled as though he'd claimed her, marked her as his in the most elemental way.

It gave her shivers to hear that cry again, even in memory. Shivers of pleasure followed by a deep, burning need to stake her own claim on him. When he returned from London, she would greet him wearing naught but those sapphires and show him the truth of what was in her heart.

Confident in her decision, she called for Mary. Her maid appeared from the little room off her own. "I need a bath. A nice hot bath with some salts to soothe my aching muscles. Then I shall dress and set about getting this house in hand with Mrs. Hedley."

"Very good, my lady." Mary helped her with her dressing gown and disappeared to see about the water. Theo picked up *Wuthering Heights* and read while she waited. Soon, she would have both her husband and his country house set to rights.

Stone looked up at the rare spot of sunshine and hoped it might be symbolic of coming good fortune. After all, with negotiations between management and their rail workers stagnating for the seventh day in a row, he could certainly use a spot of luck. For the moment, he'd settle for a simple reply from his new wife. He feared with yet another missive explaining his failure to return, she might do something rash. Well-meaning, but rash nonetheless.

Setting aside his personal worries, and with the hope that a brisk walk might clear his head, he focused on finding a way to establish common ground between the two parties. Despite the fact he was part owner—though newly so—the workers seemed to feel he might be able to strike an agreement, and management shared that notion.

A woman's scream sliced through his thoughts, and he turned to his right to see two people struggling down a shadowed alley. Again she screamed out, "Help me!"

A soldier at his core, he dashed into the narrow, darkened passage and found a woman being hit by a man. Anger sliced through Stone like a sharp blade, and he grabbed the assailant. "Stop that this instant!" he said as he jerked the woman's attacker off her person and slammed him against the wall.

The man, an ancient bag of bones, really, slid down the wall into a heap. Stone turned to check on the victim but found himself alone in a dark alley with two men. A glance back the way he'd come showed the light of the thoroughfare too far away for him to make a dash for it.

The first thug, who had a droopy eye, came at him with nothing more than his fists. Stone almost chuckled as he considered how ill-prepared the chap was for what would come next. The brute swung, and Stone ducked past him. He popped up and surprised thug number two, who seemed a bit gimpy, with a right hook as he spun around to address Droopy Eye. Face-to-face, they circled each other for a moment as Gimpy lay on the ground moaning about his nose. Stone stepped in and caught Droopy Eye on the nose with a quick jab, but the man grinned and came at him. As Droopy Eye lunged forward, Stone straightened up, stepped to the side, and jerked his arm straight out perpendicular from his body. He caught the thug at throat height, and he went down like a sack of bricks. The man wheezed as he held his throat, but Stone decided there was little point in remaining where he was. Survival was far more important than trying to bring his attackers to justice.

Besides, he was more than a little embarrassed at being taken in by the helpless-female-victim routine. It was enough that the thieves had not grabbed his wallet, though, come to think of it, they'd never made a grab for it or demanded his money. They'd simply come in swinging as though they were out for blood. He loped back down the alley and into the sunshine, where he melted into the crowd.

Of late, his life had turned into a series of high adventures. When he wasn't dealing with his new wife, he was dodging wagons, and now thieves. If he were a more suspicious man, he might wonder at the coincidences. Perhaps he needed to be more mindful of his surroundings, since it seemed civilian life had made him soft.

The two weeks of their honeymoon had come and gone with little more than a few hasty notes from Stone. The last noncommittal bit of correspondence was the outside of enough. Theo marshaled the staff, and by midafternoon had set off to Southampton to catch a train to London.

She arrived home shortly after midnight to learn that her husband was still out. Furious with her recalcitrant spouse, she entered his study with the intent to search out some clue as to what might be so important in London. They had never agreed to fidelity within the union, but she didn't want to believe her husband might be a philanderer. That would be too much to bear.

As she searched his desk, which consisted mostly of locked drawers, she could no longer contain her fears. Throughout her journey home, the voices grew louder and louder until the doubts about her marriage and her performance of her wifely duties loomed large. Had she done something to offend him? He had said he did not wish her to lie still, but could she have moved too much? Been too participatory? Heat simmered in her cheeks as she thought about all they had done together, and yet she could not deny something remained amiss.

Perhaps he saw her as little more than a broodmare? A perfunctory wife, despite their agreement to try to be amiable. Her belly twisted and turned beneath her stays, and she wanted to be sick to her stomach. But then she considered the sapphires he'd gifted her. Thought of the way she had found him staring at her in the dark of her chamber at Stonemere Abbey. As she made her way up the town house stairs, exhaustion pulled at her, aggravating her worry.

Fortunately, once in her chamber, she found Mary had again borne up under challenging circumstances. Despite her listing mobcap and the slight gleam of perspiration on her pale brow, the room was neat as a pin with nary a gown or trunk in sight. Unlike many of her peers, Theo felt a surge of gratitude at her maid's efficiency. "Please, Mary, simply help me disrobe and I shall take care of the rest tonight. You've earned your bed, plus a late-morning sleep. I shouldn't need you until midmorning."

"Thank you, my lady." Mary's tired response confirmed what Theo knew. The woman was dead on her feet. After her nighttime ablutions, Theo slipped into her bed and willed herself to sleep. Tomorrow would be the first foray into battle either for or with her husband. She couldn't be sure which yet, but whatever might come, she was prepared to go down with the ship.

Exhausted from another night of late meetings as the railway board restructured the business, Stone let himself into the foyer of his home. Parsons, his butler in town, stumbled into the hall bearing a lamp.

"I thought I told you not to wait up for me tonight," Stone said as he shed his coat and hat.

"You did, my lord. However, there was a change in circumstance that I felt you needed to be aware of upon your return."

"And that is?"

"Lady Stonemere's arrival earlier this evening, or rather last night, as it is now near dawn, my lord."

Stone groaned. He should have known she was not content when she had not replied to his last two notes. Her first reply to his initial word of extension was gracious and caring. She'd wished him well and a speedy return. Then he'd sent another one two days later and heard nothing from her. The last one had been sent two days before, so with a day for travel, she'd likely got it yesterday morning, which meant her arrival was her response. There was little doubt in his mind that he was in dun territory with his wife. "Very good. I appreciate the warning, Parsons."

He dismissed the man and climbed the stairs to find his bed. Angry wife or not, there was little he could do about it without some sleep to refresh his brain. Surely, with that accomplished, he'd figure out how to address Theo.

Morning came far too early. Stone rose from a fitful, nightmare-plagued sleep and called for Evers. In the fortnight away from his wife, his nightmares had grown worse. It seemed when he slept with her, his nights were calmer and more restful. His ever-vigilant valet, with his prematurely gray hair and perceptive dark eyes that seemed to take in everything while bearing witness to nothing, had him turned out in a trice. He plunged into the breakfast room expecting to find an irate wife waiting for him.

Instead, he found a sedate Theo calmly sipping tea as she nibbled a brioche. "Good morning, husband."

Her greeting, while not warm, was not cold. It was staid. Indifferent, even. His short hairs rose in warning that all was not as it seemed. "Good morning, wife." He pecked her cheek and took a seat next to her.

"I am glad to see you are up and about. I assumed you would sleep the day away after being out all night." Her hand trembled ever so slightly as she set the teacup back on the saucer.

She was unquestionably not as calm as she appeared. "Yes, well, my business ran into the early hours of the morning. I've only snatched a few hours of sleep so I can return from whence I came."

"I see. And is this the business that has kept you in London for the duration of our honeymoon?" She sipped her tea again. However, Stone noted the obvious strain around her lips and eyes. Not to mention that if she gripped the china any more tightly, the handle might snap clean off.

"It is." He slugged a cup of coffee in one bitter swallow and stood with a roll in hand. "I must be off. I'll be at the London and Southwestern Railway office all day, I'm afraid."

"Will I see you for dinner?"

His stomach sank. "I highly doubt it. We are in the process of restructuring things in an attempt to avoid a railroad workers' strike. I'm afraid until the matter is resolved, I shall be spending a great many hours away from home."

"Very well. I shall take pains to entertain myself." Theo nodded regally to him and continued sipping her tea.

Then she looked away from him in—of all things—dismissal. Angry, confused, and bristling to show her just who was in control, but out of time, Stone stomped out of the house and headed off to the office. He needed to end this madness immediately, and then he needed to deal with his petulant little wife. His only hope was that she wouldn't get into too much trouble alone in London.

Chapter Nine

U pon Stone's departure, Theo rose and hurled her teacup into the fireplace. The crash of the shards did nothing to alleviate her fury. Did he really believe that she would accept such hogwash? At the office? Peers of the realm simply did not work. And if they did involve themselves in trade, they did not spend long hours doing that which their managers and other employees could accomplish on their behalf.

But, she argued back, she had no proof that things were not as he described. She had no clues to suggest he might be keeping a mistress. However, that could change soon enough. If he would not be coming home for meals, then she would find this office of his and bring a meal to him. If he was where he said he would be, then she could at least rule out infidelity as an issue.

Now, what had he called the place? Oh yes, *the London and Southwestern Railway*. She rose and went to the kitchen to meet with Mrs. Beats, the cook, and arranged for a basket to be prepared for lunch. Next, she sent one of the footmen off to discover the location of the railway office so that her driver would not get lost on the way there. Finally, she went upstairs to see what she might wear for a confrontation with her husband.

Three hours later, she sat in their carriage dressed in another House of Worth creation that consisted of a series of flounces in front paired with an overskirt that gathered back at the sides. The neckline was a bit daring, with a lovely plunge that exposed her collarbones and a small bit of décolleté. The cinnamon-colored gown brought out the blue in her eyes and was the height of elegance. She couldn't imagine not turning her husband's head.

Upon her arrival to the offices, she swept in, followed by Mary, who toted the large basket Mrs. Beats had prepared. Inside, the poor clerk who greeted her stammered and sputtered as he tried to deal with a lady in a place of business.

"Please let the Earl of Stonemere know that his wife has come calling," she declared with a boldness she fabricated brilliantly.

"My lady, he's in meetings. I-I... What I mean to say is I cannot simply barge in there and interrupt such tense negotiations." The man had visibly paled at the notion of interrupting.

"Very well, then I shall announce myself. Come along, Mary." She moved past the reed-thin man with all the delicacy of a battleship. Her wide skirts parted the clerks like the prow of a ship slicing through the ocean.

She sailed toward the single closed door adjacent to the clerks' spaces and turned the knob. Inside, she found two men on their feet, shouting at each other, and her husband, with his head in his hands. Theo stopped short at the scene before her. One thought leaped to mind: *not a woman.* As the door banged loudly against the wall, all eyes turned to her. The men who had been seated rose belatedly.

Taking a bracing breath, she moved forward again as the clerk trailed in her wake, along with Mary. She walked around the long table to a flabbergasted Stone and kissed his cheek. Then she retreated to where Mary had placed the basket at the end of the long mahogany table. "Gentlemen, I do apologize for bursting in on you like this. However, when my husband informed me that he would not be home for a meal yet again, I simply could not let it pass." She smiled as the men cleared their throats. "Please, do take your seats, all of you." She lifted her brow at the quarrelsome pair, who continued to shoot daggers at each other.

Perhaps she'd interrupted at an opportune time. "Fortunately, Mrs. Beats tends to spoil us, and so I am certain

I have enough food in here to feed an army, let alone you fine gentlemen." She opened the basket and produced its contents. There were various cold meats, bread, cheese, and even a jug of ale of which the lot of them appeared in dire need.

"Theo, what gave you the idea—" Stone started, but she refused to allow him to finish.

"Now, darling, I know you are likely cross with me. But I just worried so about you locked in this room day and *night*"—she emphasized the word for his benefit—"and I simply had to come ensure you were taking care of yourself. And of course, as I expected, you are not. So, may I suggest that you men take a short recess from your labors and enjoy this fine fare?"

She dared to glance around the room, and found the men occupying themselves with anything from smoothing their suits to jotting notes in a ledger. She resisted the urge to roll her eyes at their discomfort. "Afterward, perhaps you can resume your discussions with clearer heads, if not a sunnier disposition." She stared confidently down the length of the table at her husband, who produced a baleful glare that promised retribution later. "As for me, I shall be off. I have an afternoon full of calls and other nonsense. Thank you for your forbearance, gentlemen. Stone, I shall see you at home—*for dinner.*"

Her parting shot was a gauntlet thrown. If he failed to be at home for said meal, then he would truly know the wrath of a woman. This foray would prove child's play compared to what her devious little mind would work up. She departed the railway offices with the same aplomb she had borne upon arrival. In the carriage with Mary and off to her sister's home, she collapsed in laughter. The look upon the men's faces as she'd sailed into the room and laid out luncheon was worth every ounce of retribution she might receive. And she was certain she would be experiencing some retaliation from her husband. The question was, what kind? On the heels of mirth came dread. Brazen as she'd been while storming his castle, her stomach knotted and her brow furrowed as she realized that her impulsive nature had possibly once again gotten her into trouble. And this time, it might have damaged her husband's work.

Stone watched as his wife departed in a whirlwind of cinnamon skirts. The men in the room all looked as stunned as he felt. "That, gentlemen, was the new Countess of Stonemere. I apologize for my wife's interruption; however, I believe she may be on to something. Let us take a break to enjoy the food that she has delivered, and then we can resume negotiations." Stone stood and made his way to the impromptu buffet.

Slowly, the men agreed, and they took some time to prepare plates and pour themselves ale.

Captain Chambers looked at him and smiled. "That is a clever woman you have married, my lord. I daresay she took one look at the situation and sized it up rather accurately."

Stone chuckled. "You would be correct. My wife has a knack for adventure. I fear she will keep me rather busy curtailing some of her more exciting forays if I do not stay on top of things."

The other men chuckled good-naturedly and slapped him on the shoulder. Even the union representative and the office manager had settled down from their argument long enough to enjoy the food. Half an hour later, Stone set his remnants aside and addressed the group again.

"As my wife has made it abundantly clear that I am to be home for dinner this evening, let us see if we can't come to some compromise on the hours and wages of the rail workers. We all want the same thing, for the railway to continue operations."

The men agreed, uttering a series of "hear, hears" before they got down to business. Unfortunately for Stone, he found it a bit hard to focus on anything but the fantasy of lifting those saucy skirts and helping himself to his wife's abundant charms.

Theo alighted at her sister's home and promptly knocked on the door. Fortunately, it was the time of day to come calling, not that propriety would have stopped her. She sent Mary around back, glided into the foyer, and then made her way to the main salon.

There Theo found her sister and Lady Heartfield. With her piercing green eyes and fashionably pale hair, Lady Heartfield was a stunning woman.

Theo stopped before the two women as though they were her personal tribunal. "Oh Lizzy, I've gone and made a muck of things!"

"Theo, made a muck of what?" Lizzy rose to embrace her sister.

"Why, my marriage, of course. I swear sometimes I am an addlepated fool." She sank onto the settee and whipped out her fan. Her face was flushed with embarrassment after her visit to the railway offices, and now Lady Heartfield would bear witness to her humiliation.

"What have you done?" Lizzy sat next to her and placed a supportive arm around her shoulders.

Sometimes it was hard to believe that Lizzy was the younger sister and Theo was the elder. She sighed and related the events through the last hour. At the end of her tale, Lady Heartfield and Lizzy both gasped.

"I know I overstepped by barging in, but I had to know. My imagination had begun to concoct all manner of outlandish possibilities. It's not as though Stone possesses a sterling reputation." As she retold her story, she had come to a new resolve. One born of practicality and a desire to experience more of the deliciously naughty things her husband had shown her in their marriage bed.

Lizzy gasped again. "Theo, you shouldn't say such things."

She refused to play the naïve miss. She had heard rumors of her husband's and his friend's escapades long before their engagement. There was little point in feigning ignorance. "It's true. We all pretended not to know about his little club of friends. But they aren't called the Lustful Lords because they gather to take tea and break bread."

Lady Heartfield laughed. "Very astute, dear girl. You must be practical about your husband's true nature."

"Yes, I must. Which is why I plan to seduce him." She ignored the little thrill of excitement at the notion.

"But, Theo—"

"No, Lizzy, I'll not hear it. I know that you and Carlisle are deliriously happy, but you had to show him you wouldn't break. I need to show Stone—well, that's my problem. I don't know. I don't know if he is afraid of hurting me or if he fears repulsing me, or perhaps..." She drew a deep breath and ventured her darkest fear. "Perhaps *I* repulse *him*. I did ask if my wantonness upset him, and he assured me that Mama had only part of the scenario right. Which I found odd."

"What part did he suggest she had right, Lady Stonemere?" Lady Heartfield queried.

"Oh, please, as it seems I have laid out the sordid details of my marriage before you, you simply must call me Theo."

"Very well, and you shall call me Marie. Now, what part did she have right?"

Theo glanced from one woman to the other, chewed her lip, and then blurted it out. "He said men like to be in control, but they don't wish for us to just lie there."

Marie smiled and nodded in confirmation, as did Theo's sister. "That has been my experience," Lizzy offered coyly.

"But I thought you seduced Carlisle somehow or other to show him you were as eager as he." Theo's mind raced with a profusion of questions.

"I did, but once I showed him I was game, he undoubtedly took the reins." Lizzy tucked her nose into her teacup, though it failed to hide the blush on her cheeks.

HIS HAND-ME-DOWN COUNTESS

"Quite right. Theo, dear, many men, particularly men like your husband, have a desire—one that is rather base and elemental, mind you—to possess the one they bed. To somehow mark her as theirs. For some, it is as simple as placing a ring on their finger, but for a rare breed, there is more to it. They harbor a greater need to control the world around them and those things in it. Including, in some cases, their lovers."

"Stone is rather stuffy at times. He has a difficult time being spontaneous." Theo flashed a smile. "Well, except in bed."

"Does he please you in bed?" Lizzy had ceased hiding behind her cup.

"He has the two nights we've lain together. That is what has me worried. I thought perhaps he had a mistress, but now I don't think so. Not after my surprise visit to his office. But I'm afraid I don't know enough about his life to be able to tell if I offend him in bed or if I come up short. Mayhap there is more truth in his reputation than we cared to admit and I do not garner his interest beyond the requirement to procreate?" Theo's lip began to tremble. She willed back the despair and the accompanying tears, but they both failed to cooperate. Failure was not something she had ever accepted well, and to fail at possibly the most important thing in her life—her marriage—was too much.

"Oh, Theo." Lizzy wrapped her in a tight hug as she let her tears fall.

After a few moments' indulgence, she wiped away the wetness and sat up straight. "I'm sorry for such an unseemly display, but I am at a loss as to what to do next."

Chapter Ten

T heo looked from her sister to Marie. Under normal circumstances, she was not one to take advice, but for once, she felt truly out of her depth. A sly smile curved Marie's lips, and hope blossomed in Theo's chest.

"Well, I daresay the man is holding back for much the same reasons as Carlisle did with Lizzy." Marie sipped her tea.

Lizzy blushed. "Yes, but if the rumors are to be believed, Stonemere was quite the reprobate, unlike my husband, who was more concerned about the size differences."

"And still similar issues. At the heart of things is a misguided belief that a wife cannot also be a lover." Marie focused on Theo. "If you wish to seduce your husband, you must be armed with all the erotic knowledge available to you. You will need to ferret out what excites him, what stimulates his lust, and how best to pleasure him as well as yourself. Are you prepared to take on that challenge, Theo?"

Her heart hammered in her chest. Fear of what she might learn both about her husband and herself gave her pause. Could they survive as a couple if she learned something truly abhorrent about him? Or worse, herself? "I-I don't know. I won't lie and say I'm not filled to the brim with trepidation, but I also don't believe I can survive a soulless marriage. I thought I could, but having had a glimpse of what could be possible..."

"I know it's a difficult step. I thought I might faint as I dithered over the decision." Lizzy squeezed Theo's hand in reassurance. "But in the end, he was worth fighting for."

Just under her breastbone, a tiny flame of love flickered to life. "I'll do it. You're right, Lizzy, he is worth the fight, or I wouldn't have married him despite that contract. Where do we begin, Marie?"

"I have an old friend who will be of great assistance to us. She owns a private club called The Market. An evening tour of that establishment will go a long way to teaching you all the sensual and erotic possibilities that abound. I shall arrange for us to have tea with her at Pierce House. You can meet her and explain your unique situation."

"Excellent." Theo turned to her sister. "I should think you would do well to skip tea with the owner of such a place. Carlisle would be greatly displeased should he learn of your attendance."

"Oh no. While I shall forgo the actual visit, I am beyond eager to meet such a lady. I may never have the chance to do something so scandalous ever again." Lizzy grinned unrepentantly.

"Excellent. I shall send word once the arrangements have been made. Now, I really should be on my way. I still have a number of calls yet to pay." Lady Heartfield departed the salon, leaving Theo and her sister to continue chatting.

"I do hope I can sort out this trouble with Stone. The man is an enigma. One moment indulgent and kind, the next a veritable ogre, and then, of course, he becomes someone entirely different under cover of darkness when we are alone in my room."

"Marie guided me through my tumult with Carlisle to great success, I should think she can do it for you and Stone. And I know her to be nothing if not discreet. No tales will leave her lips."

"That is reassuring, all things considered. Besides that, I do wonder how she comes to know the owner of The Market." Theo poured a cup of tea for herself.

"Do you not know who Lady Heartfield was?" Lizzy's brow wrinkled.

"No, should I?" Theo's cup hung arrested in mid-path to her lips.

Lizzy groaned. "Theo, do you pay no attention to the things I tell you? Marie was once the owner of The Market. That was before she married her childhood sweetheart, Baron Heartfield."

"Truly? I had no idea. And she is received in polite society?"

"Well, certainly not by the sticklers of the Ton. But many of the less starchy echelons have welcomed her, if not with open arms, then with the gleeful thrill of the whisper of scandal."

"Well then, I think she will be perfect for helping me in this particular situation." Theo happily sipped her tea. The clock in the hall pealed five times, causing her to sputter in her tea. "Oh, heavens. After the scene I created this afternoon, it would not do to be late for dinner. I had best be off."

With a hasty good-bye, Theo headed home.

Stone entered his study just as the clock chimed seven. His headache had yet to abate, but the cause of it was well on its way to resolution. The next few days would be used to finalize all the details, but the Herculean part of the task was complete. And, truth be told, it was in no small part due to his wife's unusual appearance at the office. Her lunch had given the men an opportunity to do business in a more social atmosphere.

It was a secret that the wealthy had learned long ago, hence the existence of White's, Brooks, and Boodles, among other clubs. Unfortunately, the representatives of the workers would never have been permitted inside those hallowed halls. Regardless, the crux of their issues had been resolved and the next few days would see them returning to normal business hours.

In addition to the railway, there were other more personal concerns on his mind. He poured himself a whisky—a much deserved one, in his opinion—and sat down in his fortress of masculinity. His study.

Of course, his wife invaded shortly after him.

"Good evening, Stone." She stopped just inside the door and hesitated as though testing the waters.

"Good evening, Theo. You are looking fetching this evening." She wore a gown of what he assumed was purple silk inlaid with two black lace panels studded by bows up either side. The bodice hugged her curves and sat just at the tips of her shoulders, offering a tantalizing display of flesh. The mounds of her breasts perched at a respectable height that did little to hide their bounty. "Do come in. There is no need to hover there."

She eased into the room with more caution than was typical of his wife. "I was worried that after my unexpected visit, you might be angry with me."

He grunted and took a drink. "I no doubt would be had your disruption not turned the tide in the negotiations."

"Oh, well. I am glad to hear that things turned out." Her pleased smile brought a rosiness to her cheeks that made his heart race a little as images of her from their wedding night barraged him. He set his glass down lest he drop it.

"That said, madam, do not make it a habit of bursting into my office in such a manner in future. I would be greatly displeased, and I can assure you it would not go well." He tamped down the urge to toss her over his knee and paddle her bottom for her impulsiveness. He imagined the rounded white flesh glowing a rosy red as he smacked her with his palm.

"Of course, my lord." Her subservient response and downcast eyes—not to mention his own salacious thoughts—heated the very blood that flowed in his veins. He reached for his drink but pulled his hand back once he realized how it trembled.

He drew a deep breath and pushed the inner beast back into its cage. His lady wife needed to be protected at all costs. Even from himself.

"Please, sit." He waved her over to one of the chairs and attempted not to watch the sway of her hips as she walked. Determined to take a sip of his drink, he reached for it again and found his hand somewhat steadier.

"Stonemere, if you are not angry with me, then is there something else you would like to discuss?" Her astute gaze took in far more than he would like. But then she pressed on. "I know today is—or rather would have been—Odey's birthday."

Stone grimaced. She was too perceptive by half. "Indeed. I was just thinking about him." He considered her calm demeanor and soft gaze. "It's strange, since I had not seen him in four or five years before he died, but I miss him terribly some days."

"I do understand. Your brother was the epitome of kindness. Despite neither of us being in love, we were—I like to believe—becoming fast friends."

Before he could reply, Parsons entered the study and announced dinner was served. Stone rose and escorted his wife to the table. The timely interruption helped him recover his equilibrium. It was both a relief and perhaps a bit of a boon to learn Theo had not been in love with his brother. The more pressing concern was what he would do with his headstrong wife. How did one rein in a woman without entirely crushing her spirit?

What did one wear to take tea with not one, but *two* notorious madams?

Theo considered her options. She rejected the yellow jonquil with the adorable bolero jacket, as it was too innocent. She wanted to put forth an air of worldliness. The red silk walking dress was too bold, too over the top for the occasion. Then she spied her navy silk walking dress with the military-cut jacket, complete with epaulettes.

That was precisely the image she wanted to convey. Responsible, worldly, and intrepid enough to seduce a former rake. Mary worked on piling her hair into an intricate chignon, then helped her dress for tea.

An hour later, Theo sat across from Marie and Madame du Pompadour with Lizzy on her right. Madame smiled and patiently sipped her bergamot-infused tea. "So, I understand you are in need of a certain type of assistance."

"Indeed. As Marie likely explained, my husband is, or was, a member of the Lustful Lords. I find myself in the odd position of needing to learn how to entertain him so I may be sure he does not stray. I have come to realize his fidelity is important to me."

"As I am well acquainted with the group of gentlemen you refer to, I believe I can be of assistance." Madame nodded confidently.

"How should we proceed?" Theo's stomach twisted in knots, which made even nibbling the tiny cucumber sandwich in her hand nigh impossible.

Madame eyed her speculatively. "First I must know how participatory you wish to be in your training."

Theo had to consciously remind herself to close her mouth. "Are you asking if I wish to take the reins, so to speak?" She couldn't control the heat that scorched her cheeks.

"Indeed. Do you wish to engage in your instruction or simply observe?"

"Observe, please. I doubt my husband would appreciate any practical tutoring provided by someone else."

"You are a shrewd woman, Lady Stonemere. Most men would object outright to any such notion. Very well, I shall arrange for you to have a guided tour through the various experiences The Market offers. Someone who can answer your questions and perhaps determine the best way to implement what you see in the course of your husband's seduction shall act as escort."

"Thank you, Madame. How soon might you be able to arrange my lesson?"

"We'll start with your first lesson on Friday evening. If you will arrive through the rear entrance just before one in the morning, there should be sufficient activity to suffice. After your lesson, we can discuss any further lessons you might desire."

"Will my point of observation be private?" Theo wavered at the thought of being seen in such a place.

"I shall provide a mask to protect your identity. Some portions of your tour will be from behind a glass wall, and others will take you into the room."

"Very well. I shall see you Friday." Theo turned to Marie. "Thank you for arranging this meeting. I can't tell you how much this means to me."

Marie rose and hugged Theo. "I fear I've grown soft in my own happiness and wish everyone to know the joy I share with Heart in and out of the bedroom."

Stone wandered out of his library in search of his wife, who was nowhere to be found. "Parsons." A niggling feeling of concern for her had taken hold and would not permit him to focus on his correspondence.

His butler appeared and then bowed. "Yes, my lord?"

"Do you know where my wife has gone off to?" Stone resisted the urge to pace the entry hall.

"I believe she is out visiting, my lord."

"When is she expected to return?"

"She did not say, my lord."

"Blast it. I swear I need to keep a private investigator on staff simply to keep up with her whereabouts." The same tingling across his neck that had saved him in battle on more than one occasion had him on edge. The one time he'd failed to heed the warning had ended in a disaster that still haunted him.

Parsons remained silent, offering no comment.

"When she returns, please let me know immediately." The helplessness ate at him, made him restless.

"Very good, my lord."

Stone retreated to his study. There was nothing in particular he could point to, just some sixth sense that gave him pause. Once she was home, he could speak to her about her day. If that failed to provide anything, then he could query the coachman.

An hour later, Parsons alerted him—rather unnecessarily—of his wife's return. As the butler departed the study, Theo burst in looking very chic in her military-cut dress. If the officers had looked like her, the rank and file would have followed them to the ends of the earth. His cock stirred as he imagined peeling off the various layers she wore.

Theo was up to something. He needed to focus on where she'd been, not what he'd like to take off her. "There you are."

She smiled an overbright smile that screamed she hid something. "Were you looking for me?"

"Indeed, I was. I wanted to confirm our schedule for the week."

"We have the Swinton soiree tonight and the Rawley ball Friday evening, should you wish to join me."

"I believe I am engaged to play cards Friday evening, but I imagine I can make time to waltz with you once or twice before departing." He offered up his attendance to see if she reacted.

"Perfect. I shall look forward to dancing with you." She lowered her lashes.

Was she hiding something from him? If she were any other woman, he would consider it flirtatious or even demure behavior. "And did you have a nice afternoon?"

"I did." Her evasive answer bothered him.

"Well, good." He had nothing else to prod her with. Damn. It seemed he would have to question the coachman.

She shot him a wary glance and bid him a good afternoon.

Stone retreated to his study just after dinner. Theo was occupied with dressing for the Swinton party, so he sent for the coachman.

"My lord." The driver bowed.

"Mr. Brown, where did you drive my wife today?" Anticipation skated over him like a swarm of flies. Now he would come to some truth. He had to if he was to protect her, and there was no longer any doubt he would protect her. She belonged to him and had rapidly become as necessary to his existence as breathing. It was an uncomfortable notion, to say the least. And not one he was prepared to examine at any length for the moment.

"I drove her to Carlisle House, where we collected Lady Carlisle, and then we drove to a home at Sixty-Nine Mayfair, my lord." The man shifted from foot to foot as though preparing to dash away at a moment's notice.

"Who did they meet with?"

"I do not know, my lord. Lady Stonemere merely bade me wait for her."

"How long was she in the house?" Stone slowly worked on releasing the muscles clamped tight along his jaw. His lovely, vivacious wife would not have taken a lover. Not only had she been innocent on their wedding night, but she was too honorable to violate their vows. He drew a breath. This must be some scheme to help an underprivileged group in some way that was wholly inappropriate.

"Perhaps an hour, my lord. Then we drove to Bond Street, where the ladies shopped, after which we drove Lady Carlisle home."

It was an answer, but not the answer Stone needed. "Very good, Mr. Brown. Thank you."

The driver bowed and fled the study. Stone made a note of the address and decided he would meet his wife at the soiree. He needed to make a stop on the way. After dashing off a quick note, he handed it to Parsons for his wife. Then he stepped outside to hail a hansom cab.

In short order, he found himself knocking on the door of the home his wife had visited earlier that day. The door opened, admitting him without hesitation, and then he was shown to the front parlor by a well-appointed butler. A few moments later, the woman he had once known as Madame Marie Marchander entered the room.

Stone's heart flip-flopped in his chest.

How did Theo know the madam-turned-baroness? Dear God, what had the woman told his wife about his sordid past? Heart racing, he rose, as good manners dictated.

"I wondered how long it would take you to appear on my doorstep. How are you, Stonemere? You look a bit pale." She greeted him with a kiss on each cheek. "It has been too long since I last saw you."

"I am well, Marie. However, I am curious how you know my wife?" Stone had no time to waste with niceties.

Marie laughed. "I see you have decided to get straight to the point. Through her sister. We've all of us become quite close."

Stone swore he would disgrace himself on the spot with the most uncharacteristic, unmanly behavior imaginable.

He was going to faint.

Instead, he sat down and drew a slow, steady breath. "How close?"

"Never fear, you dear man. Your past is safe enough with me."

Relief swept over him like warm sunshine.

"However, your reputation precedes you. While I may not have revealed anything, the Ton does love its gossip. I suggest you consider opening up to your wife before she learns the rather erotic details from another source."

"No. The others will not tell. There is no need to shock my innocent wife with tales of my lust-driven past." Stone couldn't imagine a more horrid scenario than explaining his sexual preferences to his innocent wife.

"Might I suggest you rethink that notion? It may be a course of what she sees and not what she hears."

Stone tensed, muscles locked as though he'd been dosed with a paralytic. "What might she see?"

"Stone, I tender your wife the same promise of confidence I offer you. Speak to her if you want answers. Now, I must bring this interview to a close. My husband awaits me so we may be off for the night."

"But, Marie. You must tell me." Anxiety coiled around his chest like some mythical dragon tail.

"I shall not. Go speak to your wife if you wish answers." Marie rose and left him sitting there awash in a mix of fear and worry. With a shake, he cut loose his fanciful thoughts and departed Marie's home. He had a soiree to attend.

Stone flagged down a cab and climbed in after giving the driver the Swintons' direction. Marie's warnings drifted about in his head like flotsam. The driver must have taken the long route, or perhaps he simply couldn't stand to be alone with his thoughts? He lifted the curtain, peered out the window of the vehicle, and frowned as he noticed the neighborhood looked shabby and ill-kempt. The Swintons had not moved, last he heard, and if they had, they'd not be hosting a function. His focus shifted from his disconcerting wife to the disconcerting number of incidents he had survived of late. His cab ride could possibly seem more than a mere run of bad luck if he were a more suspicious person. One might even think someone was targeting him.

While it seemed a bit far-fetched, it did appear as though he had a choice to make: see the destination at the end of his detour, or find an escape route. All things considered, he did not relish standing up his wife, and he still couldn't ascribe his run-ins as more than poor timing on his part. Determined to exit the cab as unobtrusively as possible, he checked the door and was not surprised to find it locked from the outside. With a sigh, he angled himself on the edge of the seat and used his foot to jostle the door open with one solid kick to the lock.

There was still enough street traffic that once he popped out of the carriage, he was able to slip into the flow of people and make his way back in the right direction. Once he'd walked for a while, he decided the chances of being snatched twice in one day were pretty low, even considering his recent luck. He hailed a new hansom cab and made his way to the Swinton residence. He had a wife to see and more questions than answers where she was concerned.

Chapter Eleven

T heo sat in the back row of seating for the Swintons' soiree. Where could Stone be? He had departed the house, leaving her another hasty note that told her little about what caused his unexpected departure. Had he discovered that the Swinton affair was a musicale? He had insisted early on there would be no musicales on their social calendar. As a result, she had resorted to omitting such facts when she described the various invitations they received. There would be too many missed events if she adhered to his demands. It simply wasn't done.

But still he had not arrived. Had something happened to one of his friends? Or perhaps his mother? The dowager countess had only recently come out of mourning, and at her age, anything could happen. No, his note had indicated he would join her that evening. Still, she'd been disappointed not to make her grand entrance in her new gown. The sapphire color with navy trim was simple but elegant, with pleated edges, a vee-shaped neckline, and an overlap detail on the skirt that created a wrapped effect. Without a doubt, it was her new favorite when paired with her sapphire necklace. And her husband's conspicuous absence had her forgetting about her clothing and worrying about him.

"Lizzy where could Stone be?" she whispered as the first performer took her seat at the piano.

"He'll come. No need to worry pointlessly." Lizzy turned to listen to yet another halting rendition of Beethoven's "Moonlight Sonata."

Theo repressed the sigh that strained to escape. Then a warm presence settled into the empty seat on her right. Startled, she looked up to see her husband's dark countenance. He said nothing as he stared at her with a mixture of brooding worry, confusion, and a spark of anger. Annoyance over her omission of the nature of the evening's events should not have resulted in such a swirling mix of emotions.

Something was wrong.

But then his gaze drifted over her gown and the stones at her neck, and his expression cleared. He reached over to pluck her hand from her lap and tuck it under his arm. It was as if he'd pulled off a mask and replaced it with a more pleasing version. Theo was mystified.

They sat—suffered, if her husband was to be believed—through six more mediocre performances of voice and instrument. Once the gathering was free to move about, he guided her into the gardens for a breath of fresh air.

"Good evening, Theo." His gaze roamed over her person in an intimate caress.

"Hello, Stone. Where did you run off to tonight? As I recall, we were to arrive together." Curiosity got the better of her. If he dubbed her a nosy harpy, then so be it.

"You remember the Earl of Brougham? He requested I join him at White's for a bit. He came across some investment information he thought would interest me."

"Really, Stone. And you'd have me believe such information would compel you to rush off and leave me a cryptic note in explanation?" She arched a brow in disbelief. "Honestly, if you do not wish to tell me where you went, you simply need only say so."

He sighed. "Very well, I had an urgent errand to run, and I do not wish to discuss it."

"There, now, was that so hard?" Though still curious to the point of agitation, she was much happier with the honesty of his latter statement than the untruth of the former.

"No, in truth, it wasn't." He hesitated as though considering something. "Theo—"

"There you are, Lady Stonemere." Lady Swinton glided into the garden. "We are organizing a second round of music. Would you honor us with a song?"

Theo flushed. Dear God, was the woman mad? Obviously, the marchioness had never heard her sing, which wasn't surprising since she *did not* sing in public.

"Oh—Lady Swinton, I—" Theo pressed her fingertips to her temple in distress.

Stone intervened, to Theo's relief. "Lady Swinton, I'm afraid my wife is not feeling just the thing. I brought her outside for a breath of fresh air. If you will excuse us, I believe I shall escort her home."

"I am sorry to hear you are not well. Of course, you should retire for the evening. My cook has a wonderful tisane I simply could not live without. May I fetch the recipe for you?"

Theo winced. "That is very generous of you, my lady. However, Mrs. Beats has her own recipe she swears by. I can only imagine the uproar if I appeared with another formula."

Lady Swinton nodded sagely. "Too true. Staff can be so difficult to manage at times. Well, off with you. Perhaps next time you might honor us with a performance."

"I shall consider it," Theo demurred and latched on to her husband's arm. Whereupon he ushered her into the house and out through the front door.

Safely tucked into their carriage and headed home, Theo tried to study her husband by moonlight. In the last hour, he had swung wildly from dark and brooding to pleasant and amenable to solicitous and caring. Her head spun with the effort to keep up with him. "Thank you for intervening with Lady Swinton."

"It was clear if she had pressed, you would have been forced to do something drastic, like fake your death. Am I to understand you are not musically accomplished?"

She couldn't see him very well as the moon had slipped away into the dark, but she could hear the smile in his voice. "I daresay I am an accomplished assassin of all things musical. And yes, faking my death was a consideration." Theo couldn't suppress her mirth.

"Well then, as your husband and protector, it was my duty to save you from such drastic measures. What remains to be seen is how you shall escape in future."

The carriage pulled to a halt. "Why, don't you see the obvious solution?"

"I'm afraid I don't." Stone exited the vehicle and turned to help her.

"I shall not attend any musicales in future." Theo grinned and swept past her husband to enter Denton House.

His chuckle followed her into the house.

His wife was full of surprises. Perhaps she would understand his sullied past? Perhaps she even shared some of his proclivities? The notion appeared so far-fetched, he discarded it before it even fully formed. No, things were best left as they were. Even if she had become aware of his history, there was no reason to air the details and potentially embarrass her. Or worse, repulse her.

Upstairs, they retreated to their separate rooms. Once naked, he slipped his robe on and approached his wife's chamber. Sinking his cock into her depths might go a long way toward easing his concerns and doubts.

She called out for him to enter, and he found her in a delectable state of dishabille. With her hair tumbled about her shoulders, her chemise proved the only barrier to her many charms. And there, still encircling her neck, were the sapphires he had given her. Yes, tupping his wife would ease his concerns. Or so he hoped.

From where he stood, he beckoned her over with the curling of one digit, which she responded to effortlessly. "Remove my robe."

A silent nod preceded the requested action. Nude beneath the now-missing garment, he watched as her gaze roved over his chest and then lower. Her breath hitched in the sweetest demonstration of his effect on her. Then her hands followed the path her gaze had traveled, punctuated by the occasional press of her lips to his skin.

Desire flared through him. "Wife, I do not think I can be gentle tonight."

"I don't recall asking you to be gentle, husband." She continued to explore his body, pausing here and there to caress each battle-carved scar that pocked his skin.

He wanted to push her away from the sight, but her touch was so sweet, he could not make himself end the delicious torture. Not yet.

"What have you done to your body?" Her concern poked at the soft spot deep in his core.

How did she slip past his hardened defenses so easily? He groaned as she kissed and nipped at his stomach, then down his hips. When her hand wrapped around his turgid length, his hips pumped forward in an instinctive twitch. He shook with the desire to push his cock past her honeyed lips and thrust into the source of such sweetness.

The first swipe of her tongue caused his heart to stop and restart. Never had he imagined his wife doing such a thing. It was scandalous enough that he had kissed her so intimately, but he had not anticipated such reciprocation. Then he thought no more as her mouth opened wide and covered the tip of him.

He moaned. "Oh God. Feels. So. Good."

And with each word of encouragement, she pushed lower onto his shaft, taking more of him into her warm, wet mouth. Then her hands decided to explore. Her dainty fingers trailed down to his inner thigh and over his stones. The flicker of sensation jolted him, and he fisted his hands, all the while curbing the desire to sink them in her silky hair. Because once there, he would hold her head as he pumped into her mouth in a debased mimicry of sex.

His body hummed with a need he could not have prepared himself to control. In a last-ditch effort, he pushed her away from his cock, felt the loss of her heat when she was pried off the tip. She dropped to the floor, where she lay sprawled in surprise. Wild with the need to be inside her, to mark her, he flipped her over onto her hands and knees, knelt behind her as he shoved her chemise up, and plowed into her from behind like the animal he knew himself to be.

He gave the beast some leash and thrust into her over and over again until the slap of flesh on flesh punctuated by an occasional grunt was the only sound to be heard. He gripped her hips and buried himself deep with each long stroke. She moaned and pushed back into his hips as her form started to shake. Her climax slammed through her and reverberated into him as her channel clutched at his cock in a fierce paroxysm.

Their bodies slickened with sweat as he pounded into her until she was spent and could barely hold herself up. Then he allowed his orgasm to take him over the edge. Pleasure zipped up from his balls to his fingers and toes, causing them to curl. With each pulse of his climax, he howled with pleasure as he came deep inside her. His limbs still tingled with the effects of his release as he lay with his chest plastered to Theo's back and struggled to catch his breath.

Once reality pierced his lustful haze, he cursed silently. What had he done to his wife? How would she ever forgive him for treating her so roughly? He withdrew from her quim and helped her find her legs as she stood. When he saw the rug burns on her hands and knees, he could not contain his self-disgust.

"Oh Christ, Theo. What have I done to you?" he muttered, and then hefted her into his arms. He deposited her on the bed and helped her slip between the sheets.

"Stone? It was lovely what you did." And then she drifted off to sleep, exhausted from such strenuous lovemaking.

And it was all his fault. The baseness of his needs and the desire to control, to dominate his partner. His wife. He was a wretched man unfit for a woman as fine as she. And with her attempt to ease his fears, she confirmed he was also corrupting her with his taint. Women like Theo were not raised to be handled so forcefully, but they were taught to accept their husband's demands. Her willingness to accept his rough treatment must be some corruption stemming from him. She certainly wouldn't actually enjoy such attentions.

He strode from her bedroom and shut himself away in his chamber. He shook with the realization that he could not control his lusts enough to make proper love to his wife in a dignified manner. In an attempt to claim her, to allay his own fears, he had instead opened Pandora's box.

Chapter Twelve

T heo hesitated at the top of the stairs on her way down to the breakfast room. She ached everywhere—her knees, her thighs, and deep in her core, where she was sure Stone had left his brand on her body. The stairs were daunting, but she smiled and pushed through. Weakness was not to be tolerated. She'd loved every minute of her night with her husband. How he'd let her explore the terrain of his frame, then flipped her over, and finally shoved into her body. Her center heated and softened at the memory.

The first step down resulted in a medley of aches flickering to life. Her legs seized and her breath stalled. After that, each step got easier as she worked the kinks out of her muscles. Finally, at the bottom, she swept into the morning room to find it deserted. Double damn. She had been disappointed to wake in the dark of night alone. But she had cheered herself with the notion of sharing a cozy breakfast.

She had been thwarted, and it was not an experience she relished.

Her frustration had simmered as she sat down to breakfast, but by the time she ate and set out to run her errands, she had pushed her turmoil aside. And when she stood outside her pride and joy—the one thing in all her life that she she'd done right—nothing else mattered.

The children who were fortunate enough to have found their way to The Benevolent Foundling Home for Boys and Girls were those who had been thrown away by Society or otherwise forgotten. Usually, Mrs. Richter, her headmistress, got word of a child in need, but occasionally one simply appeared on their doorstep. Theo had once considered establishing a board to help fundraise and otherwise oversee the home, but every time she attended a function thrown by the women of Society, she knew it would be a mistake. So, she continued to sponsor the home herself, and thanks to a number of wise investments, she had more than enough to cover the home in addition to her other personal expenses.

A boy scampered across the paltry space they called a yard and tripped over a small bush he couldn't see as he tried to catch a ball. Theo took a step toward him, worried he might have injured himself, when he popped up from the ground with the ball in hand. "I caught it, you blighter! You owe me half your dinner portions tonight."

Mrs. Richter walked out in time to hear the boy's announcement, and his foul language. "Jimmy, we'll not have such talk here. And Harry will eat his own portions. Neither of you have need of more."

The two boys looked at her, one with a smile and the other looking very put out. Theo had to work hard to curb her amusement.

"Lady Stonemere!" Mrs. Richter spotted her standing on the sidewalk and bustled over.

For a moment, Theo wasn't sure to whom she was speaking. She was still adjusting to her new title, as well as to her new husband. "Good morning, Mrs. Richter. I see the children are doing well."

"Indeed, they are. Quite well, in fact. Our younger class is inside having lessons while the older children are exercising off some energy." She took Theo's arm, and they started toward the front steps of the house.

But Theo stopped their progress. She couldn't help but stare across the fence at the open land that remained unused. "Has Mr. Hafferty had any visitors by to look at his land, by chance?"

Mrs. Richter shook her head. "I and the staff have kept an eagle eye for visitors, but nobody comes by but the caretaker once a month."

"I promise, Mrs. Richter. I will get that land for us. I am bound and determined those children will have an open area to run and play where there aren't hazardous bushes and too little space."

"I know you will, Lady Stonemere. Perhaps now with your new title, he'll consider your offer?"

Theo grinned. "What a capital idea! I shall take another run at the old goat today. Now, tell me how the children are doing. Are the new clothes holding up better?"

As promised, on her way home, Theo made a point to stop by the Hafferty Brothers' Mercantile. How two brothers who barely spoke could work together escaped her, but somehow they managed to do just that. She spotted the elder Hafferty brother directing the shop assistant on a ladder against the wall of shelves. He was assisting a customer, so she simply smiled and waved at him as she went in search of the younger Hafferty. Although she thought of them as older and younger, they were both ancient by anyone's standards.

Determination pushed her forward as she approached the younger brother, the one she'd labeled an old goat. "Good afternoon, Mr. Hafferty."

The old man looked up at her, a smile flitting about his lips until he recognized her. "You again. Lady Lawton—"

Drawing up to her haughtiest tone, one she'd heard her mother use with unruly staff, she stared the man down. "If you don't mind, it is Lady Stonemere now."

He frowned at her interruption. "Young lady, I would not care if you were the queen herself. I am not selling that land to you."

Frustrated beyond good manners, Theo demanded, "Whyever not? I have made you a fair offer. Is my money not good enough for you?"

The old goat snorted. "Women have no business doing business. They belong at home. I will not sell to you or your man of affairs. My ridiculous brother may choose to encourage such hoydenish behavior, but I shall not. Besides, he had no business selling our family home."

"Mr. Hafferty, it is not as if I tore your family home down. I have repurposed it, filled it with children, laughter, and love."

The old man's face turned beet red. "You have filled it with rabble."

"Have you no heart? They are children!" Theo turned on her heel and stormed from the store, frustrated that he refused to sell to her for such heartless and chauvinistic reasons.

Furious that she would never be able to give her children the space to run and play, she stomped into her carriage and ordered the driver to take her home. She was in no mood to make social calls or shop.

Stone sat at his desk working his way through the stacks of correspondence that came with his duties in Parliament. Theo had been home only a few days, but her presence was often felt in the house. Today turned out to be no different. The front door slammed shut with a furious *bang* and then his wife barged into his study. For minutes, she said nothing directly to him. Instead, she simply paced the floor and muttered to herself until she stopped and drew a deep breath. "Why is it that men see women as little more than domestics?"

Stone stopped and considered his wife for a moment. "While I know some men treat women as though they have little intelligence and even less intrinsic value, I suggest that not all men treat women in that way. If you could offer a bit more detail as to your particular situation, perhaps I could offer more valuable insight into the male mind."

Theo nodded and primly took a seat across from where he sat. "Very well. As you must be aware after the marriage contracts, I own a home and small piece of land that houses an orphanage. Next to the home is another plot of land that once was a single parcel. I was able to purchase the house and land at an excellent value; however, the owner of the other half of the land refuses to sell to me."

"And I assume you are given to understand that the reason this person refuses to sell to you is because of your sex?"

"He has explicitly stated this as well as a family squabble as the reasons he will not sell." Theo's anger seemed to be fading with the sharing of her problem. The deep wrinkles in her forehead were smoothing out, and her jaw seemed to be less tense.

"In my experience, everyone has a price. Have you tried offering him an amount well above fair market price?" Stone would have certainly doubled the fair value if he wanted the land badly enough. From across the desk, the sound of a sniffle drew his attention. His wife dabbed at watery eyes that, while not filled outright with tears, proved she was far more emotional about this piece of business than he had initially suspected.

"I cannot afford to offer him such an amount. If I were to do so, there would be nothing left to fund the orphanage for the rest of the year. And, on general principle, I shouldn't have to pay more merely because I am a woman."

"I would suggest you have to pay more merely because you do not possess the land in question. Can you not fundraise for the monies needed for the annual budget of the orphanage?"

"I do not wish to have a bunch of pinch-faced Society women making my orphans unhappy. Inevitably, when boards are formed and Society ladies take over, the object of their charity suffers from an overwhelming barrage of rules and expectations. By sponsoring the home myself, I can ensure it is run with love and care and the children are allowed to be what they are: children."

"I see. Well, it seems you and the land owner are at an impasse. I could certainly offer to help make up the difference in cost if you were willing to accept my assistance."

She paused for a moment or two, most likely considering his offer, but then shook her head. "I shall find another way to accomplish this. I do appreciate your offer, Stonemere. But this is an endeavor I began on my own, and I shall finish it that way."

"As you wish, but should you change your mind, the offer stands." Stone found himself curious to see how she might turn the rather hopeless situation in her favor. He sincerely doubted the man who had refused her offer knew the lengths his wife might go to in order to accomplish a thing.

In fact, he truly didn't know, and now his curiosity bade him to watch the situation more closely. Perhaps it would be good if he knew exactly what his wife was up against. He assumed she was dealing with an old-timer who did not share his more modern views of the world and women. But just to be safe, he decided to have his man of affairs poke about a bit. Ensure Theodora wasn't dealing with a more sinister character.

"Thank you, again, for the offer, and for listening. I'm not normally so easily thwarted, but that man seems to be able to twist me up just so." She glanced at the clock on the shelf nearby. "It is getting late. I should go check on dinner and change. I shall see you then."

"Indeed." He rose as his wife departed. Who would have known that the woman who seemed so retiring initially would turn out to be such...a brick? He couldn't think of another term that fit his wife so aptly. Every day she offered him a new facet to her, a new piece to the puzzle. A strange sense of contentment settled over him.

Stone arrived at Carlisle House early Friday morning. Morning visits were not due to start for another hour, but he harbored little concern. The question of his wife's adventures and the possibility she might discover more about his licentious past gnawed at him. He and Carlisle had been acquainted prior to their connection by marriage, and as embarrassing as the whole scenario might be, he needed to lean on his brother-in-law's ability to compel his wife to reveal what occurred at Lady Heartfield's home the day before.

He was shown into the library and left to stew for half an hour. His own fault, of course. He could have sent a note over warning of his visit, but something told him his quarry would slip away if he did so. Instead, he waited, until finally, the Marquess of Carlisle appeared. "Good morning, Stonemere. To what do I owe the pleasure of this early-morning visit?" One black brow rose toward his hairline, adding an edge to Carlisle's already stern features. The man barely topped six feet in height, but his barrel chest and thick arms lent him a menacing quality that Stone was sure his tailors worked very hard to counteract, though with little success.

Stone drew a calming breath. "My apologies for the hour, but I have need of your assistance in eliciting some information from your wife about her whereabouts yesterday while in my wife's company. I fear without your help, I shall be shut out of some pertinent details." Stone eyed the decanter of scotch. Just a sip might ease his nerves.

"Well, I am sure Lizzy will be happy to assist if there is something of concern. I'll have her join us." He tugged on the bell pull and, once a footman appeared, sent him off to retrieve the lady of the house.

She appeared dressed for an outing, her paletot and bonnet on. He'd been spot-on; she was looking to escape.

"Yes, Carlisle." She stepped inside the door but did not cross to join them. "I was just on my way out."

"Lord Stonemere had a question or two for you. Could you stay a moment?" Carlisle gestured at the companion chair to the one Stone occupied.

Theo's sister stood in the doorway for a moment before resignation wiped the smile from her face. "Of course. How may I be of assistance?" She removed her bonnet while she took the seat and peered at Stone with a daunting innocence considering his intended line of questioning.

"I believe you accompanied my wife to call on Lady Heartfield yesterday. I wanted to know who else attended your visit." He decided to drill right to the heart of the matter.

Lady Carlisle blushed and stared at her hands. The silence stretched out until Carlisle had enough. "Lizzy, whom did you see yesterday?"

Theo's sister gasped and glanced up to lock gazes with her husband. Stone recognized the unspoken command he had given his wife. The immediate shift of power was both electrifying and heady to watch. It made him wonder if Lizzy's sister might be as susceptible. He had seen inklings of such obedience, but he had not dared to believe it a real response. It seemed far more likely he'd imagined that which he wanted to see.

"Carlisle." She paled. "Please." Her plea was a mere whisper.

"Dear, it will be best if you answer now." The unspoken discussion of the punishment to come settled heavy in the silence.

"Yes, my lord." She turned to face Stonemere. "We met with Madame du Pompadour."

Carlisle emitted an outraged gasp as Stone's breath caught in his chest. Good God, he was doomed. "About, what?"

The woman blushed profusely and dropped her gaze. "Th-Theo arranged to have a tutorial i-in all things erotic."

Carlisle groaned as Stone continued his attempts to breathe.

Carlisle asked the next obvious question. "Lizzy, when and where is this tutorial to occur?"

"Tonight, at The Market." Her murmur stabbed Stone deep in the heart, deep in that soft core he tried to protect.

"What is this lesson to consist of?" Stone managed to rasp the question out from between clenched teeth.

"Oh, she is only planning to watch, my lord. She specifically insisted she would not want to engage in anything...physical."

"And what is the purpose of all this? Why is she having a tutorial?" Stone wanted the answer, and yet terror of the truth stole his breath and made his heart gallop.

Lady Carlisle stared at him, her brow creased with confusion. "Why else would a married woman wish to learn such things?" She glanced from one man to the other, and Carlisle looked as lost as he felt. "To seduce her husband."

And with that simple statement, air returned to his lungs, blood returned to his extremities with a tingling rush of sensation, and the wheels of his brain clicked back into working order. To seduce him? Priceless.

He grappled to find a reasonable response. On one hand, the fury that she would go into such an establishment alone scorched the pain of the perceived betrayal. On the other, it was a heady experience to realize she wished to seduce him. That his wife desired him so much, she would put forth such an effort. Should he paddle her or reward her? Perhaps both before the night concluded. "Thank you, Carlisle, Lady Carlisle. I believe I have intruded enough on your morning."

"I'm sure you can find the way out." Carlisle rose from his seat behind his desk, circled around to where his wife sat, and placed a hand on her shoulder to keep her from rising or fleeing, Stone surmised.

"Quite. One last thing... Can you please ensure your wife does not inform my own of this meeting?"

"Consider it done." Carlisle turned to the diminutive woman who sat with strength and pride radiating from her, defiant to the end, much like her sister.

"Good day." Stone turned to leave.

As he departed, he caught the steely order from man to woman. "Bend over the desk and lift your skirts, Lizzy."

Stone imagined having an identical conversation with his own wife in the near future. But first, he needed to visit Madame Celeste du Pompadour.

It took a mere twenty minutes to reach The Market due to its convenient location. Settled near Maple Park, slightly north of Oxford Street, it was quite easy for its clientele to reach. Stone had his driver drop him around back and then knocked on the kitchen door.

A maid opened the door and promptly let her jaw flop open upon finding a gentleman and not a delivery boy. "My lord?"

"I need to see Madame du Pompadour immediately." He stepped inside, pushing past the dumbstruck wench.

"But she's asleep, my lord."

"Wake her. This is of the utmost urgency." Stone started toward the front of the house. "I shall await her in the main salon."

"Yes, my lord." The girl scurried off to find her mistress as he went in the direction of said room.

Twenty minutes later, in elegant dishabille, Celeste appeared. "Lord Stonemere. I should have guessed it was you." She grinned and sat down on the chaise across from him.

"Celeste, I am here about my wife."

She chuckled. "Quite a little hoyden you married yourself to."

Stone ground his teeth. "Be that as it may, you must call this evening off."

"No, I do believe she—and you—will benefit from tonight's lessons."

"This is unacceptable. I cannot have my wife parading around an establishment such as this. She would be ruined." Stone rose from where he sat and paced the length of the room.

"Please, Stone, do give me some credit for protecting the innocent when possible. Your wife will arrive masked, in a hack, and then enter through the back door. She will be escorted through the private hallways and provided a view via the various windows we have for such pleasures." She paused, drew a breath.

"I was going to give her the option of watching in person in the Bacchanalian room, but I can see from your rather piercing glare that I should rethink such an offer."

"You're bloody right you will rethink such an option. I shall not allow her to be here unescorted. I shall act as her guard."

"Good heavens, do you think she will be ravaged upon entering my establishment? I assure you, I only allow such games with known participants who are willing and eager for aforesaid play. As I recall, you should know this since you have participated in the ravishing of similar participants." She raised a brow.

"You know too much for my own good."

"When you join The Market, you are assured confidentiality in your private business. Even had your wife asked me about your past liaisons—and she did not—I would not tell her anything I knew."

Stone sighed. He'd not meant to question Celeste's integrity.

"But I would strongly recommend you consider revealing the nature of your past in relation to this establishment. It is not uncommon knowledge, and were she to hear it from someone else or see something that might raise questions, you would not appreciate the outcome, I think."

"I'll consider your counsel. Now, about tonight. I shall come dressed for the role, masked and all. What time should I arrive?"

"No later than half past midnight. She will be here a quarter hour after that."

"I intend to take my wife home to deal with her. However, nothing ever goes as planned where she is concerned. Can you have the blue room with the spanking bench available should I need a private place?"

"Of course, my lord. The Market would be happy to accommodate you and your wife this evening." Celeste gave a regal tilt of her head, no simpering miss there. No, she had blossomed into a stunning woman, and wore the mantle of madame with panache.

"I shall see you tonight, then." He nodded and departed The Market. He loathed the deception required, but refused to allow Theo to venture down this path without some protection. Certainly, he could lock her in her room tonight, confront her, and forbid her attendance. But then his lovely wife would not speak to him. And he damned well liked hearing her talk. He liked the things she said, he liked the things she did with her mouth, and he wasn't ready to give all those up in a single idiotic move.

No, far better to indulge her curiosity while being able to control the situation. Then at home, he could raise the issue of her lack of trust in discussing such things with him. Of course, that would make him a brilliant hypocrite, but there you had it. He should confess his sordid past, yet he wasn't sure he could. Perhaps after tonight, he might find the stones to do so.

Chapter Thirteen

F riday came much faster than Theo had expected. If her choice of gowns for tea with two madames had been difficult, it was absolutely unnerving to select a gown to wear to a brothel.

After considering her options, she decided to go with a frock of deep red, almost a maroon, trimmed with black edging and bearing a simple pleated hem of organza. The gown offered a delicious dip into a vee above her breasts and pretended at modesty with a matching organza fichu, a bit of fabric she could easily remove with a precise yank before entering The Market.

Satisfied with her choice, she rang for Mary and gave her directions for her evening wear, which included the deep-hooded cloak she usually wore in late fall. Mary simply curtsied and took off to see to her duties.

Theo sipped her tea and worked to quash the flare of guilt that attempted to rear its head. Despite her husband's enthusiastic activity two nights prior, she remained certain something wasn't quite right. Why had he disappeared after their intimacy? Why was she always left with the sensation she was on the cusp of discovering something truly wonderful?

There was no room for doubt. Doubt would not ensure her husband's undying love and fidelity. Doubt was a dream killer, and she refused to let her dream of marital bliss die.

Resolved to follow through on her plan for the evening, she rose and prepared for the evening to come. By the next day, she would be ready to launch her campaign of seduction.

Stone remained unaware, but a war would be waged, and she would be the victor.

After a flurry of activity to get ready, she found Stone waiting at the bottom of the stairs. He watched her with an eagle eye as she descended to his side.

"You look particularly enchanting this evening." He bowed over her hand.

"As do you, Stone. Well, I should say—you do look dashing this evening." Goodness, she needed to pull herself together. She hadn't fumbled so badly in front of him since they were practically strangers. Why should she now?

"Shall we?" He held out his arm, and they departed for the Rawley ball. It was mid-Season, and the balls came fast and furious. Everyone tried to outdo one another with the biggest crush of the Season. It was all rather silly, and yet here they were dressed to attend yet another such attempt.

At least she only needed to endure until Stone decamped for his club. After his departure, she could slip away to learn all the things she needed to seduce her husband. Or at least some of the things she needed. She couldn't possibly arrange to disappear like this more than once. Stone was far too observant not to notice such absences.

They rode quietly in the carriage until their turn came to arrive. As each ball became bigger, the lines to arrive grew longer. The long wait made one consider a more pedestrian mode of arrival, if only walking were not so unfashionable and the venues so far. They entered the grand town house and climbed the stairs to the ballroom. After being announced, they entered the ball with enough time to join the first waltz.

Stone took her into his arms and swept her into the dance. She loved to dance with him. He rarely spoke, but led with a firm hand. However, tonight he dispelled the notion that he might not chat.

"And what are your plans for this evening, wife?" A distinct air of speculation tinged his question.

Had he felt her flinch? Damn, could he know of her post-ball plans? "I would imagine they are much as usual."

He smiled at her. "I shall be departing for my club a little later. Should I send the carriage round to pick you up after?"

"No need to trouble yourself. I am sure I can manage a ride home with Lizzy and Carlisle, or someone else if they are unavailable."

"Very well. Do be careful as you flit about this evening." The music ended, and Stone escorted her off the floor and deposited her with her sister.

Theo was deuced glad to be rid of her husband for the evening. He disappeared into the cardroom, and she knew he would head out shortly from there. As he departed, she turned to see Lizzy looking a bit pale. "Are you unwell, Lizzy?"

"Not at all. How are you tonight?" Lizzy bit her lip, as though nervous.

"Much calmer than I ought to be. I am curious, mostly. I do hope I can glean something useful without having to make multiple visits."

Lizzy gasped. "Theo! I thought this would be just the once."

"As did I, but the more I think on it, the more doubtful I grow about that thought. Honestly, Lizzy, did you learn to dance in one session? To knit in one go? How can I expect to learn"—Theo glanced about them—"all that I need to know in one night?"

Lizzy groaned and pressed her fingers to her temples.

"I shall, of course, do my best, and perhaps it will be enough. But, I reserve the right to continue my studies if needed to accomplish my goal."

"Oh, Theo. I would dare to venture that one trip will be sufficient. Your husband will be quite capable of answering any questions you might have. At least, based on what Carlisle told me, I would expect that to hold true." Lizzy blushed, and Theo was certain it had nothing to do with the warmth of the room.

"What precisely did Carlisle tell you about my husband?"

Lizzy slashed a furtive glance about them, "We had best step onto the balcony, where we aren't likely to be heard—or seen, for that matter."

They made their way through the crowd and stepped into the cool night air. It was brisk but refreshing after the oven-like temperatures of the ballroom. Theo was desperate to know what her sister had to share. "Come on, then. Spill the beans. What did your husband tell you?"

"Well, as you know, Stone was a member of the Lustful Lords. It turns out he was the founder of the wicked little band of men. And it would seem he led them into all things debauched."

Theo wanted to growl at her sister for dragging out the telling of the details. "And?"

"And they all engaged in very naughty things. They have participated in orgies and shared women. Some of them treat the women like slaves, and they make them service them in every way imaginable. Carlisle wouldn't tell me everything, but he did indicate that they often play at The Market. I imagine you might see some of them tonight."

"Oh my. Sharing? Orgies?" Theo whispered the naughty notions and felt the blood drain from her face. To her great mortification, it all rushed to her loins, where it gathered to pulse and throb. Such unspeakable acts, and yet her blood heated at the notion of such behavior.

"Carlisle even mentioned that one of the group was a-a"—Lizzy glanced around again and lowered her voice to a whisper—"sodomite."

"Oh, well. That couldn't be Stone." Despite the cool air, Theo's cheeks heated. But she was certain her husband could not be him. And yet, her curiosity was piqued. What would it look like, two men together? Would she find the vignette stimulating or off-putting? Perhaps she'd find out soon.

"Either way, I would think you will discover quite a lot with this night's business."

"Hmm...it does sound like that would be true." And damn her soul, she looked forward to it all.

Stone arrived at The Market in the nick of time. It seemed as if every man in the cardroom wanted a word with him as he tried to make good his escape. He had just slipped inside the back door and stepped into the shadows when his lovely lady wife appeared.

He could hear voices pitched to a low murmur, and then her cloak was removed. The deep red gown he had deemed lovely earlier suddenly looked indecent as her breasts all but spilled from the neckline. He thought back to when they danced and distinctly recalled a bit of fabric across the vee of the neckline that no longer veiled her cleavage.

While the gown was still conservative for a brothel, he struggled to control his outrage at her wanton display. Her body belonged to him. It was his to bare or cover as he saw fit. And he did not see fit at the moment. She would need to learn that such decisions belonged to him. With a steadying breath, he reminded himself he would be able to intervene should it be necessary.

"Miss Fanny Hill, may I introduce you to Miranda? She will be your guide tonight, and Thor here shall be your protection." Celeste waved at him where he lurked in the shadows.

"Protection? I had not realized I might need such a thing in this place." Theo sounded worried.

"Merely a precaution. You truly have nothing to fear from The Market." Celeste darted a glance at him, and he could almost hear her thoughts about what his wife should fear in terms of him.

"Very well. It is nice to meet you both." She inclined her head. "Please lead the way."

Miranda took her arm, and they entered the bowels of The Market, Stone trailed a few steps behind. Their first stop was a window onto the main salon. "This is where the ladies and gents might meet before retiring upstairs. If you'll watch, you can see the art of flirtation. The bat of the lashes, a deeper lean in that allows a better view of her breasts."

"I'm afraid I don't fully understand. He's my husband; do I need to do such things?" Theo sounded curious and a bit surprised.

"Women often forget that sex, even for men, starts well outside the bedroom. Men enjoy the art of flirtation as much as women do, and in particular when they know where it will lead." Miranda smiled at Theo.

"Ah, so despite all that we are taught by Society, as a wife, I should be teasing my husband. How very enlightening."

The ladies watched, while Stone hovered over them, as women continued to flirt and preen for the men. Soon one gentleman had his hand diving down the bodice of a woman who merely winked at him and seemed to coo as he groped her. Stone watched, indifferent to such blatant displays in what was meant to be a civilized setting.

"We should move on." Miranda led Theo upstairs, and then they exited the back passages to enter the hall of windows. It was the hall set aside for the voyeurs. They went to the first room's viewing area and took a seat. Inside, Stone watched as a man and a woman kissed.

Theo seemed equally as unaffected as he was by the tame display. Even as the man pushed the woman's bodice down and suckled her breasts, it was basic play. He had shown her more adventure in their few couplings.

"This will be the most familiar view tonight. A straightforward display of sexual activity between a man and a woman," Miranda murmured.

They watched on as he moved quickly to thrusting his prick inside her as her legs were tossed up around her ears. "Perhaps we could move on? I believe I am in search of a more advanced education," Theo ventured, and Miranda nodded her agreement.

He resisted the urge to growl at his precocious wife. Next, Stone followed them to a room that revealed a man with two women. This stirred his juices. As they watched, one woman slipped down over his shaft and the other straddled his head. The two faced each other and leaned forward to kiss while the man serviced them from below.

Theo's breath hitched and grew labored as she watched the women kiss and then fondle each other. It was, in fact, affecting Stone in a soon-to-be obvious way. He considered bringing his cloak back over his shoulders to hide the ridge of his erection from her, but then decided it was better she learn how such things affected men.

Chapter Fourteen

T heo found herself torn between burgeoning lust and
  utter discomfort that such a fine specimen of a man
hovered over her as she watched the blatantly erotic displays.
Her husband would be furious if he knew she'd witnessed
such things in the presence of another man. Well, he'd likely
be furious if he knew she was there at all, but needs must.
Under the current circumstances, it had become imperative
she comprehend how to pleasure him and how to keep him
tied to her bed—perhaps even literally, should it be required.

Next, they rose and shifted to another room. There they
watched a man strung up by his wrists as a lash flicked across
his back at the command of a beautifully dark and exotic
woman. "Oh." Theo gasped as they sat down. Her buttocks
tingled with each snap of the whip.

Miranda chuckled. "Do not fear. He is enjoying every
moment of his punishment. Let me explain." Miranda
pointed to the woman wielding the whip. "Miss Lash is an
expert wielder of all whips and paddles. Her subject attends
The Market to be punished for his trespasses each week. He
gives over control to her, admits his wrongs, and takes the
punishment she dictates to help him feel better."

"Does she always whip him?" Theo's voice hitched softly.

"Not always, but mostly. Tonight he must have been very
bad, for she has commanded a round of figging as well as
lashes."

"Figging?" Theo didn't understand.

"See how his cheeks are clenched? Look carefully and
you will see a nub poking out from between. It is ginger

root that has been pared and shaped for insertion into his bum. It causes a fiery burn inside, and as each lash of the cat-o'-nine-tails falls, he can't help but clench tighter around the root, making it burn more."

"A-a-and he likes this?" Who could have imagined a man enjoying such a thing?

"Oh yes. He's quite ecstatic. In fact, I believe you shall see just how much he enjoys it if we tarry a moment more." Miranda nodded toward the display.

Three more lashes fell over his arse, and then he cried out and shook violently. Theo watched, confused, until she saw Miss Lash reach down and pump his rod much as she herself had done to Stone the night before. Only this man ejaculated his seed all over the floor.

Theo could not stop the images of herself in a similar position from popping into her head. And the telltale excitement that percolated inside had her squirming in her seat. Could Miranda tell? What of the brute looming over them?

"On to the next display," Miranda announced, and marched out of the space.

Next, they found a room with a group of men and women. Theo heard the guard grunt behind them as though he disapproved of their viewing such a thing. How ridiculous, considering what they previously witnessed, so she ignored him.

Behind the glass, three men and three women gathered in two groups. One group had a fine-looking fellow with blond hair treating two women much the same way as the earlier display, except, to Theo's shock, one of the women was on the bottom. The other woman straddled her head and ground her pussy against the other's mouth while the man fucked the one on the bottom. It was arousing and outrageous, and Theo made herself tear her eyes away to look at the other group.

Her breath grew labored as she watched the next group of two men, one dark and one lighter. They took turns pushing their cocks into the woman. While one occupied her lower down, the other filled her mouth. This had Theo's thighs rubbing together as her nipples pressed into her chemise and corset. Every shift of her weight, every movement jostled them slightly and sent sparks of desire straight to her hot, wet center.

She whipped out her fan.

Stone watched in silent shock as his sweet, innocent wife took in Linc and Wolf's activities.

Activities he'd once participated in.

Her fan worked hard to cool her pink cheeks as her chest rose and fell. From his vantage point over her shoulder, it appeared her breasts would spill out any moment. He wanted to catch them for her and then squeeze those ripe nipples until she squealed in pained delight.

His cock throbbed inside the tight leather breeches he wore for the occasion. He'd donned an old pirate's costume, sans the accessories, to offer some kind of menacing presence. Covered in black from head to toe, he hid in the shadows of his hood and mask.

But damn his black heart, he wanted to toss Miranda out and bend his wife over so he could take her right there. The idea tempted. Too much so. "Leave us."

Miranda instantly obeyed his command, even as a confused Theo rose to follow her.

"Ah, ah, ahhh. You, my sweet, will stay where you are." He pitched his voice lower than normal, adding a soft Irish lilt. But the steel tone of command remained, and his wife obeyed. So, she was not so unlike her sister, then. Hope burned within his chest right where he had been told his heart should be.

"Please excuse me, but I really should go." Theo again tried to rise and leave.

"You have been a very naughty girl, haven't you?" He blocked her departure.

"Me?" she squeaked.

"Yes you, pet. You have been a very bad girl. Does your husband know where you are?"

Even by the low lighting in the viewing room, he could see that she paled. "W-who are you?"

"Who I am is not important now. Please address the question. Does your husband *know* where you are?"

"No." She choked on the word.

"What would he say if he knew you were in a place such as this?" Stone didn't have to work hard to convey his displeasure.

"H-he might be angry. But I swear it was well intentioned. He would understand that. I think." She bit her lip and dropped her gaze.

Did she suspect who he was? He let the soft brogue slip away. "Yes, I think he would. However, he might also understand that many of your scrapes start out in such a way, wouldn't he?" He reached for her, pulled her into his arms, pressing her breasts against the muscled plane of his chest, and secured her wrists in one hand behind her back.

"Oh no. Stone." She wilted against his chest.

"Shhh. Now do not fret, pet. We will make all right soon enough." He needed the room he'd arranged. Not one of the viewing rooms, but one of the private spaces. He snatched the laces from his pirate's shirt and secured her wrists. Then he tossed her over his shoulder and went in search of the blue room. And make no mistake, they would come to terms.

Theo tamped down her panic. While Stone was not happy about her presence there, he did not seem irate. Though the fact that she was currently arse over ears and being carried through a brothel might suggest that she should retain a bit of her trepidation.

A door opened and closed. Lights turned up, and then she was on her feet. Hands still bound, she took a step back from the man she believed to be her husband. "Stone?"

"Yes, Theo, it is me." Visual confirmation came as he pushed back his hood and removed his mask to reveal the emerald-green orbs she had come to love.

"I can explain everything." She stepped toward him. Could she make him understand? Perhaps he already did?

"No need, wife. Your sister explained it all this morning."
He quirked a brow in punctuation.

"She told?" This idea dismayed Theo more than the
knowledge that Stone knew of her plans at all.

"She had little choice in front of her husband. I would
hazard a guess that they have much the same relationship
we shall." Stone slid his cloak off his shoulders and let it flow
to the floor.

"They do? We shall?" Theo swallowed and stepped back.

"Quite so. And just as Lizzy received her punishment this
morning after I departed, you will receive yours now."

"Punishment?" The word squeaked out, even as her pulse
thrummed. She grew light-headed when she reflected on the
man who had been bound, whipped, and—she swallowed
again—figged.

Stone captured her wrist and pulled her against him. "Easy
now. I can see you're imagining the man from earlier. That
is not how I intend to go about things—yet. If you enjoy it or
benefit from such activity, we may consider it. But for now,
we shall start simply. A basic spanking for a wayward wife
will more than suffice."

"Thank you, my lord." She struggled to get the words past
her parched throat and leathery tongue.

"Mmmm. I do like the sound of that on your lips. But,
when we are alone, I prefer you call me Master. Is that clear?"

Theo nodded.

"Say it, pet. Say, 'Yes, Master.'" He led her to the bed.

"Yes, Master." Water. She would kill for something liquid.
"May I have something to drink, Master?"

"Very nicely done. You may." Stone glanced around the
room and then spotted a pitcher of wine and a few glasses.

He walked over, poured a glass, and brought it to her. He
held the crystal to her lips and let some of the ruby liquid
slide down her throat. It tasted divine and wet her mouth.

"Now, we need to prepare you for your spanking." He
glanced around the room and focused on a piece of furniture
Theo had never seen before. It was oddly shaped, much like
a bench, but too tall and narrow to be comfortable. Stone led

her over to it and had her lie down on her stomach along the length of the padded seat. Then, to her relief, he untied her hands.

Oh, fleeting joy.

Doubt assailed her when he secured her arms to either side with leather straps that buckled. Then she felt a similar latching down of her ankles. "Stone? What are you doing?"

"What are you to call me, pet?" He sounded stern, harsh even, to her ears.

"Master." Fear made her voice higher pitched than normal, almost squeaky.

"Very good. This is a spanking bench. Many upper-crust houses have them for disciplinary purposes with servants and children. It is easier for you to take the spanking if you cannot fight me. Also, I do not want to injure either of us."

"Are you sure this is necessary? I promise I won't do anything like this again, Master." To her horror, she could feel telltale wetness seeping from her eyes. She was crying.

"Oh, pet." He sounded so sweet when he called her that. "I'm afraid it is necessary to help you remember not to do such things. But never fear, you will feel better about it all once this is over. I promise you will feel amply punished, and I shall not feel the need to be mad any longer. Do you trust me?"

Did she trust him? She paused for a long, agonizing moment and considered the question. Deep inside, a small flame of warmth sprang to life. She did trust him. He had never intentionally hurt her and treated her only with care—sometimes too much care. "If it will help, Master." She rested her forehead against the padded bench and closed her eyes.

Stone raised her skirts and found the drawers she usually wore beneath them. "In the future, you will not ever wear these. Do you understand me?" God, his cock ached. His wife lay strapped to the bench as she quivered in anticipation and fear. Never had he imagined doing this with the woman he'd married, but she so sweetly complied, submitting to his will until he was rapidly losing the ability to imagine *not* doing it with her.

He found the slit in her drawers, reached inside, and rent the fabric until it hung from her hips and thighs in ragged remains. Her cunny glistened with desire. He wanted to kneel before her, splayed on the makeshift altar, and feast. But first, he needed her to understand she could not do such things as meeting with a madame and visiting brothels without consulting him. There were consequences for her actions.

"Please count for me, pet. Ten swats and this will all be over." He rubbed her buttock, and she flinched. He rubbed the other side until she relaxed, and then he drew back and struck with lightning speed.

"One," she yelped.

"One what, pet?" He rubbed the afflicted area.

"One...swat?" Theo sounded unsure, and he knew he needed to explain.

"One, Master. Always finish with Master so I know whom you are addressing."

"Yes, Master. That was one, Master."

"Excellent." He smacked the other cheek.

"Two, Master."

By eight, tears streamed down her face and her juices dribbled down her thighs. Stone wasn't sure he could finish the punishment before he buried himself in her pussy. If he took her bent over, each thrust would imprint the memory of the spanking on her.

He landed the next to last blow across both cheeks.

"N-n-nine, Master."

And then the last.

"Ten, Master." The relief was evident in her tone and the way her frame relaxed.

He rubbed the rosy-red area again. "You did very well. While I would like to say this is the last of such events, I am certain it will take a few more reminders for you to fully comprehend what you should and should not do without discussing it with me. Now, we must make up."

He leaned over, kissed her on the cheek near her mouth, and then moved away. He circled back to where her arse tipped up to give him the best access, and knelt down. Using his tongue, he scooped up a dribble of her juices from her inner thigh. She tasted as sweet as he remembered.

Then he followed suit on the other side. Her legs quivered, but she remained silent. He grabbed her red bottom and spread her cheeks wide, ignoring her groan at his touch. He knew his hands would rouse the burn, but if she proved to appreciate a bit of pain with her pleasure, she would learn to like the sensation. Even crave it. Then he slid his tongue from her clit to her rear hole in a long, leisurely swipe. She gasped but had no path of retreat.

He repeated the motion over and over again until she futilely tried to push back into his tongue. Their mutual excitement escalated, and he pressed two fingers deep into her quim while he licked her clit. She squirmed but went nowhere as he manipulated her pleasure.

"Stone," she cried out, and he smacked her stinging rear.

"Say it." His command rang out in the room.

"Master," she whimpered and pressed against his fingers still lodged inside her. She could barely move, but she took what little she could get.

"That's it. Do you want to come?"

"C-come?" She continued to wiggle.

"Orgasm. Do you want me to make you feel good?" He urged her on and twisted his fingers deeper inside her.

She moaned again. "Oh yes. Please, Master. Please make me come."

Her begging did him in. He latched on to her clit, stuffed a third finger inside her, and pushed her over the edge. She screamed out her pleasure in long wails of excitement punctuated with a plea to her master. To him. Satisfaction curled in his belly like a dram of whiskey.

As she came down from her peak, he notched his cock against her cleft. "Hear this, pet. You are mine." He thrust into the warm grip of her cunny. "You belong to me, this pussy belongs to me, your pleasure belongs to me, and your arse belongs to me. Do you understand this?" His muscles trembled with his restraint.

"Yes, Master." Her voice was loud and clear and so goddamned sweet.

He couldn't hold back any longer. He had not intended for this to occur tonight, but he couldn't stop his natural response to his wife's temerity and her excitement. He fucked her hard then. Gripped her throbbing cheeks and pumped into her until his every muscle vibrated with his own orgasm. Eyes sealed shut, he saw fireworks that would rival Covent Garden's display. He continued to thrust into her until his prick softened and she had succumbed to another wrenching orgasm.

Sated for the moment, he slipped from between her thighs and reached for her straps. Once she was unbuckled, he helped her rise and stumble to the available bed. They lay side by side for a bit. Her skirts tangled around his boots as he wrapped her in his arms.

"Master, while I'll agree that I am without question yours, I would also stake my own claim on you. You, my lord, are mine. I own you, your pleasure, and all it entails." Then she pressed a kiss to his chin followed by one to the exposed flesh of his chest.

Delight spread over him like a fine cloak and warmed him. They belonged to each other. "Yes, Theo. I also belong to you. Never doubt it."

They lay there, quiet in the aftermath of what they had shared, and reveled in the peace. Never had he experienced such utter calm and contentment.

After a space of time that he could neither count—nor did he care to—he rose from the bed. "Come, my lady, we should return home. I had intended to conduct this interview there, but as you can see, I became carried away with events."

"Yes, Master." She made to rise.

"Sweeting, my lord will do in company, and Stone at home. Master will be reserved for the bedroom."

"But we are still in a bedroom, Master." Her eyes twinkled with pleasure as she rose and smoothed her skirts.

Stone couldn't contain his laughter. The cheeky wench was right.

They gathered their things and quietly slipped out the back of The Market. Stone wanted to get his wife home where she belonged.

Chapter Fifteen

Theo rose and stretched the next morning to find more new muscles sore from her trip to The Market. She could not have planned for a happier ending had she tried. There was no doubt she'd discovered the elusive something that had been missing from their private moments, and she'd helped her husband see that she was up to any challenge he might pose in the bedroom.

Unfortunately, her bottom would be sore all day. Perhaps she should forgo her afternoon visits? She feared she might wince with every move and draw her friends' notice. Her cheeks warmed at the notion of explaining why her bottom pained her.

No, that wouldn't do.

She was mid-stretch when the adjoining door to Stone's chamber opened. He strolled to the bed, leaned over, and kissed her. No tepid good-morning peck, either. He half lifted her from the bed, sank his fingers into the mess of her hair, and possessed her mouth much as he had her body the night before.

It was an unparalleled kiss good morning, good afternoon, or good night.

As he set her back on the mattress, he sat on the edge and smiled. "Good morning, Theo. How are you feeling?"

Squirming under the regard of her too-handsome husband, she found her wits still scattered as she took in his chestnut-colored hair and rich green eyes. Her cheeks heated as she tried to form a response. Would she never cease to blush? "A bit sore. You seem to be in fine fettle this morning."

"I am indeed, wife. And what are your plans for today?"

"I think I shall laze about the house and not even receive visitors. Some parts of me are sorer than others, and would make for an awkward time of visiting." She stared at him pointedly, which made him laugh.

"Ah, I see. Unfortunately, I believe you need to visit your sister today."

Theo was sure she didn't have any plans to visit Lizzy. She was very diligent in managing her calendar. "I do?"

"You do. You see, you owe both her and Lord Carlisle an apology for pulling her into your antics of last night. I am certain she received a spanking equal to yours for her part in events. I gathered Lord Carlisle does not relish doling out such punishments, though he clearly feels it is sometimes necessary. You should note we are of similar minds on this topic."

"Oh. Very well, I suppose I shall go round to visit my sister and tender my apologies. I should be able to manage a quick apology to both."

"Oh, my sweet. You are new to these things, aren't you?" He kissed her nose.

"Well, you know I am, Stone." Her brow creased.

"You shall go, take tea, and have a nice long visit with your sister. It is the final part of your punishment, and then all is forgotten."

"But I thought—"

"Do not question me on this, pet. Punishment is never complete until you have addressed those you've wronged in the course of your shenanigans. Just be grateful I am not requiring that you adhere to your normal routine to include a ride in Hyde Park, and then afternoon visits." His stern tone had her thighs quivering and her bottom tingling.

Her body's unusual reaction to him would take some acclimation. How could she both dread yet relish something so heartily?

"Yes, Master. I am very grateful and shall be sure to linger over tea with Lizzy today."

"Very good, pet. I am off to the House of Lords for a horrendously boring session and have a few errands to run. Do be home when I return this evening, as I have plans for us tonight."

"Of course, Master." She couldn't help the little thrill of anticipation that spiraled down her back.

"Oh, and please be sure to move your things over to my chamber. You may turn this into a sitting room or dressing room, but you will sleep with me from here on out." He kissed her soundly again and then strolled out of her room.

She let her toes curl as she hugged this new command to her breast and reveled in her husband's change of demeanor. Then she decided to ring for a bath of Epsom salts to help ease her aches and pains.

Later that morning, Theo stood in her sister's private sunroom and waited for her. She needed a moment after the carriage ride over. She could have sworn Stone bade the driver to run over every pothole and bump in the road.

Her sister appeared looking fresh and happy. There was no sign of her having been spanked. Nor did she remember any sign during the ball the night before. Instead, Lizzy rushed in and hugged her tight. "Oh, do tell me what happened last night."

Theo followed her to the settee, where they sat together. As they took their seats, they both winced. Theo giggled. "I, uh, see you've suffered the same results of last night as I did."

"Indeed. Do you forgive me for telling? I really had no choice. It only would have made things worse." Lizzy blushed and dropped her eyes.

"Oh, I understand more now than I did last night. I assume you were spanked sometime yesterday?"

"Oh yes. Right after Stone left, I received twenty swats for various infractions. Of course, afterward, I was taken care of in the most delightful ways. But I tell you that is the last meeting with a madame I shall ever arrange for anyone." Lizzy nodded in emphasis.

"Yes, well. I have to say I'd happily do it again if it achieved the same results. But let me tell you what occurred." Theo told her sister the entire story, right up to the end of the spanking. The rest was, of course, far too private to share.

Lizzy blinked. "Oh my, he sounds even more commanding than Carlisle."

"I daresay I need it more than you. I am forever getting into trouble. I shall strive to avoid such things, but in the past, that has not proven a successful strategy."

"Well, perhaps together we can keep you out of trouble." Lizzy grinned.

"I find that highly unlikely." Carlisle walked in and bowed to them. "Please do not stand on my account. Sit." He flashed a knowing smile at them, the beast.

"I am glad to see you, Carlisle, as I am to tender my apologies. I am very sorry if I got Lizzy caught up in one of my scrapes. I do have a knack for such things. But I shall endeavor to keep her out of any future mistakes."

"Thank you, Lady Stonemere. I do appreciate the effort. If you two will excuse me, I only wanted to make myself known to my wife. I am home from the House as we let out early."

"Oh dear!" Theo jumped up. "Sorry, Lizzy, but I must get home right away."

Lord and Lady Carlisle's laughter chased her out of the house as she bounded into her carriage and called for the driver to take her home.

She walked into the town house and found her husband had not yet returned. Relief coursed through her as her poor abused bottom still ached. No need to revisit that lesson so soon.

She quickly handed over her outer garments and headed upstairs to see after Mary's progress in moving her things to Stone's chamber. As usual, Mary had all well in hand. Theo

FHIS HAND-ME-DOWN COUNTESS

strolled around and tried to imagine how she might utilize the newly vacated space.

She realized the afternoon sunshine was lovely in there and that it would make a fine personal sitting and dressing room. She asked Mary to have her writing desk brought up from storage along with some other furniture for the room. She would leave her dressing table there as well and give it dual use.

As she contemplated a color change to the room, big warm hands wrapped around her waist and hauled her up against a far bigger and warmer chest.

"Good afternoon, Theo."

Mmmm, she enjoyed how he nuzzled her neck. "Good afternoon, Stone."

"I am happy to see you followed directions very well today. I understand you had a nice long visit with Lizzy. I assume you apologized to Lord Carlisle while you were there."

"I did, just before I dashed home. I see you finished early."

"We did. Then I ran a few errands, and here I am. I would very much like to have a private word with you."

Theo followed him into his—well, their—chamber. He sat down in a wingback chair by the window and patted his lap. "Come and have a seat."

"Of course." She perched on his lap without a wince, as the throb had begun to subside, and he wrapped his arms around her.

"I wanted to speak of last night and how our relationship has changed as a result. There are topics we should speak of so that we are both content in how things develop."

"Very well, what would you have me know?" Theo tried to ignore the butterflies flitting about in her stomach.

"I am a dominant man. After years in the military, I expect to be obeyed. There will come occasions where you will break my rules and will, therefore, need to be punished. Punishments can take on many forms. Spanking will be one. I shall always discuss with you what your punishment will be and what you are being punished for prior to meting such things out."

"Thank you for the reassurance." Theo snuggled closer to him.

"I shall also never punish you in the heat of the moment. I do not wish to hurt you or scare you in such a way that it would break the trust in our relationship. Neither of us wanted to marry, but I believe we are finding our way to a better-than-average marriage, and I would not jeopardize that."

Theo nodded solemnly. "Agreed."

"Good. Do you have any questions about anything you saw or experienced last night?"

Theo stared at the floor, unable to voice her questions. Flames licked her cheeks, and she was sure her skin had turned red.

"Ah, I see there are questions, but you are not ready to ask them. I wish you would ask me, but I shall wait until you are ready." He drew a breath. "One last bit of business. As we explore the kinds of things you saw last night and other things I would enjoy doing with you, I need you to understand that I shall push your boundaries. It is human nature to reject new and different things, so I would like us to have a phrase or word that you may use when you absolutely cannot continue on with what we may be doing. Keep in mind, you may not use it for punishment, but you may use it any other time you need to stop everything."

"What kind of word? I'm not sure what I should use." Theo tried to push her nerves aside and focus on this opportunity to give her some way to control things even as she surrendered herself to her husband. The notion made her both giddy with desire and utterly terrified.

"I think something that would not come up under intimate circumstances, like a color or an animal, might be best."

"Oh, how about Zeus? I should think he wouldn't come up under such circumstances."

"Very well, Zeus it is. I would like to hold you a bit longer, and then I shall let you dress for dinner. We have an invitation to the Grishams' tonight for dinner and cards."

Theo groaned. A long night of nothing but sitting. How would she ever survive it?

Chapter Sixteen

July 1860

S tone strolled along Bond Street on the way to his jeweler. He had it in mind to buy a pair of sapphire earrings to match the necklace he'd given Theo. After her stunning revelation the previous night, he wanted to reward her courage. As she had sat curled against him on their bed, she'd looked up at him with a wariness that had disturbed him at the time. But with a little patience and trust, she took the leap and told him what he had already suspected. The pairing with Linc and Wolf had excited her, made her fantasize about what it might be like. And to his great pleasure, she shared those deep, dark thoughts with him, which gave him the opportunity to find a way to make her fantasy a reality. As a result, he was terribly excited at the prospect—hence, his trip to the jeweler.

Traffic was heavy, as usual, so he seized the rare opportunity to dash across the street. He was midway across when a hack appeared out of nowhere. With a Herculean leap, he damn near made the sidewalk. Instead, he managed to slip off the edge of the sidewalk, bumping a man as the public coach rolled by, and clipped his shoulder. The man he collided with reached out and grabbed on to him. With a firm yank, he was hauled to safety with little more than a sore shoulder to show for the incident.

"Those damn hacks are becoming a public safety issue," the man said as he steadied Stone.

"Indeed," Stone agreed as he got his bearings. "That was bloody close to the walkway. I must thank you for hauling me forward when you did. I might've landed beneath that hack without your quick thinking."

"Not at all. Nothing any man wouldn't've done." He clapped Stone on the shoulder and grinned. "I daresay it took me back to my military days."

"Well, thank you for your assistance. My carriage is at the top of Bond Street. May I drop you somewhere?"

"Thank you, but that's not necessary. I was just on my way to meet my wife at the haberdasher's."

"Very well. And thank you again for your assistance." Stone turned and decided he would stop at the jeweler's another time. White's seemed like a good destination. After all, a drink would help settle him after yet another near miss.

A week later, Theo and Stone sat in the library enjoying a quiet evening at home. He was reading the same passage for the third time when Theo's soft giggling shattered his concentration again.

Thwarted, he finally gave up on the political treatise he'd spent the last hour attempting to read. Setting the pamphlet aside, he relaxed in his chair and watched Theo enjoy her novel. She seemed to alternate between gasps, groans, and giggles. He considered how much he had enjoyed exploring his wife's newly awakened desires and hearing her groan and gasp for much different reasons. And though they had discussed much, she had mentioned one particular pairing from The Market, the lone woman with two men. Perhaps this was a particular pleasure he should consider offering up to her? His whole being tightened in annoyance at the notion of another man touching his delicious little wife. Pushing the thought aside, he returned to his previous enjoyment of her occupation until—at some point—she became aware of his scrutiny and looked up from her book.

"My apologies, Stone. Was I too loud?" She bit her lip in a seductively innocent gesture.

"Not at all. I enjoy watching you." His heart thumped steadily in his chest.

"That's a bit odd, but I must say I was enjoying my novel. The heroine had just purchased a high-perch phaeton with a handsome matching set of cattle. I fear I am rather jealous of her freedom to drive her own vehicle." Theo sighed.

"What would you do with your own vehicle?" Stone tried to picture his wife sedately tooling through Hyde Park. No, not his Theo.

"Well, drive it, of course. I could take it to my fittings, go visiting, or stop for an ice at Gunter's."

"You would require driving lessons. However, I don't see a reason you couldn't take the cabriolet if you'd like to go for a drive." Stone sipped the brandy that he had all but forgotten while suffering through reading that ridiculous pamphlet.

"Lessons are not required. I've driven my parents' country wagon, as well as a phaeton or two in my time." Her lips tipped up at the edges in the hint of a smile as her eyes sparkled with the glitter of confidence.

"Nonetheless, before I trust my vehicle and cattle to you I shall see you handle them." He stared at his wife and considered just how besotted he'd become. Without a doubt, she would drive too fast if she didn't end up out-and-out racing. "On second thought—"

"No. You've made the offer, and I accept. When might I display my driving skills for you?" She leaned forward, earnest as ever.

Stone sighed. Resigned to what he knew would come, he gave in. "We can go for a drive tomorrow afternoon in Hyde Park."

"Hyde Park?" She made a little moue of disappointment.

"Yes, Hyde Park." He stood his ground.

"But I thought you wanted to see me handle the reins? I could fall asleep and the cattle would simply follow the parade of other carriages. There's no skill in managing them there."

While her pout was adorable, the petulance he found less so. "Pet, do we need to discuss this in a different manner?"

Her eyes widened as a flare of lust lit her gaze. She hesitated, as though considering her options.

"Theo, if you wish to be spanked, you need only ask," he offered casually.

"Hyde Park would be lovely." She nodded and eased back in her seat.

He chuckled. "Come, pet. I believe it is time to retire."

Theo wetted her lips with a slow erotic slide of her tongue. Ah yes, she was as interested as he in indulging in some private time. And if they didn't make it upstairs soon, he would be locking the library door and engaging where they were.

She tilted her flushed face up to him and focused her desire-darkened blue gaze on him. "Perhaps we could stay here, Master?"

Curiosity gripped his bollocks and squeezed. "Oh?"

"Please, Master." She rose and sauntered closer to lay her hand on his chest and lowered her gaze. "I have a particular fantasy about your desk."

The ache in his groin bloomed to a throb as he imagined her bent over his desk while he plunged into her. "My desk, eh?" He paused for effect. He had decided to stay the moment she suggested it. "I believe you should tidy things up a bit, then."

He turned her around and patted her backside in encouragement. She moved to his desk, tucked the inkwell away, and straightened up the paperwork.

Stone eased up behind her, eschewing the safety of the locked door in favor of the thrill of possible discovery. Her hair remained up from the day, which exposed the delicious length of her neck. Unable to resist, he leaned in to nuzzle the soft skin. She arched into his lips and pressed her backside against his groin.

Wrapping his hands around her hips, he then slowly dragged them up her torso to trace over her ribs before snaking around to cup her breasts. She ground into him with a sensual rotation of her pelvis, and he bit her where her neck and shoulder joined. With a moan, she tried to push her breasts more firmly into his grip.

Good God, she was a hedonistic baggage, and he loved it.

"Master, was the study not properly dusted?" The rasp of her voice paired with her docile words pushed him closer to the edge.

"It was, in fact, not dusted to my satisfaction, in addition to the mess you made of my paperwork in the process." He reached over and knocked the neat stack of pages onto the floor.

"Please, Master. I'll do better, I shall."

"Oh, we'll see to that, pet. I am quite sure you will be clear on my expectations by the time we are through." He reached up and roughly yanked on her bodice. The sound of rending fabric and pinging buttons made him wince. He'd pay for that later.

"M-master?" The pleading note in her voice spurred him on.

He said nothing as he reached into her corset and pulled out one of her breasts. Unable to resist the urge, he pinched her nipple and bit her neck again as he lifted her other breast free. Then he licked the column of flesh once, twice, before he latched on and sucked her neck. Her pebbled nipples plumped beneath his fingers as she whimpered under his touch. Desperate to be deep inside her, he released her breasts and pushed her chest flat against the desk.

With a jerk of the ends of his necktie, he had the neckcloth loose. Her breathing shifted to a labored sawing of air as he looped the fabric around her wrists at her lower back. Once she was securely bound and at his mercy, he rucked her skirts up until her creamy thighs and backside were exposed.

"Now, I do hope you will follow along, pet. When dusting my office, you will be more careful of the things placed on my desk. Please count each blow for me."

Theo tried to regulate her breathing, but desire had the best of her. Her thighs were slick with her juices, and she waited, eager to feel the first blow. The bloody problem was that Stone had discovered how much she enjoyed a good spanking, and he would often draw out the first blows until she begged him to hit her.

He waited. And waited. And waited more.

Crack. His palm met the flesh of her bum, and she cried out. "One, Master." *Yes!* She silently cheered as the heat bloomed in one cheek and sizzled straight to her clit.

"Please keep in mind that while I do not wish my things disturbed, I do not want to live in filth either." He landed the next whack.

"Two, Master." She struggled to breathe through the pleasure-pain as her body warmed and softened. She wiggled her fingers to keep the blood flowing and awaited the next strike.

"However, having a wanton baggage such as yourself on staff keeps me happy, so you will be spared dismissal without references." He landed the next two blows in succession.

"Three and four, Master." Her focus spun off, deserting her when she needed it most.

He rained more blows on her tingling arse, and she sputtered, unable to recall where she left off in the count.

He knew how difficult it became for her to concentrate. "I believe that was five and six, pet."

"Y-yes. Five and six, Master," she croaked out through her parched lips.

"Four more, pet, and then all will be forgiven." He paddled her backside in four consecutive blows.

She had to breathe to control the orgasm that pounded at her core. Her thighs quivered, and drawing air became a chore. "Seven, eight, nine, and ten, Master." She cried as he shoved his fingers—was that two or three?—deep into her cunny and stroked her.

There were times she swore someone had provided her husband a map of her body. He seemed to always know exactly where to stroke and how hard to push her. No man could ever make her feel as he did.

He withdrew his fingers, released his trousers, and shoved his cock into her wet heat in a single pulse-pounding stroke.

She couldn't muffle her cry of satisfaction as he tunneled deep inside her.

He wrenched her arms up a bit as he took hold of her bound wrists and levered her against the flat surface. Wordlessly, he hammered into her until she could hear nothing but the slap of his thighs against hers and feel nothing but the slide of his prick deep into her swollen flesh.

Her hips banged against the desk with every stroke as he groaned behind her. Then the crest of erotic delight broke over her with the force of a speeding train. She screamed her release until her throat grew raw and her legs could no longer support her weight. Had she not been pinned between her husband's loins and the desk, she would have slithered to the floor in a boneless mass of skin and muscle.

"Theo, you delicious wench." The rumbled words tripped across her heart as he lost himself in her. He swiveled his hips and lunged into her until he shook with the intensity of his climax. "God, yes!" His cry of completion released a series of shivers up her spine that were pure pleasure.

Stone lay slumped over her as he returned to awareness. "Christ," he muttered, and eased up from her lush form, where she lay squashed against the desk.

His wife patiently waited while he let his softened cock slide from her heat. It was shameful that he wanted her again already. Shameful and unrealistic.

He released her arms and rubbed them a bit to get the blood flowing again. "Are you well, Theo?" Worry always nagged at him after a particularly rough bout of lovemaking. Somehow, his resilient little wife always came up smiling and ready for more.

"Mmmm...better than well. Amazing comes to mind, Master." She smiled as she settled her skirts in place.

He kissed her, trying not to swallow her whole while he expressed exactly how satisfied he was with their life. Suddenly, the door swung open and one of the maids burst into the room.

Theo gasped.

"Oh! Milord, milady." The girl bowed and curtsied and attempted to back out of the room.

Theo stepped away from the circle of her husband's arms but remained in front of him in an effort to preserve his modesty, even as she held her ripped bodice together. "What did you need, Katarina?"

"The coals, milady." She waved the coal bucket wildly, sloshing the briquettes about in the metal container.

Theo stilled her face into a mask of calm. "Please." She waved the girl on even as he muttered a curse behind her and pinched her bottom in retaliation.

It was but a moment of noise and fuss before the girl scurried from the room. As the door closed behind the poor wretch, the pair of them dissolved into laughter. Stone tucked his penis away and Theo scooted out of reach. He imagined her bottom was plenty warm as it was.

"You are an evil wench to leave me literally dangling while the coals were replenished." Stone glowered as he moved around the desk to return to his original seat.

Theo laughed. "It served you right for leaving the door unlocked." She aimed a gimlet eye at him.

"I plead innocence. Had you not tempted me so greatly, I would have remembered to lock the door." He could no longer claim sleep deprivation. Since he'd installed his wife in his bed, his nightmares had faded. Most nights, he slept soundly with her tucked snugly against him, though he'd neglected to discuss either the nightmares or their abatement. After all, it might be momentous to think of himself as a whole man again, but he could not share such important news without first shaming himself by revealing the aforementioned weakness to the woman who should feel nothing but safe and protected with him.

"Pish. You chose not to turn the lock. You had plenty of time to do so." Theo's amusement bubbled over her efforts at control.

"Very well. I'm caught out. But you must admit, it was all great fun." He grinned like a little boy on Christmas. He could not have imagined being so happy with one woman, let alone one of his own social standing.

Theo picked up the reins and urged the horses forward into a sedate walk. As they rounded Queen's Gate onto Rotten Row, she quickened the pace to a tame trot. She worked hard to control the urge to give the horses their heads and let them run. They were as antsy as she.

An interminable hour of trotting only to stop and chat with another passing rig or some dandy who tried to make walking fashionable had her on edge. Her driving skills had been earned in the country where it was de rigueur to let the cattle run as they would like.

As they returned home, Theo ventured a conversation. "So, did I pass muster, Stone?"

"Quite satisfactory, Theo. Though I am sure as soon as I leave you alone, you shall go tearing down Bond Street and cause a horrid scandal." He grinned, unrepentant.

"Do you think me so low? Bond Street? Why, I shall go tearing down St. James's Street in an affront to all masculinity, or do nothing at all." Her declaration had him doubled over in laughter.

As he recovered from his mirth, he straightened up. "In all seriousness, Theo, if I hear of reckless behavior at the reins, you will be punished."

His stern tone sent shivers spiraling down her spine. How was it she reacted so readily to him? The merest hint of his command had her sitting at attention and ready to please. That was, unless she wished to earn a punishment. "Yes, Stone."

Her imagination roamed to more licentious ideas as they pulled around to the mews. Over the weeks, they had discussed the various things she had witnessed at The Market the night he learned exactly how deep her wantonness ran. Still, the image of the woman and two men remained with her, taunted her in the dark of night when she allowed her deepest fantasies to roam free.

Despite having voiced her curiosity to her husband, she could never ask for such a thing.

How did one tell a man who had given her so much pleasure that she might wish for something more? That the idea of a cock in her pussy as she swallowed another sent her into paroxysms of ecstasy? And still, a concern nagged. Was the idea more appealing than the reality? While she had seen the woman's enjoyment, a niggling doubt lingered. Would she enjoy such a thing? More importantly, would her husband?

"By the by, I've invited the Earl of Brougham to dine with us tomorrow night." The intrusion of the announcement was both a dash of cold water on her lusty thoughts and served to draw her back to the moment in which she was to be handling the vehicle.

They drew to a stop, and one of the stable hands grabbed the bridle while Stone dismounted from the cabriolet. With a sure-handed swiftness that stole her breath, he whisked her down from her perch. His gaze warmed as he let her slide along his chest and legs until her feet touched the cobblestones.

"Tomorrow? Stone, you should have told me sooner."

"I meant to tell you last night, but something distracted me." He winked at her and then ambled up the front steps.

Chapter Seventeen

Once Stone had discovered the idea of two men servicing her tickled some sort of fancy for Theo, he knew he wanted to offer her the experience. And yet he had struggled with the question of sharing his wife. Though his best friend could be the only choice, he still found the notion challenging. He and Cooper had shared women many times over the years, starting as early as Eton, when they had to scrape the cost of one up between them. It seemed his father had not considered prostitutes part of a young man's necessary expenses.

But Theo? She was special, and though he wanted to indulge her every fantasy, the idea of sharing her with anyone had his hackles rising. Yet, he would muddle through for the sake of her bourgeoning sexuality. To crush her erotic curiosity now would be like putting a prized racer out to stud too soon.

So he'd dug deep and asked Cooper to join him as he received a special gift he had ordered for his and Theo's private use. As they set up everything, he planned to broach the idea of exploring what he believed to be Theo's deepest desire. He wanted to fulfill it for her.

He had ordered some custom-built pieces similar to those from The Market right after their first night, and today they were to be delivered. It was only three items, but they would occupy one of the many chambers upstairs. Of course, the door would be locked, and only Peter, a footman, would be permitted into the room to clean and polish the wood. If the bed needed to be made, the footman would supervise.

Once the delivery men unloaded the crates into the room, Cooper helped Stone unpack and set everything up. He had purchased a very fine spanking bench, a St. Andrew's Cross, and a throne upon which he might sit and spank his wife when lesser punishment was needed, or just for fun.

The room also contained a relic of a bed from the 1700s. It was old and built to accommodate four or five sleepers. He'd acquired it a few years back from an old inn that shut down. He'd had a new mattress stuffed and new sheets made for it. The bed offered plenty of space for him to maneuver, and should Cooper decide to join them, they could easily all fit.

The possibilities suddenly seemed endless as his wife's acceptance of his control settled into his bones. Tonight he planned on introducing her to their new room, a new toy, and possibly a whole new experience.

"Cooper, I was wondering if you might be up to some of our old antics?" Stone dragged the bench into position.

His best friend coughed and sputtered. "Is the ball and chain chafing so soon?"

"Gad, no." Stone couldn't help the light burn that rode high on his cheeks. "I believe my wife might enjoy the idea of welcoming two men into her bed."

Cooper raised an eyebrow. "What leads you to believe such a thing? Aside from the fact I am assembling a St. Andrew's Cross in your spare bedroom."

"Of all the sights she took in that night at The Market, the one thing she seemed most curious about was Linc and Wolf with the little brunette. I believe she is curious about what it might be like, and, being the accommodating husband I am, I would like her to have that experience."

Cooper laughed outright.

"It's not that funny, Cooper."

"Oh, but it is. Whoever gave you the idea that you were accommodating?" His friend chortled to the point of snorting.

"Do be serious. I am asking you to help me." Stone paused. Lowering his voice, he admitted, "I don't think I could stand for anyone else to touch her." He stared at the floor, unable to look up and let his friend see how difficult the entire proposition was for him.

"Bloody hell," Cooper muttered. "Are you sure you want to do this?"

"Not at all, but I want to give her the opportunity if she wishes it." They set the last of the furniture into place, covered the pieces—except the bed—with Holland covers, and locked the door behind them.

"I've never known you to be this attached to a woman. If you believe you can handle this, I shall be your third. But you must promise me that if the situation becomes too much, you will cease things and let me leave. I'd not lose you as a friend." His friend's loyalty was the primary reason Stone thought he could manage this one night for his wife.

Cooper slapped him on the shoulder in the closest thing to a hug they would ever share.

"I promise. And thank you for this, Cooper. As I said, it will be up to my lady wife if this occurs or not."

"Agreed."

They retired to the billiards room to await Theo's return from a visit with her sister. Dinner would be a casual affair with just the three of them. In the meantime, a few friendly wagers would entertain them.

Theo arrived home to find the men occupied with table games. She greeted her husband and then retreated upstairs to change for dinner. She opted for a silk-and-cotton gown covered in an alternating pattern of flowers and dots underlaid by cream-and-blue banding.

The dress emphasized her neck but entirely covered her chest and arms. It was a demure dinner dress meant for a simple evening at home. She joined the men in the study to wait until dinner was served.

"Good evening." She had met Cooper only the once at her wedding, and then, of course, she had seen him the night she visited The Market. He was a handsome blond devil with big, soulful brown eyes and the physique to rival any Greek god as depicted in the National Museum.

They both bowed. "Theo, you remember my friend Robert Cooper, Earl of Brougham. Cooper, my wife, Theodora Denton, the Countess of Stonemere."

"Lovely to see you again, my lady." Cooper bowed over her hand.

"Please, call me Theo. I know how close you are with Stone. You are all but family." She clasped his hand in hers.

"Then by all means, call me Cooper or Brougham."

Theo looked him over, squinted with one eye closed entirely, and then grinned. "Cooper, it is. You simply aren't a Brougham."

They all laughed and enjoyed a drink before dinner as Cooper regaled her with childhood stories of her husband. Soon enough, the dinner chime sounded, and the two men escorted her into the dining room.

Stone directed her to sit at the head of the table as he and Cooper each took a side. They continued to chat and laugh through dinner until Theo rose. "Well, I shall leave you two to your port."

"Dash it all, I think I'd much rather continue this convivial little group. We should move to the study, where we can indulge in a drink while still enjoying ourselves." Stone rose and assisted her.

"If you wish, Stone." Theo couldn't hide how pleased she was to continue their evening of frivolity. Soon they were in the study, reminiscing about their childhoods. Theo relayed a story of playing Poor Pussy with the village vicar back home. Her mother had been selected to be the kitty, and when she had reached the vicar and meowed pitifully, all while her face grew bright red, the poor man couldn't keep a straight face. Instead, he laughed uproariously and wound up the poor pussy.

The men laughed with her until their sides hurt. Theo thought for certain Stone's might split open.

"I have a wonderful idea," her husband said suddenly. "Why don't we play?"

"Play what?" Theo asked, still a bit befuddled from her mirth.

"Why, Poor Pussy, of course." Stone schooled his features.

"A capital idea," Cooper chimed in.

"Absolutely not," Theo countermanded the men. She would not crawl about the floor in such a ridiculous manner. Not to mention, with some of the more erotic experiences she'd shared with her husband, the use of the word "pussy" had a whole new connotation for her that would make the game feel more awkward than it might have to start.

"Oh, come now, pet. I'd like to play Poor Pussy. And you can have first go." He winked.

The nerve of the blasted man. She could have first go, as though he were doing her a favor. "Oh, I wouldn't want to stand in your way, my lord."

"You may call me Master, pet. Cooper will not be offended by such intimacy, would you?"

"Not at all." Cooper sipped his brandy.

Theo tamped down her surprise at Stone's openness. She hesitated, long enough that were they alone, she would have earned a punishment. Her gaze darted from one calm face to another. "As you wish, Master."

"Excellent. Now, on your paws, Poor Pussy." Stone's tone brooked no resistance.

Theo couldn't restrain the sigh of resignation as she sank to her knees and then dropped forward onto her hands. She started with Stone, being more comfortable with him than his friend. She crawled across the floor to where he sat and dropped her bum to her heels. She curled her hands like paws and meowed.

Straight-faced, Stone looked at her and said, "Poor Pussy, poor Pussy. I think you can beg better than that."

Theo wanted to curse the man for not having said it a third time. She sighed and tried again. This time, she rested her "paws" on his knee and meowed mournfully.

"Oh, much better, but not quite close enough." Stone winked at Cooper.

Blast him, he would pay for that. This time, she worked her way between his thighs and rubbed her cheek along his inner thigh while mewling piteously. His prick lengthened in his trousers as her breath fanned over his groin and her cheek rubbed him through the fabric.

He inhaled sharply and released it slowly. "Poor Pussy, Poor Pussy, my Poor Pussy." His face remained steady and unchanged.

Theo frowned and realized she had to move on to Cooper since there was nobody else to turn to. She hesitated.

"Now take yourself over to Cooper and beg him as prettily as you did me that last time," Stone ordered.

Her stomach flip-flopped. Granted, she found him attractive, but she had never been so intimate with a man other than Stone. She glanced at her husband, uncertain.

He smiled his encouragement and then raised a brow at her continued hesitation.

She sighed and crawled over to the blond Adonis. As before, she eased between his open thighs and laid her head on his leg. His cock hardened, and again she found herself rubbing her face against a fabric-covered cock—just not her husband's. In an unexpected turn, she found her thighs grew damp with her desire despite the blush that warmed her cheeks. She closed her eyes, drew a breath, and meowed. The ragged sound that emitted from her throat couldn't have sounded less like a cat.

"Poor Pussy, Poor Pussy—" Cooper hesitated and glanced at her husband, who must have nodded to go on. "Poor Pussy." And then he smiled.

Theo worked very hard not to return the smile and won out. After a moment, she jumped up and proclaimed, "Ha! You're the Poor Pussy."

Cooper grinned and dropped to the floor from his chair. "Very well, if you insist." He turned and winked at Stone, then made his way over to where she had taken her seat. He neared her skirts, crept closer, reached out to grasp the hem exposing her trim ankles, and waited.

Confusion and surprise held her still as she took in the image of such a handsome man practically peeking under her skirts. Theo shot her wide-eyed gaze at her husband, who responded with a calming casualness. "If you're not interested, you need only say the word."

Chapter Eighteen

"I don't understand. Are you suggesting...?" She looked at Cooper, who had raised the hem of her dress slowly to her knees.

"Indeed, pet. Is it not something you are curious about? Something you wanted to experience for yourself?" Stone appeared calm and collected as he waited for her response.

In contrast, her heart raced as though she'd run through Hyde Park under her own steam. How did he know? What had she done to reveal how deep her curiosity ran? Damn her too-observant husband. He was proving too keen by half, and she found it both delightful and terrifying. She swallowed. Unable to speak, she nodded.

"Then let the Poor Pussy make you smile." Stone leaned forward as though he sought a better view of what would come next.

Her face flamed while her thighs parted as if of their own volition. Cooper lifted her skirts all the way to her waist, exposing her lack of bloomers. Strong hands gripped her hips and pulled her forward to the edge of the chair.

"Hold your skirts up for him, pet." The command made her all warm inside.

Gathering the material, she crushed it in her fists as Cooper slid his tongue along her slit. She groaned as he unerringly found her bundle of nerves and swirled around it. He continued to delve deeper into her core while Stone rose and moved around her chair and behind.

Her husband reached down and opened the back of her gown until he could reach inside her bodice and seek out her breasts. Deft fingers plucked and pinched her nipples while an unfamiliar tongue explored her folds. Cooper traced up and down her pussy, circled first her nub and then the entrance of her channel.

When Stone bent over and latched on to a breast to suck hard, she exploded. Her cunny spasmed around Cooper's tongue as her juices flooded him. She whimpered and arched into Stone's mouth on her breast as Cooper carried her up to the peak of bliss and slowly back down to the reality of two men catering to her pleasure. Her head spun even as she ached for more.

Stone pulled back from Theo's pebbled nipple and smiled at her dazed expression. She looked lovely and sated. Then, a movement lower down caught his eye, and his heart lurched. Ah yes, Cooper was with them. He drew a sharp breath of air and gripped the arms of the chair. He had invited him to join them, and to his satisfaction and displeasure, Theo had concurred when given the chance. How could he feel two such emotions at once? It made little sense to one who had always indulged in pleasure with the same singlemindedness with which he led a charge on the battlefield. Despite his confliction, he would follow through with this—even if it killed him.

"I think perhaps we should adjourn upstairs." He stepped away from his wife and Cooper. His friend took her hand and helped her rise on wobbly legs.

Stone slid up beside her and took her other arm to help steady her. Together, they led her upstairs, but as they reached the door of the newly prepared room and stopped, Theo questioned him. "Master, why are we stopping here?"

"I have multiple surprises for you tonight, pet."

She blinked. "All right, then."

"I can only imagine you will enjoy everything Stone has in store for you, Theo." Cooper rubbed her hand, which sat tucked under his arm.

"He does seem to know my deepest, darkest desires. Even those I have not voiced." She let her gaze rove over Stone in a visual caress that warmed his heart and settled some of the tumultuousness of their adventure.

He unlocked the door and swung it open. "Wait here." Then he stepped inside and turned up a couple of lamps. He sat on the throne, anticipation with a bit of uneasiness thrumming through him, and bade his wife and friend enter.

Theo's gaze sought and found him immediately. Her eyes widened and her lips parted as she spied him lounging on the imposing wood throne. It was beautifully carved with dentil moldings, ball-and-claw feet, and other ornate details that softened the look of the black walnut. The dark wood was finished with a black stain that only deepened the color and made the scarlet cushions all the more startling.

In a move that had the throb in his cock intensifying, Theo dropped to her knees with a whispered, "Master."

Behind Theo, Cooper groaned in a similar state of distress.

Watching his wife submit to his needs so willingly was without a doubt one of the most erotic things Stone had ever seen—and the woman was fully clothed.

"This is my throne. It is where I shall sit when I deem it necessary to mete out punishment or when I provide you direction." Stone rose and walked over to the first covered item. He slipped the sheet off the furniture and waited for Theo's reaction.

She did not disappoint.

A soft gasp escaped her as she looked at the padded bench. Her tongue slipped out to moisten her lips. "A-a spanking bench?"

Most households had them, but typically they were not so well appointed since they were used for household discipline. "Yes. When you are in need of a proper spanking, we shall make use of the bench. As you are aware, it has a myriad of other very pleasurable uses as well." He grinned as he pictured her strapped to the bench while he took her from behind again. "You may come and inspect it."

Theo rose and walked over to the bench. She ran her fingers lightly over one padded leg rest until she touched the leather strap that would buckle her leg in place. Her breathing grew shallow and rapid as her skin flushed.

Yes, his wife very much liked the idea of the bench.

"Cooper, if you would remove the other cover?" Stone seemed to have startled him from his own reverie with his request.

"Of course." Cooper yanked on the cover across the room, which caused Theo to turn from her inspection of the bench.

She inhaled sharply through her nose as she reached out to grab Stone's arm. "M-Master?"

Her entire body had tensed as she spied the St. Andrew's Cross. Stone had expected a stronger response from the torture device. Little did she know the delights that awaited her on the cross. He stepped up behind her, snaked an arm about her waist, and cradled her against his chest. "Tell me what you are thinking, pet."

"I-I'm scared." The whispered words of fear poked at his dominant heart and made him want to protect her even more.

"Pet, have I ever given you a reason to believe I would cause you harm?"

"No, of course not," she declared with a firm resolve that was far more than he had expected.

"Then, what scares you?" He needed her to tell him. To acknowledge the roots of her fear so they could move past it.

She stood mute.

"Pet, you will tell me what is distressing you this instant." He needed her to speak.

"Please, Master. Do not make me say it." She turned her eyes up to him as she leaned sideways in his arms.

He struggled with the urge to kiss her but managed to quell the desire. It was rare for Theo to outright disobey him, and he recognized they needed to deal with the situation immediately.

"Theo, you will explain yourself or suffer twenty spanks as punishment for disobedience." He dredged up his most commanding tone in hopes he could help her break the bonds of trepidation. He had not intended to use anything but the bed tonight; however, he would not let her fear fester.

"Please, no, Master." She straightened up and let her head fall forward in defeat.

She would rather take the spanking than tell him. He shook his head. "Cooper, come help me undress Theo."

His friend walked over from the cross, and they worked on removing her dress, then her petticoats and crinolines, and finally her corset and chemise.

"Leave her stockings and garters." Stone helped her over to the bench, and together, he and Cooper got her into position and strapped down her legs and arms. Stone glanced around the room. "Bloody brilliant. I hadn't planned on needing to punish her tonight. I suppose my hand will do. Pet, do you know why you are being punished?" Stone took in the sight of his wife splayed along the padded bench, legs spread, and pussy open to his inspection, as well as her plump cheeks lifted into position for swatting.

"Yes, Master. I refused to tell you what scared me."

"Correct, and in so doing, you have earned twenty spanks." He rubbed one cheek and then the other.

"Yes, Master."

"Cooper, please keep count if you will." He hesitated. "Theo, you may stop this at any time if you wish to tell me."

"No, Master."

Stone sighed. "Very well."

He slapped her right cheek.

"One." Cooper's baritone rumbled off the stroke.

Stone landed eight blows by the time Theo's tears started. Cooper glanced up at him, almost as desperate to stop things as he was. But Stone knew he had to follow through. Theo needed him to be strong for both of them. Two more cracking swats landed, and she gave in.

"I liked it, Master," she cried out.

Stone stopped mid-swing and moved around to her head. "Liked what, pet?"

"The torture device. I-i-it excited me, and I felt ashamed and scared that I wanted you to tie me to it." With her admission, her tears fell harder.

"Pet, look at me." He tipped her face up so he could see her tear-drenched eyes. "I am incredibly pleased it excited you. It does the same for me, and I relish the notion of tying you to it while I have my way with you."

"Y-you do?" Confusion stopped the tears but creased her forehead.

"Of course I do, pet. Why else would I have had it made? All better now?"

"Yes, Master." She offered him a tremulous smile.

"Good, I'm proud of you for telling me. We won't use the cross tonight, but we will try it out in the near future." At her little moue of disappointment, he chuckled and added, "I promise."

It made him happy to know she was as enticed by the cross as he. With a nod of his head, he and Cooper unbuckled her wrists and ankles before helping her stand. Stone scooped her up and carried her to the bed, where he set her down.

Hovering over her, he rubbed her arm and leg on the left side while Cooper took care of her right. The massage morphed into petting as their hands roamed up over her shoulders to tease her breasts. With a moan of contentment, she arched into their hands as they rubbed and stroked her body. Leading the way, Stone bent lower and sucked on a nipple, all the while continuing his caresses. Cooper followed suit, causing her to cry out in pleasure. As she writhed beneath their attentions, Stone drew his hand down to spread her thighs. Relaxed and lost in the sensations, she complied with his nonverbal request for access and spread her legs. With access granted, he stroked her slick pussy, sliding a fingertip over her folds and around her swollen nub. Cooper joined in Stone's explorations, swirling his fingertip around the drenched opening of her channel.

"More, please, Master," she begged him.

Stone released her nipple long enough to reply, "More what, pet?"

Her hips bucked against their hands while her head tossed back and forth. "So empty."

Stone pushed a finger inside her, sliding to the third knuckle, and released her breast again. "Is that good, pet? Do you need more?"

She clenched around his finger and whimpered. "Fill me, please, Master." Her breath hitched on the plea as her breathing grew more rapid.

Cooper lifted from her other breast. "May I?" With Stone's assent, he slid a finger inside her as well.

Theo squealed in delight and fucked herself onto their fingers. As the first wave of her orgasm hit her, they simultaneously latched back on to her nipples and sucked hard and then pumped their fingers in and out of her sheath. She rode wave after wave of pleasure, until the grip of her cunny slowly lessened around their fingers. Certain that she was satisfied for the moment, they pulled their fingers free and released her nipples to allow her a few moments of recovery. As she came around from her blissful stupor, she looked up at Stone and smiled. "Thank you, Master."

Stone laughed. "Not so quick, my pet. There is far more to come. Are you ready to continue?" He couldn't resist stroking her cheek as he waited for her reply.

She nodded, but then spoke. "Please, Master."

"Very good, then." Stone helped her sit up, and then he and Cooper stepped back and stripped. Theo watched as they removed each piece of clothing, her interest in both men evident, though Stone was pleased to find her gaze returning to him more often than not. When they were both naked with cocks hard from pleasuring her, Stone considered what she might enjoy. She had proven an avid disciple of his rod, so he thought that might be a good place to start. "Pet, on your knees."

She eased off the bed and sank to her knees as he had requested. The subservient position appeared to thrill her if the glow in her blue eyes was proof. And then she licked her lips as she eyed their shafts. So he moved closer and offered his length to her. She looked up as though requesting permission, and, with a nod from him, she wrapped her delicate fingers around the base of his shaft and engulfed the head in her mouth. Stone couldn't control the groan that escaped him as her heat surrounded his erection. To his left, Cooper stood with his own hand wrapped around his shaft and watched.

Stone thrust between her lips, pushing deeper into her mouth and throat. She choked and sputtered around him but refused to pull back. But then he took the choice away from her and withdrew. "Do not forget our guest, pet."

"No, Master," she concurred as she seized his length. After a brief hesitation, with one hand still wrapped around his cock, she took hold of Cooper's shaft and leaned forward. Trepidation had her gaze darting back toward Stone as she hesitated, but then she sucked the tip of Cooper's cock into her mouth.

"Focus on him, love," Stone urged her as she tried to balance her loyalty to him with her desire to experience something—someone—different. Stone decided to make it easier for her. "Stop for a moment." He pulled away, went to his pile of clothes, and dug his necktie from the heap. Then, with deft movements, he placed her hands behind her back and lashed them together. "Now, all decisions are mine. All you need to do is open wide, pet."

And with that, he circled back around and pushed his cock into her waiting mouth. She latched on and sighed in contentment as he pumped his hips until his balls brushed her delicate chin. Then he withdrew and signaled for Cooper to take a turn. His friend repeated the movement, pushing deep into her mouth and throat. His cock was slightly thicker but a bit shorter than Stone's, so taking Cooper was different for her. She gagged a bit but pushed past the momentary challenge.

Soon they set up a rhythm where one would slide in and out of her mouth a few times and then they would switch. Even as he struggled with watching Cooper sink his cock into his wife's mouth, he could also see how much his wife was enjoying sucking both of their cocks. They continued the pattern until Stone thought his balls would explode with need. He wanted to come, but he wanted to do so deep in his wife's cunny. He withdrew one last time and then helped Theo rise, though her hands remained bound for the moment. Her lips were swollen from sucking them, and her gaze glassy with desire. Despite two orgasms and a spanking, she seemed to be ready to come for him once more. Eager to see that happen, he directed Cooper to untie her hands. While his friend did so, Stone leaned down and kissed his wife. She responded, eager and sweet until her hands were free and she could latch on to his bare shoulders.

He pulled away and turned her toward the bed. "Up you go, pet." Eager for whatever he had planned, she scrambled onto the bad and looked at him for further direction. Stone decided he needed to be inside her, to feel her wrapped around his cock. "On your hands and knees, please. Arse toward us."

With her soaked pussy on full display, they admired their handiwork. She was wet and swollen with need. Stone grabbed her still-rosy bottom and leaned in to drag his tongue along her wet slit. Her sweet-tart taste burst over his tongue, drawing a groan from deep within his chest. He looked over his shoulder and caught Cooper watching, desire in his own gaze. Stone waved him over. "Taste her. She's so bloody sweet."

Cooper leaned in and lapped at her folds, eliciting a shudder from Theo. After a few moments, his friend drew back, his lips wet with Theo's juices, and Stone had to fight off a rogue surge of jealousy. Ruthlessly controlling the unwelcome feeling, he pointed to Theo's head. "Have her suck you off while I pound her sweet cunny. You may come in her mouth if she is willing."

Satisfied that Cooper was taken care of, he notched his prick at Theo's quim and pushed forward. She moaned and pushed back to meet him as he slid into her hot channel. He gave her a moment to adjust to his invasion, and then he pulled out until just the tip remained.

Theo sensed the blond Adonis's presence more than saw him, since her eyes were closed while she relished the feel of Stone's cock buried deep inside her pussy. When she opened her eyes, she found the purplish head of Cooper's cock in her face. Just as it had happened at The Market when she watched the three lovers, the notion of being filled with cock caused her body to heat and soften.

Stone shuttled in and out of her quim while Cooper nudged her lips. "Suck it, Theo." The strange baritone caused shimmers of lust to sparkle through her.

"Take his cock in your mouth, pet." Stone's command spurred her to action, and she opened wide to accept the erection.

As she swallowed him down, Stone thrust into her pussy, and she could no longer think straight. They consumed her as surely as they filled her and pleasured her. Cooper groaned, pumping in and out of her mouth in time with Stone, who had also reached around to rub her clit. Deep savage shudders of bliss started where his fingers touched her and intensified until her body surrendered to the tidal wave of carnality that crashed over her.

She groaned as her orgasm broke and the men continued to use her body. Before long, Cooper shouted his release and tried to pull away. Theo refused to let him go and hung on to his hip with one hand as his salty seed flooded her mouth.

Thrown over the edge, Stone exploded inside her with a powerful stroke that seated him deep in her cunny. "Theo," he bellowed, and then collapsed over her back.

They lay in a heap as they recovered. Cooper reached over and kissed her lightly on the lips. "Thank you, Theo." Then he rose from the bed, dressed, and slipped from the room.

Stone lay there holding his wife in the quiet room. Many emotions buzzed within. Tired, but more than ready to retire to their room, Stone crawled from the bed and carried his wife with him.

As erotic as watching her with another man was, it had been an equally torturous undertaking. Now that it was over, he wanted to beat his chest and cry out to all and sundry that she was his. Yet he would never have denied her the experience, the utter abandonment of having two lovers who catered to her every need.

But now that he had survived, he wanted—no, he needed to imprint himself on his luscious little pet. Determined to remind her of their bond, he carried her back to their bed, laid her down, and suckled her breasts. As she roused to his loving, he moved lower. With a few swipes of his tongue, she was awake and ready to take him again.

He spread her thighs and plunged in to the root of his cock. With each successive stroke, his balls slapped against her arse. "Mine, woman. You are mine."

His declaration became a chant as he slid into her over and over again. He cradled her in his arms, letting his weight rest on his forearms, and he made possessive, demanding love to his wife. Their climax came with a synchronicity that had Stone's legs turning to pudding as her cunny clutched at his length. He imagined the warm spurt of his cum marking her inside and out. The need to claim her in the way of master and slave made him crazy with its persistence. Perhaps a bracelet or collar of some kind could be fashioned for her. Or perhaps she'd wear the sapphires at all times for him?

"Thank you, Stone. This night was an amazing gift." Her softly uttered appreciation speared his heart and solidified her control over him.

He would do anything for her. Kill anyone who tried to take her from him. Somehow, his unwanted bride had turned into the one woman he could never live without. "You are welcome, Theo." *I shall never let you go.*

He slipped from her body and snuggled as close to her as he could manage. They drifted off to sleep wrapped around each other.

Chapter Nineteen

Stone woke with the sun despite their late night. He stretched and made to rise when Theo snagged an arm about his waist and tugged him back toward the bed. "Don't go," she murmured.

He chuckled and tumbled back into bed. "I did not intend to wake you."

"Mmmmm. You didn't. I was luxuriating in your warmth when you deserted me."

"My apologies. I thought you were sleeping and merely aimed to let you rest. After last night, I assumed you needed it." He lay back down and settled her so she draped half on his chest and half off.

"I merely need you near me. Stone, I want you to know that while I appreciate the gift of last night, you are the only man I want in my bed."

The worry that had clutched at his heart the night before, even after they had made love alone, released its treacherous grip. "Ah, wife. I am very glad to hear you say that. While I wanted to indulge your curiosity, let you explore some of what is possible, it was a night I'd prefer never to repeat."

She smiled at him. "Excellent." Then she nibbled her lower lip again as color rose in her cheeks. "Though I do not know how I shall ever look Cooper in the face again."

"Cooper would never treat you with anything less than the respect you are due. I would never have invited him into our bed if I did not trust him implicitly." Stone dragged his knuckles along one pretty pink cheek.

"Well, I shall endeavor not to turn into a complete blushing simpleton in his presence, though I fear that may be a challenge."

Stone tamped down his jealousy. She was a bit embarrassed over what they had shared. She was not infatuated with his longtime friend. In desperate need of a switch in topics, he reached for something easy and mundane. "Do tell me, what are your plans for today?"

"I believe I am scheduled to receive callers this afternoon, and then tea with my sister and Lady Heartfield."

Stone couldn't control the urge to run his fingers through the golden silk of his wife's hair. The strands sifted through his fingers like water. "Must you be chummy with Lady Heartfield?"

"Stone, it is not as though we discuss you whenever we visit. You are rarely, if ever, a topic of conversation." Theo sat up, clutching the sheet to her breasts. "She was once someone you trusted. Why should that trust have changed? She did not reveal anything of your history to me." She reached over and laid her hand on his chest, as though reassuring him.

When the sheet slipped down around her hips to leave her breasts exposed, he struggled to focus on the conversation. "Very well. But I do ask that you be careful whom you meet of her acquaintances. No more madames and such."

Theo laughed softly and stretched, lifting her breasts high and exposing her softly rounded belly for his delectation. "Agreed. Though you are becoming quite the hypocrite, aren't you, my lord?"

"Be that as it may, I do not wish you to be tarnished with my former reputation any more than you are by virtue of our marriage." His gaze drifted to her rosy nipples that puckered under his scrutiny as she released her stretch.

"Yes, Master." The husky tone would have given away her quick shift from morning conversation to desire-fueled action if her use of "master" had not. Without discussion, she delved under the covers and sought out his rapidly thickening rod. Marriage was a far more pleasant state of being than he could have anticipated.

A few days later, Theo strolled out the front door and clambered up into the cabriolet. Reins in hand, she set out for a drive through Hyde Park and then to shop on Bond Street. With the tiger clinging to the back of the vehicle, she raced through the park in a rush of excitement. She simply adored driving fast. The rush of the wind, the thrill of the speed. It made her feel wild and alive, not unlike how she felt when kneeling before her husband.

Spying her sister, who had come out for an early afternoon ride before the truly fashionable crowd took to Rotten Row, she stopped to chat.

"Hullo, Lizzy." Theo grinned at her sister's surprise.

"Oh, Theo, tell me you did not take Stone's cabriolet for a drive without his permission."

Theo tutted at her sister. "Of course not. Stone gave me permission to drive his team and vehicle whenever I like. They go very fast, Lizzy. It's much better than driving Mother and Father's old carriage or that wagon the house staff used. I should have taken Father's rig out for a drive sooner."

"He would never have allowed that," Lizzy pointed out.

"He would likely never had known. He barely noticed me as long as I did not turn up lame," Theo countered.

"You may be correct. However, one would think your husband realized your penchant for recklessness after your jaunt to The Market." Lizzy rolled her eyes.

"He trusts me to handle myself and the team. Really, it's not as if I'd do anything foolish."

"Good afternoon, Lady Stonemere." A familiar dapper young man pulled up in a phaeton.

"Good afternoon, Denton." Theo offered him a jaunty nod in greeting.

"I don't believe I've made the acquaintance of your lovely companion." The golden brown of his hair gleamed in the sunlight like the pelt of a mink. His golden eyes danced with mischief as he glanced at Lizzy.

"This is my sister, the Marchioness of Carlisle. Lizzy, this is *Mister* Hugh Denton. Stonemere's cousin."

He reached across the space between his carriage and Lizzy's horse to take her hand in greeting. "Lady Carlisle, a pleasure to make your acquaintance, though it seems I have done so too late to claim the heart of such a lovely lady."

Theo eyed the man curiously. He appeared rather taken with her sister, who replied with all due courtesy. "A pleasure, Mr. Denton."

His attempt to dazzle her sister over with, he switched his attention back to Theo. "That is quite a stunning team and vehicle you are driving, my lady."

"Thank you. My husband has excellent taste in horseflesh." Theo resisted the urge to preen.

"Too bad such fine beasts are subjected to a sedate trot through the park." His unapologetic grin teased Theo with a hint of mischief...and she so loved mischief.

"I am quite capable of providing the cattle the necessary exercise."

The glow in his eyes warmed. "As handsome as you look atop that rig, I can't help but think those cattle are more than any lady could handle."

Theo guffawed good-naturedly—though he had called her driving skills into question. "You play at being a bounder, sir. But, I daresay I can handle my team better than you yours."

Lizzy gasped.

He chuckled. "Why, that sounds like a challenge. Would you care to place a small wager on that? Say, fifty pounds?"

Theo hesitated. She had nearly forty pounds to hand, and she would bet Lizzy could supply the rest. "Done. Shall we set the course?"

Lizzy gasped again. Was she breathing at all? Were her sister's laces so tight she'd faint as soon as Theo took off?

"Lady's choice." Denton bowed gallantly despite being seated and managing his team.

"Theo, you can't do this," Lizzy pleaded.

"It is done, Lizzy." She turned to her competitor. "Queen's Gate to the North Gate."

"We'll need a starter and someone to spot the finish." Denton glanced around. "Hail, Brougham."

Theo was sure her entire head had caught fire. The one bloody person that had to be trotting by was the Earl of Brougham. *Damn and blast.*

"Good day, Denton, Lady Stonemere, Lady Carlisle." He tipped his hat at each in turn.

"Excellent timing, Brougham. We need someone at the finish line to judge the winner, and I hope the ladies will excuse me if I declare Lady Carlisle biased."

"Oh, are you racing Carlisle?" Cooper looked about for Lizzy's husband.

"Not at all, I'm racing Lady Stonemere." Denton failed to hide his pleasure at the surprise on Cooper's face. Theo wanted to drive away and pretend the whole episode had never happened. She suppressed a groan, desperate to escape. How had she gotten herself into this scrape?

"Lady Stonemere?" Cooper blanched. If he'd been a woman, Theo was sure he'd have fainted.

"Quite so. I intend to show Lord Denton that not only can a lady handle a vehicle, but she can do so better than he." Theo tilted her chin up and refused to look into the eyes of the handsome man who had pleasured her ruthlessly a few nights earlier.

Cooper sighed. "Where is the finish line?"

"The North Gate. Lizzy will see us off at Queen's Gate." Theo nudged her cattle forward as they became restless. It was as though they knew what she was about.

"I shall await you there." Cooper nodded and then turned and trotted off on his chestnut.

"Excellent. Shall we assemble at Queen's Gate?" Denton tapped his reins and left Theo to turn her vehicle around.

After dispatching her groom to accompany Lizzy's maid for a short stroll, she and Denton set up at the start and waited for the signal from Lizzy. With the drop of a handkerchief, the race was on. Denton took an early lead, but Theo knew where she would take control. With his higher-sprung phaeton, she would be able to careen around the corner onto the north path and breeze past Denton, who would need to slow down to prevent tipping over.

She stayed close to him, and with the first turn, surged ahead. After the final turn onto the north path, she was well in the lead and leaving him behind. His cattle had worked so hard in the first part of the race that they had little stamina left as they hit the final stretch. Still, in the end, he was nipping at her heels as she crossed the finish line and burst onto High Street. With a quick jerk of the reins, she avoided a dray cart and three street urchins attempting to earn a few pennies.

Once she pulled back around, she found Lizzy and Cooper both fuming at her. "I won!" Her pronouncement fell flat as the pair glared at her. Then Denton pulled back around as well, and they relented in their demeanors.

"Good show, Lady Stonemere." Hugh acknowledged her fine driving and paid his debt before he bid them all a good day.

"Well, it was a lovely drive in the park, but I must collect my groom and be off. I do have errands to run." Theo waved and urged her horses away from the site of her latest catastrophe. Or at least it would be once Stone heard about it. And with Cooper as a witness, there was little doubt in her mind that he would hear of the race.

After retrieving her groom, she drove to Bond Street. She might as well enjoy her first and last outing in the cabriolet.

Chapter Twenty

S tone was relaxing by the fireplace when Parsons announced a guest. "The Earl of Brougham to see you, my lord."

"Show him in." Stone steeled himself for his first visit with his friend since they'd shared Theo.

Said friend stormed into the study, his face a mask of fury. "Stone, what the hell are you doing turning your wife loose on London like that?"

Stone shot out of his chair. "What the devil are you talking about?"

"You gave her your cabriolet to drive?" Cooper sputtered and huffed in agitation.

"I allowed her to take it out for a drive." He groaned. "What did she do?"

Cooper snorted.

"No, wait. Just tell me who she raced." He pinched the bridge of his nose between thumb and forefinger.

"Denton."

"Dear God." He collapsed into his chair. "How awful was it? Clearly, she's not hurt."

"Awful? The bloody wench trounced him. She beat him handily and took fifty pounds in the process. But you should have known better than to let her alone in that vehicle. She's far too reckless."

Stone had known this would happen. He'd almost reneged on his promise to her. But he'd wanted to trust her to be careful. It was clear that had been a bad idea. "I know. I had hoped if I trusted her a bit, she would prove to be worthy.

Clearly, I am too besotted with my own wife to know what's good for her."

"Well, the worst I should expect will be the gossip. Though I doubt Denton will be touting his loss at the hands of a woman. But it was the middle of Hyde Park. Someone will have seen the race and will make mention of it." Cooper poured himself a brandy.

"Yes. It seems Theo will be facing the cross a bit sooner than either of us expected. Thank you for letting me know about the race. I would have been much angrier to have heard it through the grapevine."

"Yes, well, since I played witness, I knew you needed to hear of it. Do be sure to give her a good swat for me."

Stone grinned ruefully. "Certainly. By the by, do you have a moment? Been meaning to run something past you."

"Of course." Cooper settled into a nearby chair.

Stone sighed and pinched the bridge of his nose again. "Well, I feel a bit silly, but I seem to have grown rather accident-prone. In the last few months, I have tripped and fallen in front of two moving vehicles, gotten caught in a snatch-and-rob carriage, and was attacked in an alley while attempting to rescue a lure."

"Sounds as though you either need to be more careful, or something more nefarious may be afoot. Any ideas who might prefer to see you under the ground?" Cooper took another sip of his drink.

"No. I can't imagine who dislikes me enough to wish me dead. Either way, I shall endeavor to be more careful. And if anything new comes to light, you will be the first to know."

"Very well. Stay safe, my friend." Cooper tossed back his drink and departed.

Stone remained seated and stared at the flames in the fireplace. His wife had turned out to be more trouble than he had ever imagined.

Theo opened the front door and peered around the solid wood obstruction. Lucky her. The foyer was empty. She eased the door closed and turned around to sneak upstairs. Without a doubt, Stone would have heard about the race by now. She had been approached by no fewer than three ladies on Bond Street while shopping to offer their congratulations.

She had one foot on the stairs when the silence shattered. "Theodora Denton, in my study."

She cringed. Double damn. Word had obviously reached him. She turned and walked into his study.

"Attempting to sneak in, were you?" He sat behind his desk.

"Um." Her heart raced as indecision warred within. Should she make a run for it and lock herself in her sitting room until he calmed down?

"I know you were. Just as you know that I am aware of your afternoon excursion." He rose and paced around the desk.

She nodded, unable to force words past her parched throat.

"Please explain to me how you wound up behaving so recklessly after our conversation about how important the vehicle, cattle, and—most importantly—you are to me?"

Anger radiated off his towering body. She'd cocked it up. She had suspected, but now she knew just how badly she'd done so. She swallowed and wet her dry mouth. "I stopped to chat with Lizzy when your cousin Denton joined us. Well, it all started out friendly enough, I suppose, but then he suggested that a woman couldn't handle a team. It was a challenge I could not let pass, not only for myself, but for all women."

Stone turned his back on her, which made her stomach rise up, twist, and belly flop in her torso.

"I'm very sorry, my lord. I promise the cattle were never in jeopardy, and there is nary a scratch on the paint." She bit her lip to quell its tremble.

"Go upstairs to our private room. You know which room I mean. There you will strip and kneel in the corner to await my pleasure."

"Yes, Master." She scurried from the study, up the stairs, and into the new room. There she hung her dress and paletot in the wardrobe that had been added since her last visit. She struggled with the rest of her undergarments but finally managed to free herself. With only one corner available, she knelt there naked but for her stockings, as was his usual preference.

An eternity might have passed as she waited. Perhaps it had only been ten minutes, but her knees ached and her heart pounded with such force that she was certain she would have an aneurysm. His heavy footsteps thumped down the hallway, and then he entered the room. The creak of wood bearing a significant weight indicated he had taken a seat on the throne.

"Come to me, pet." His command startled her, but she stood and approached him immediately. "Kneel, please." He waited for her compliance. "Do you know why you are to be punished?"

"Yes, Master." She nodded. "I was reckless, I put your cattle and your vehicle in danger, and myself at risk." A tear slipped down her cheek as the guilt of her rashness settled on her chest like a weight. It was how she always felt after each scrape. Usually she hid in her room and cried until the feeling passed, but Stone had not allowed her such retreat.

"Most importantly, you put yourself at risk. Beyond the possessions and the horses, you could have broken your fool neck. Come here."

Stone pulled her back to her feet. He could see the misery etched on her face as she realized how rash she'd been. He took pity on her, enough so that he would not strap her to the cross as punishment. By all accounts—and he had heard more than one over the course of the late afternoon at his club—she had acquitted herself well. Poor Denton appeared the cad for goading her into such a display, even if it hadn't been malicious.

"Yes, Master." She stepped up beside him and hesitated.

"Bend over and settle your hips across my knees." He helped her get into position. "You will take twenty spanks as punishment for your disregard for your well-being. This is not about the carriage, nor the cattle. This is simply about you risking your neck. Do you understand me?"

"Yes, Master." Her muffled response was enough.

He could no longer delay the inevitable. He landed the first swat and paused.

"One, Master." Her voice waffled with the sting of the first strike.

Then the second. "Two, Master."

The next four came in a flurry of quick slaps. Her bottom was nice and pink, and she counted for him without his direction to do so. While the need to spank her made him unhappy, her capacity to remember that he preferred someone to count was gratifying.

The next four strikes of his palm came in an even distribution across the meat of her backside and increased the color to a bright pink. Heat radiated off her flesh now as he continued on to an even dozen. Just over halfway, and he could hear her tears between her accountings.

"Almost done, pet. Eight more and you will be clear of your misbehavior. Do you promise to never again put yourself at risk in such a manner?" He rubbed her inflamed flesh.

"I promise, Master." When her voice cracked, he almost stopped the punishment.

He much preferred pleasuring her to punishing. But if she was to respect him and his authority over her, then he must follow through with this onerous task. He shifted the next four strikes to the cuff of her bottom. They fell slow and hard to ensure as she sat for the next day or so, she would remember this lesson. He ranged the last four blows from the top of her bum down to the newly spanked cuff.

Theo cried, though she never thrashed, fought, or otherwise attempted to prevent the spanking. She accepted her punishment with the grace and poise he had come to admire her for. When it was over, he helped her stand, gave her a sip of water from the pitcher he'd placed in there earlier, and settled her on his lap.

"How do you feel after your first real punishment?" He tried to hide his worry that he'd been too rough with her.

"First? Master, you spanked me our first night in here." Her face flushed at the memory.

"I did, but that was less punishment and more an aid to help you past your fear. It is the motivation that determines if it is punishment or discipline. Discipline is a way to help you push your boundaries or remind you of what they are. Punishment is the result of wrongdoing or poor behavior. The other more significant difference is that I do not enjoy punishing you, whereas I shall always thrill to watch you respond to discipline."

"I'll have to mull that over a bit before I can fully understand the nuances of each, Master." Theo's brow wrinkled as it always did when she thought hard about something.

"There is no rush. Once you are sure you understand the difference, we should discuss it to make sure we are in accord." He pressed a gentle kiss to her forehead.

"Yes, Master." She sighed and settled closer against his chest.

"Now that the ugly part of the night is over, you will refrain from speaking again until I grant you permission. Simply nod your understanding."

She dipped her head forward in acknowledgment.

"Good. Stand for me, pet. I want to introduce you to something we will both enjoy." He stepped toward the St. Andrew's Cross but drew up short when she did not move. He glanced back to see her eyes wide and her chest rising and falling in rapid, shallow bursts. "Theo, I promise you will not be struck again tonight. Do you understand?"

She nodded.

He tried to ease her forward, but she remained rooted in place. "Are you still ashamed about your desire to be tied to the cross?"

She nodded.

"And do you remember what I told you the other night?" He pitched his voice low and warm to soothe her.

She nodded and let her gaze lock with his.

"I am as eager as you to tie you to the cross. I intend to restrain you and make you orgasm until you are too weak to stand on your own. Then I shall lay you down and make love to you until dawn." His cock throbbed after painting her a picture of what the evening held in store.

She drew in a long, slow, and very deep breath. Then she nodded and smiled at him.

"You please me beyond measure, pet." This time when he stepped toward the apparatus, she followed.

He placed her so that her back pressed against the wood beams and then used the buckles on each extension to bind her at the wrists and ankles.

Theo drew a deep breath and sighed as he let his fingertips trail up her leg. Her thigh quivered and her flesh prickled with goose pimples. He reached the apex of her thighs and dipped the tip of his finger into her folds. Her juices coated his skin and made him weak with the need to taste her. With a wicked smile, he lifted his hand to his lips and sucked the digit. Her sweet-tart flavor burst over his tongue as he savored the taste.

He looked up to find she avidly watched his every move. Lust gleamed in her eyes and sparked a reciprocal feeling within his own breast. It still boggled his mind how desperately he wanted this woman.

He reached between her spread thighs and gathered more of her feminine essence. As deliberate as any artist, he painted each nipple with her juices. Then he leaned over and sucked one until she moaned and pressed her peak deeper into his mouth. Satisfied with her response, he switched to the other side and repeated the process.

When he reached down to find her thighs damp with her cream, he dropped to his knees. More her supplicant than her master, he wedged his shoulders between her legs and parted her labia. With her tender pink flesh exposed to his gaze, he eased closer. Hungry to have her musky taste on his tongue, he leaned in and licked her from her channel to her clit.

Theo muttered something that sounded like the start of "Master," but since she was under orders not to speak, he dismissed it as faulty hearing. As he delved deeper into the matter at hand, his cock gave him an angry throbbing reminder that he had kept his own needs at bay for far too long. And still, he remained determined to melt her with pleasure.

He swirled his tongue into her pussy and pumped in and out in mimicry of what he would soon do with his cock. She thrust her hips and tried to grind against him. He recognized she was close to the edge, so he swiped up and over her clit until she screamed with her climax. He drank her in and ruthlessly worked her back up to another peak. She broke on the dying waves of her first crisis. Her knees softened as she flooded his mouth with her pleasure. Still not satisfied, he continued to thrash her sensitive nub, forcing her to yet one more climax. This time, her body resisted his demands, so he took one wet finger and pressed against her tight sphincter until she relaxed into the pressure. As he slid in to the knuckle, she yielded, and she fell over the edge once more. Her voice hoarse from her bliss-driven screams, she could only whimper as the orgasm ravaged her.

Content with his efforts, Stone worked to release first her ankles and then her wrists. Her limbs weakened by satisfaction, she sagged against him as promised. Shaking with his need to be inside her, he hefted her up and carried her to the bed.

Having settled Theo on the mattress, Stone stripped to the skin and lay next to her. The way she cuddled closer to him caused an odd warmth to suffuse his chest. Having had very little experience with any pleasure outside the physical realm in the past five years, it took him a moment to recognize his state of happiness. The sense of rightness that came from caring for her, tending to her needs.

With his prick eager to be warm as well, he took but a moment to savor the heretofore forgotten emotion. Could it be love? He pushed the notion aside, certain his desire played tricks on him. Then his amorous side took over, and he embarked on a deeper exploration of his wife's form. He let his hands stroke over her ribs and down to the flare of her hips.

She curved into a delectable backside that begged for attention of any type. He caressed her pink cheeks and gave a gentle squeeze that garnered a response from his pleasure-drunk wife. She silently slipped her hands up his chest to loop around his neck and then pressed her breasts against his chest.

"I see my pet is recovering from her stupor." He wanted to bury himself inside her, but he also wanted her awake and coherent enough to enjoy their lovemaking. Because, despite the equipment, the rules, and his overbearing nature, it would be something gentle and tender. And that was something he had never done before.

Still bound by silence, she pulled his face down to hers and plunged her tongue into his mouth. Though she initiated the kiss, he immediately took over and ravaged her tongue, teeth, and lips. He tasted and touched every part of her mouth as they shared their air, their joy, and their very souls.

Then he rolled her over and sank into her cunny with a swift, sharp thrust of his cock. She moaned and shook beneath him as he breathed through the initial rush of bliss. Ever so slowly, he withdrew to the huge swollen tip of his shaft and hovered. As he pushed both himself and her to their breaking point, he knew without a doubt he could never touch another woman, let alone master one. He was as much a slave to Theo as she was to him.

With a groan, he drove back into her channel and proceeded to pound into her depths with a fierce determination born of his newly discovered tenderness. As she exploded around him, her hips jerked up to meet his powerful thrusts. He pumped into her over and over until his own release burst through him in a jolt of cosmic sensation that would have brought him to his knees were he not already there.

Never again would he share her. Never again would another man be allowed to touch her as he touched her. Theo was his wife, his slave, and the physical embodiment of his heart.

Chapter Twenty-One

T heo rolled over as someone swept open the drapes, blasting her face with sunshine. "Mary, close those curtains, or I shall dock you a week of pay."

"How very shrewish of you, pet." Stone's sardonic tone caused her to roll back over and crack a single eyelid.

"It's you." Surprise had her heart fluttering beneath her breast.

He raised a dark eyebrow. "And who am I, pet?"

A wave of disappointment in herself pushed her stomach down near her knees as she sat up, the sheet clutched to her breasts. "You are my master."

"Very good. Do try to remember that, or I shall have to assist you." He stalked toward the bed with a determined stride that sent frissons of excitement and trepidation sliding through her from head to toe. "Do you often threaten to withhold pay from your maid?"

Somehow, her stomach had shot from her knees to her throat in the blink of an eye. "No...err...yes, Master."

His upper lip quivered, but she wasn't sure if it was in derision or because he resisted the urge to smile.

"What I mean is, I often threaten her, but she is well aware I do not mean it. I tend to be a bit querulous in the morning, Master." While she knew Stone would never hurt her, she was learning to dislike disappointing him.

"Well, this is something new I have learned about you. Unfortunately, I believe today you shall have good reason to be peevish." He sat down on the edge of the mattress and cupped her face with one hand. "You see, pet, today you must go and visit your mother. Then you shall make a stop to visit your sister. After that, if you have time, you will need to visit my mother, as well." He leaned forward and placed a kiss on her forehead. "After those visits, you may either come home or address any other business you have a need to attend."

Theo repressed the desire to sigh heartily over the itinerary he had laid out. Visiting both of their mothers in one day? With an aching bottom? Well, at least Lizzy would be able to commiserate. "Yes, Master."

"Now, I suggest you arise and prepare for your busy day. I have a number of issues to address with my man of affairs and shall be closed away most of the day." He had walked across the room and opened the door to leave when he turned back and caught her rising stiffly from the bed. "I shall enjoy knowing you think of me with every seat you take today."

"Yes, Master." She wanted to hurl every epithet known to her at his head as her bottom flared to life again.

The door closed, and she cursed with her first true step. "Son of a pox-ridden whore."

"I do believe the dowager countess would object to such a characterization." His laughter followed the statement as he strolled down the hall.

She should have known he would listen through the door. Shaking her head, she managed to get to the privy as Mary appeared.

"Good morning, my lady."

It seemed cruel that Theo's maid enjoyed mornings so much, but there were many who did. Why, she had yet to fathom. "A bath, please, Mary. I do need a good soak with some salts before I can bring myself to visit Mother. I think I shall see her first."

"Of course, my lady. Do you have a dress you desire to wear today?" The sounds of cabinets opening and closing could be heard as Mary went about her day.

"The clover-green walking dress will do nicely. And my oldest petticoats, as well. I fear anything rougher than a feather would be too harsh today."

"Very good, my lady. I shall be back shortly with your bathwater. Your dressing gown is on the bed."

Once Mary had left, Theo made her way over to the bed and found her robe. She pulled it on and then decided that sitting to wait for her bath was far less desirable than standing.

Stone walked up the stairs to his cousin's rooms and rapped smartly on the door. A moment later, he was shown into the nice—though not lavish—apartments. With only one servant to act as butler, maid, and valet, Hugh managed, but not with the same level of comfort as Stone had when he was at university.

"My lord." Hugh emerged from the sleeping chamber, fully clothed as though he had been about to depart. "To what do I owe this honor?"

He sat down across from Stone on the other small sitting sofa. "I am certain it cannot be beyond your expectation that I might visit after yesterday's incident in the park."

Hugh paused from tugging at his cuffs and looked up at Stone. "Oh, that." He chuffed. "A bit of fun between cousins-in-law."

Stone stared at him, his temper rising at his cousin's intentional obtuseness.

"I daresay no one shall even hear of it. Certainly not from my lips," Hugh said.

Of course, they wouldn't, not from the one who'd lost to a female. His countess had handily trounced his cousin, but that did not rate. "Oh, I am quite certain you shall not mention your loss to my wife. But I fear it is the wagging tongues of every dandy, fop, and chit who also happened to be strolling in the park at the same time who shall be your doom."

"Doom?" His voice squeaked like a rusty hinge.

"Perhaps doom is a bit strong. But word of both the race and your subsequent loss have already made the rounds of White's." His cousin paled a bit, but he forged ahead. "I have already addressed this issue with my wife. However, I feel it is appropriate I convey to you the level of my displeasure. So let me be crystal clear on this point: if you feel the need to race through Hyde Park again, you will find some other man's wife to challenge. Or, better yet, I suggest you find a man. But if you involve my wife in such antics again, our next interview will be far less civil."

Hugh stood, his hands balled into fists as though he resisted the urge to punch Stone. A laughable notion at best. Then he relaxed his hands and pasted on a smile that rankled more than any other action or words could have. "Well, I think you've made your point. And while I do sincerely regret involving your wife in such indelicate activities, I might suggest you worry about taming that hellion you made a countess, and less about who I may or may not lose to in a future race." He strode toward the door and opened it wide. "If you will excuse me, I have an appointment I must get to."

Stone rose, still perturbed, but short of punching the man in the face or calling him out, he had little recourse. As he departed his cousin's flat, he wondered when it was he'd lost his edge as an officer. There was a time he could make grown men cower in fear with a mere look.

Regardless, he doubted his cousin would make the same mistake twice. Nobody wanted to be known for losing a carriage race to a woman.

Theo shifted in her seat for possibly the twentieth time in the last hour. Of course, each time she fidgeted, her mother gave her that look. The one that once upon a time struck fear into a little girl's heart.

"...and then Lady Fairbottom fainted dead away in the middle of the musical. I do believe it was the sour note from the poor Morton chit that caused it." Lady Upton cackled, oblivious to the byplay between mother and daughter.

Determined to make her escape, Theo set her tea down and rose. The relief from standing was short-lived, however, as walking had proven almost as painful as sitting. "Mother, I fear I must be off. I have two more stops to make before my day is done."

"Oh, are you visiting the Dowager Countess Stonemere?" Her mother thoroughly enjoyed running in the same circles as Lady Stonemere. Their family had held the earldom for over two hundred years. It might be a lesser title than her father's, but it was old and prestigious.

"I am. Stonemere particularly asked me to check in on her. I do hope you ladies enjoy the rest of your afternoon." Lady Upton and another woman Theo had already forgotten the name of tittered as she swept from the room. Unfortunately, her mother was right on her heels.

"Dear, can you and Lord Stonemere join us for dinner next Saturday?" Her mother looked so hopeful. "En famille, of course."

"I believe we are available. I shall have to consult my calendar to be sure. Now, I'm off, Mother." Theo kissed her on the cheek and departed the house before she had to accept some other invitation to one of her mother's silly salons. Theo had frequently suffered through salons hosted by her mother that were a parody of the real thing. The women would gather about, and once one person said something that sounded reasonably intelligent, they all agreed until someone had to leave.

At her next stop, Theo gratefully sank onto her sister's sitting sofa and leaned onto her hip. Lizzy giggled at her sister's rather obvious predicament. "Oh dear. I daresay Stonemere learned of your adventure yesterday. Did he not?"

Theo dropped her chin upon her fist as she leaned against the armrest of the chair she'd chosen. "Of course, he did."

Lizzy looked pointedly at her sister. "You knew when you accepted the challenge things could go badly with him."

Theo sighed. "I did. But that rotten Lord Brougham tattled to Stone. We should never have involved him in the wager."

"Yes, well, I'm glad he was there, and that Mr. Denton paid up once you trounced him." Lizzy defended the rotten scoundrel. Maybe if she knew what had occurred between her, Stone, and Cooper, she'd feel differently about his betrayal. Theo certainly did.

"The thrill was in the race and the win. I wouldn't have given the money a second thought." Theo was not much of a betting woman, probably because she often lost when she did wager.

"It is the principle of the thing, Theo. A man—or woman—of honor always pays his or her debts." Lizzy seemed more scandalized by Theo's disinterest in the money than by the actual fact of the race.

"Yes, well, I have my doubts about men and their honor." She rubbed her tender bottom.

Lizzy giggled again. "You poor thing. Are you terribly sore?"

Theo grinned. "It was worth it. Everything that came after was absolutely amazing. I'd take the punishment a thousand times over for the pleasure that followed."

Lizzy's eyebrows rose. "Well, just don't go getting into trouble just so Stone has a reason to spank you."

Theo laughed. "No, no. He has assured me I need only ask if I would like to be spanked."

The women fell into a fit of laughter before settling down to discuss the rest of the day's gossip. Two hours later, after a stop with the Dowager Countess of Stonemere, Theo headed home. She had intended to visit the orphanage, but neither time nor her backside would permit any further stops. Once home, she sank gratefully into a hot soaking tub for the second time in a day. As her aches and pains eased with the heat, she relaxed and planned a nice quiet dinner at home for her husband.

Chapter Twenty-Two

S tone had just returned home from White's after having lunch with Cooper and Flint. He left early when his stomach became upset, and now that he was home, he was glad he'd departed. As he went to sit behind his desk, his arms and legs trembled like a leaf in the wind, and when he took his seat, a clammy sweat broke out on his forehead while a chill skittered down his spine. Deciding he needed to lie down, he tried to rise again, but his stomach chose that moment to revolt. He barely made it to his feet before tossing up his accounts in a nearby planter.

After a short while, he was able to make his way back to his desk, where he rang the servant's bell. Mrs. Beats appeared, and upon seeing he did not feel well, she immediately marshaled the staff. Before long, Stone found himself ensconced in his bed with Evers and his wife fussing over him.

"Theo, this is simple food poisoning. Please, stop fretting. I will be fine by morning." Stone was certain his worrying wife might drive him mad. And, most importantly, he needed to sort through events in his head. When he considered all the various accidents and near misses he'd escaped of late, it was getting harder and harder to deny that something foul was afoot.

"Do you recall what you had to eat today?" She stood next to his bed, her hands clamping tight only to shift and repeat the motion.

"I had halibut for lunch. I am sure it was simply a bad piece of fish. Do go on and eat your own dinner. Evers and Mrs.

Beats will see that I am cared for, and then I plan to sleep. All this has taken quite a toll." He yawned, his energy waning with each passing moment.

His wife looked mutinous. "Absolutely not. I am your wife, and I shall see to your care."

"Theo—" He yawned again.

"Stone, sleep for now. I shall be here when you awaken, and we may argue about your care then."

Exhausted and unable to argue further, he drifted off to sleep.

The next morning when Stone awoke, he found a sleeping Theo perched in a chair, fully dressed with multiple locks of hair hanging about her face. He moved to sit up but found himself still feeling poorly.

Theo sat up and yawned as she stretched. She looked delightfully rumpled, and, if he were honest, it touched him deeply that she cared enough to linger at his bedside. She glanced over at him and, upon realizing he was awake, turned a concerned gaze upon him. "How are you feeling this morning, Stone?"

"Better." He fibbed because she looked as exhausted as he still felt.

"Excellent. Why don't I go see about a breakfast tray for you?" Her eyes sparkled with a desire to help.

He wanted to groan at the idea of food, but decided to agree with her. "That would be excellent. If you'd send in Evers, I will clean up a bit so I can...eat."

"I am so glad you are feeling better. I must say, you scared me terribly yesterday." Theo rose and came over to the bed. With a gentleness that suggested she did not fully believe his story of feeling better, she leaned over and kissed his still-damp forehead. She departed, and as she opened his chamber door, Evers slipped in as though he knew his presence was required.

Alone with his valet, he quickly dashed off a note to Cooper alerting him to his predicament. Perhaps a trip to Scotland Yard was in order after too many coincidences. Then again, he and Cooper could look into a few things first. Possibly substantiate his thoughts before filing a report.

Besides, it seemed this incident would fall into the same failed category as all the others. Whether it was by luck or some other factor, he seemed to have survived what appeared to be an intentional poisoning. After all, Cooper had had the same lunch and had not been feeling poorly when they parted.

Exhausted from the correspondence and the effort expended with Evers's assistance to set himself to some rights, he fell asleep again before his wife returned with breakfast.

Two weeks spent caring for her recovering husband slipped past before Theo realized it, and she had yet to visit the orphanage. It still concerned her that food poisoning could have laid him so low, but in the end, he had recovered with some rest and her own careful ministrations. Of course, in that time she had begun experiencing her own upset stomach, which had at first worried her that he was sick with something contagious. But, determined to complete her visit to the orphanage despite the regular morning queasiness, she stopped by the library, where she often found Stone after breakfast. Some days they would sit companionably and each deal with their correspondence. Other days he locked himself away with his man of business and took care of pressing matters.

This morning, he sat hunched over the desk, scratching out a letter to someone, his head bent in concentration. The morning sun shone through the giant window behind him, framing Curzon Street and even catching a bit of Curzon Chapel, and shot sparks through his dark hair. Little glints of gold and flame danced about what were normally very sedate, dark strands of hair.

Smiling, Theo stepped in the room and drew Stone's attention. "Do you have a moment to discuss a few invitations?"

He looked up and grinned at her. "Certainly. What entertainments do you have at hand?"

Theo sat down and sifted through those she knew were coming up soon. "We have an invite to the Hawksbury house party."

Stone groaned. "I detest house parties. How long is this one?"

Theo shared the sentiment heartily. For all that she enjoyed the country, she much preferred Stonemere Abbey to most of the modern, overly adorned country homes of the Ton. "A week, but I daresay we can go for the weekend festivities in a fortnight and not stay the full week. I'll let Lady Hawksbury know that business keeps you from arriving sooner."

"Very well. If you believe we should attend." Stone's deferral to her wishes socially boosted her confidence and reminded her that she was, in fact, his partner in many aspects of their marriage. In all the important ones, she preferred to be his pet, submissive to him in a far more traditional sense than she ever imagined.

"I do. I heard yesterday that Lord Townsend will be in attendance for the ball, and I believe you were working on securing an investment from him for the railroad."

Stone chuckled. "Indeed, my perceptive wife, I am. And you are right, it is a wonderful opportunity to mention our endeavor once more."

"I shall reply this morning before I go out. We also have an invitation for a musicale at Lady Devon's that I shall be making our excuses for, but the Marquess of Downing is holding a ball next weekend. It should be a frightfully stuffy event, but Mother and Father will take note if we do not attend."

"Then, by all means, add it to our calendar. Any further mandatory entertainments?"

"That should be all. Since we are so newly married, we can escape many of the lesser invitations. Have you anything for me?"

"I am afraid not. Once I finish this correspondence, I shall be off to White's. But I shall return home in time for dinner as usual."

"Excellent. I believe Mrs. Beats is planning roast pork for dinner." Theo rose and headed toward the door.

"Wife, I believe you have forgotten something." Stone rose from his seat and rounded the desk.

Theo wanted to ignore the nerves fluttering in her belly as he approached. Then he leaned over and pointed to his cheek. "I believe a kiss on the cheek is a customary sign of affection."

Theo flushed, thrilled that he wished to observe such customs. With a grin, she stretched up and placed a peck on his cheek. But before she could sidle away, he wrapped an arm about her waist and hauled her into his chest.

Then he tipped her face up to his and kissed her gently on the lips. "But I think I prefer a kiss on the lips to one on my cheek. Do remember in future, pet."

"Yes, Master." Her breathless reply slipped out as he released her from his arms.

With a lightness to her steps she could only credit to her husband's attention, she headed up to her writing room to reply to the various invitations before her visit to the orphanage.

As it happened, it was afternoon before she was able to escape the house and visit her children. She watched as they ran about the desperately tiny square of green adjacent to the large house they lived in. It was impossible not to look at the larger square of green on the other side of a fence that divided what had once been a single estate into two separate plots of land. One brother had been eager to sell, the other not at all. And so she bided her time until the day the holdout changed his mind.

"Lady Stonemere, 'tis always lovely to have you join us." Mrs. Richter greeted her as warmly as she always did, even before her marriage to Stonemere.

"I do enjoy seeing the children flourish. It reminds me that all is not horrible in the world, though perhaps it would be a little cheerier if I could pry that plot of land from that obstinate man's hands."

Mrs. Richter snorted. "Curmudgeonly old sod. He chased little Bell out of his yard after their ball flew over the fence and refused to return it." She shook her head. "I do hope whoever bought the property is kinder to the children."

"Bought the property? Whatever do you mean?" Despair stabbed right through her corset and into her heart. She had been waiting for years for an opportunity to buy the remaining piece of land.

"I heard from the old man himself that someone came to him and offered an outrageous sum, far more than it was worth, to buy the land. The man looked positively gleeful as he acknowledged how he gouged the new owner."

Theo harrumphed. "Well, if they pressed the old man, it serves them right to overpay for the land. Why, it's barely big enough to build a house on, certainly nothing ostentatious. And this neighborhood is not exactly an address of note. I wonder who could have afforded to purchase the land without regard for their future investment." Theo's curiosity had her bidding Mrs. Richter farewell as she headed off to Mr. Harrington's office to set him on the trail to discover who'd stolen her property right out from under her nose.

Stone sat contentedly in the library and sipped a glass of scotch as he waited for his wife to return home from her outing. She was always in an excellent mood after she visited her orphans, and he hoped to capitalize on that mood this evening. He looked forward to a night of sexy fun with a woman who matched his own appetites perfectly.

The front door slammed shut with a resounding *boom* that echoed through the house as though a portent of doom. A moment later, Theo stalked into the library, pulled her adorable top-hat-styled bonnet off and slammed the poor confection down on the table, absolutely crushing it beyond repair.

Stone sighed. It seemed as though someone or something had his wife's tail feathers in a ruffle. And that was never a good thing, as he had come to learn. "Good evening, Theo. I take it your day did not go as you intended?"

"I am simply furious." She practically vibrated with her emotions.

"Come, my dear, sit and tell me what has you so up in the boughs." Stone's gut clenched. Could she have discovered what he had done?

She flopped onto the settee across from him. "It's the orphanage." She clenched her fist and banged it against the arm of the small couch. "That old man who refused to sell me both pieces of property to spite his brother has had the audacity to sell the parcel to someone else after I have made multiple offers over the last few years."

"I do hate to point out the obvious, Theo. But it is his property, and he has the right to sell to whomever he chooses." Stone gulped, having to swallow past the lump in his throat. He had no idea she would be so upset if she found out about the sale of the property, and damn it, just how did she discover it? He'd made the old geezer promise to keep it quiet.

"Yes, but you know I want that land for my orphanage. The children need room to play, and as of yet, I have been unable to convince the old curmudgeon to sell. It pains me they have so little room." Theo sniffled.

The tears gathered in his wife's eyes almost broke his resolve to hold the truth back. He had planned it as a belated wedding gift for her, but his man of affairs was coordinating some necessary changes to make the land suitable for the orphanage before he presented his gift. What he needed now was time to finish preparations for the full surprise. "I do hate to see you so disappointed. Perhaps we can find some way to cheer you up?"

"It is a lost cause. I am simply devastated."

"Come now, Theo." Stone rose and switched to the space next to his wife on the settee. "Perhaps something good will come of all this? One can never be sure of what the future holds." He reached out and gathered her into a gentle embrace. She leaned into him, snuggling in his arms as though she could find no better haven for comfort.

"I cannot imagine how this might turn about." She sat up and looked at him with eyes full of emotion. Disappointment swirled with hope as she considered how she might best adapt to her new circumstances. "Perchance I shall simply have to set about finding a new location for my orphans?"

"I daresay you should not jump to action so quickly. Some unexpected boon may present itself if you bide your time. Not unlike our fortuitous marriage." He leaned in and snared her pursed lips in a kiss meant to tempt, tantalize, and, most importantly, distract.

She sank into the kiss, letting her form melt against his as they sprawled on the settee in a heap of fabric and limbs. While it had been a last-ditch effort, kissing his wife seemed to accomplish his primary goal. And, lucky sod that he was, the bonus was proving to be an ardent embrace from his lovely wife.

But then she broke their entanglement and drew back to stare him directly in the eyes. "I know what you are about, husband."

That blasted lump of guilt was back. "You do?" he all but croaked in reply.

"Indeed. You are distracting me with your very fine amorous skills. And while normally I would abhor such tactics, today I shall allow it. But do not think this will work in future."

He considered her serious tone and the slight lift at the corner of her mouth, which suggested she repressed the urge to grin at him. "I shall keep that in mind, wife."

"Very well, then, I daresay this is where you should sweep me upstairs and take me to bed if your plan is to be certain of success."

"I see. You have this all thought out. Perhaps, instead, I shall take you upstairs and paddle you to distraction, pet." He had to dig deep to find his stern, disciplinarian tone.

Instantly, her lashes drooped and a dash of pink bloomed on her cheeks. "If that is what you wish, Master."

He groaned. The woman knew just how to twist him in knots. Whereas before he'd been thinking of a little fun in their bedroom, now she had turned his head toward much more dominant thoughts. Thoughts of bending her over the bench and spanking her arse red as he fucked her deep. And despite the early afternoon hour, he would follow through on the images in his mind, because he strongly suspected his lusty wife was thinking of a similar distraction. "Upstairs, in our private room, naked. I shall be along shortly."

She stood up and, with a nod, dashed off to do his bidding. Almost all was right with his world. His wife was both spirited and submissive, the railroad had settled back into normal business routines, and his nightmares had greatly receded. The only concern now lay in the frequent accidents he'd had of late. He needed to address the issues soon, but for now, his wife awaited him. Needed him. He carried a strange sense of satisfaction with him as he headed upstairs.

Chapter Twenty-Three

August 1860

S tone couldn't help but watch Theo as she dozed in the carriage on their way to the Hawksbury house party a week later. She had remained gloomy for days as she waited for her man of affairs to solve the mystery of the "Land Thief," as she'd dubbed the buyer. Guilt twisted in his gut, creating a nauseous feeling that his wife seemed to share of late. At first, he'd thought she was coming down with an illness as she appeared a bit green most mornings, but then in the last few days, she had returned to her normal chipper self. However, these were not the only pressing concerns.

Less than a day's drive, Hawksbury Grange was close enough to London to allow for a shorter weekend visit. Its proximity did nothing to ward off Stone's concerns about the many accidents he'd recently been having. And the thought of possibly entangling Theo in the matter—even by accident—rankled. But by hour four, he'd settled down after a distinct lack of calamity. No broken axles, no rogue wheels, and no startled horses.

Instead of watching for assailants to leap from behind every bush or bend in the road, he now focused on his lovely wife. How had he been so fortunate as to marry the one woman strong enough to be both his countess and his lover? He couldn't fathom it, but he knew he would take further advantage of it while they were at the house party.

Other than bending Lord Townsend's ear about the railway, his main goal was to teach his wife some new naughty games. He fully intended to take her for a private picnic and make love to her in the great outdoors. He could just imagine how the dappled sunlight would decorate her pale skin as he kissed her from head to toe. The image of her breasts bared in the wide open had his cock stirring in anticipation.

Yes, his marriage had been more fortuitous than an actual love match. He liked spending time with his intelligent wife. Enjoyed hearing her take on political issues and business ventures he pondered investing in. Often as not, she had a perspective on things he had not considered himself. He felt a tug in his chest, just under his breastbone, that once more reminded him of emotions he'd long ago shut down.

The carriage jolted, and his wife woke up with a start. She sat up as they hit another bump, and this time landed in his arms. "Really, darling. You needn't arrange to have potholes in the roadway just to gain my attention."

Theo blushed and then wiggled against him, settling down. "Don't be so arrogant, my lord. How do I know you didn't have those potholes placed there to create this very scenario?"

He growled, his restraint wearing thin after his lusty musings. "Because, pet, I would simply take what I want without the need of artifice or games." And then he swooped in and kissed her. Slipped his tongue past her lips to explore the warmth of her mouth. It occurred to him they had yet to have a go at sex in a carriage, and this provided some rather excellent opportunities.

Theo sank into his body, a sweetness in the move he had not expected from his independent wife. Lips still firmly locked, he shifted his free hand around to her back, where he worked the laces loose. When he had enough undone, he broke their heated kiss. "Sit up and straddle my lap, pet."

"What naughtiness does my master have in mind?" Her query came out in a husky voice that had his cock growing even harder. She did as he asked, pushing her skirts out of the way so her thighs pressed against the sides of his.

"Very naughty things come to mind. Now, if you would please take hold of the straps on each side of the windows..." He pointed to the two leather loops dangling from the ceiling of the conveyance on his side. A matching set hung on the other side of the small space to accommodate passengers seated opposite.

"Yes, Master." Theo followed through and slipped a delicate hand and then wrist through each loop. Being a taller-than-average woman, her arms easily spanned the distance while thrusting her breasts forward and into his face. With a pleased grin, he reached inside the neckline of her dress and lifted her breasts from the confines of her corset. In the cool darkness of the carriage, her nipples puckered into tiny berries ripe for plucking. He leaned in and wrapped his lips around one nub. She moaned as he sucked gently on the already swelling flesh. Satisfaction surged through him, mixing and swirling with his own lust to create a heady cocktail to pump through his veins.

Then he shifted to the other tip and repeated the attention. With her legs spread and her body wedged against his, her pussy rubbed over him with each mindless grind of her hips. Her passion stole his breath and reminded him how lucky he was to have her to wife.

"Master, please..." she begged. While she still may not be able to say what she needed, he knew. But it was too soon to allow their fun to end. They had at least another hour before they arrived at Hawksbury, and he intended to make it an enjoyable ride. For both of them.

Theo's breath caught as Stone sucked harder on her nipple, sending jolts of delicious electricity down her frame. She figured it was far too early for him to give her release. He tended to enjoy drawing things out. But she also knew he loved hearing her beg, and as lust rode her hard, she had few qualms about doing as he preferred. In the end, the pleasure would be worth the effort.

And my, was there effort. Her thighs shook with the strain of holding her weight up. Her arms burned from the stretch and strain of unused muscles. And her pussy ached for that which only he could give. But then he shifted her skirts about as he sucked her nipple and burrowed his hand beneath her dress.

"Open to me, pet." His demand, rough and wanton, speared straight to her core.

Spread and waiting, she could feel him search for her slit and silently praised herself for sticking to his demand she forgo the troublesome bloomers. To be honest, she'd done so out of habit, not out of any anticipation of what might occur. How she could have failed to realize a trip with hours ahead would leave ample opportunity for them to explore, she couldn't be sure.

"You are not wearing bloomers. Such a good pet." The rumble of his pleased voice did things to her. Unspeakable things, and she loved it.

"Take me, Master." Urgent need overrode any sense of delicacy, both for her and for him.

His fingers caressed her soaking slit, matching the pulse of his mouth on her breast. And when he slid two digits deep into her hot core, she nearly melted from desire. He pumped in and out of her, pushed her to the brink of orgasm and then stopped. "Would you like to experience the pleasure of riding a man while traveling in a carriage?"

Excitement shivered through her, one part lust and one part anticipation. The forbidden quality of sex in their carriage as they rolled down the road tantalized and enticed. Clopping hooves of outriders and the occasional call between their coachman and their groomsmen added an air of risk that stirred her juices and made her feel all the more wanton for loving it. "Please, Master."

"Then mount your ride, my lady. I believe the road is about to get bumpy." Stone pressed his cock against her opening and guided her down as she released her handholds on the straps. The incredible sensation of being filled and stretched had her light-headed with desire. And then they hit their first bump. The jolt sent them both bouncing on the seat, though for her, mostly on his pole.

They both groaned in pleasure as they did, indeed, hit a rough patch of road. Theo relished the control Stone granted her as she lifted up and slid back down his cock until her orgasm ripped through her with little warning. "Yes,

Master!" Her cry echoed through the carriage, and without a doubt, every one of their attendants heard. Her only saving grace lay in the fact that Mary and the other house staff rode in a carriage behind them and likely did not hear.

Beneath her, the man she was coming to love and treasure pumped into her until his own climax rolled through him. Together, they fell into a rumpled pile of exhaustion. Theo couldn't help but doze as her husband wrapped himself around her as though she were the most precious thing in his world.

"My lord, we have entered the grounds of Hawksbury," one of their riders called out, causing them both to stir.

She sat up and moved to cross back over to her side of the carriage when Stone stopped her. "Best stay here beside me so I can play lady's maid. Though I fear your dress and hair may be beyond repair." His wry grin told her he didn't regret their interlude any more than she did.

"I daresay I can brazen through. I can't imagine others haven't passed the drive to Hawksbury in a similar fashion." She grinned and, together, they worked on setting each other to rights.

Twenty minutes later, Theo swept from the carriage and onto the front drive of Hawksbury Grange to discover, to her horror, that not only were the Marquess and Marchioness of Hawksbury there to greet them, but so were her parents and Stone's mother. She leaned into her husband and hissed, "For heaven's sake, we aren't the royal family. Why are they all here standing about?"

"Not sure, but I'd say you best get to brazening through, or one of our mothers is going to melt on the spot. Though come to think of it, that would redirect everyone from staring at you." His ability to joke at that moment had her lost between hilarity and frustration.

She thwacked him with her fan and attended to the requisite greetings. "Lord and Lady Hawksbury, how kind of you to greet us when you have so many other guests at hand."

"I do like to welcome each of our guests during these intimate little gatherings. Family and friends are so important." And then Theo found herself in the arms of Lady Hawksbury. Well, it was better than her remarking on her very rumpled appearance.

"My lord." She curtsied and moved on to her mother and father as Stone brought up the rear. "Mother, whyever are you out here waiting for us?" she whispered.

"Lizzy and Carlisle are just behind you. They sent word earlier when they had to stop at an inn after having wheel trouble." Her mother eyed her up and down, one brow arching. "Perhaps you should have considered having carriage issues prior to arriving."

Theo blushed but brazened it out. "I can't imagine what you mean." And then she moved on to greet Stone's mother. "Dowager Stonemere, I am so pleased you were able to come."

"Well, my dear. You do look pleased, but I suspect it has little to do with my presence." The dowager winked at her and patted her arms as Stone sputtered and coughed behind her.

Oblivious to her guests' dismay—and in some cases amusement—Lady Hawksbury ushered them all into the house.

Chapter Twenty-Four

After Stone and Theo settled into their room, he went in search of the men at the house party. There was time before dinner for a drink and some conversation. To his great delight, he found Cooper among the gentlemen gathered in the billiards room for a friendly game. His best friend leaned over the table and took his shot. The ball missed and Cooper lost, which freed him up for a chat.

"It's damn good to see you, Cooper." Stone leaned in to whisper, "I thought this party would be a dreadful bore."

Cooper laughed and grinned. "Oh, it has been. The days are long and tedious, especially the entertainments. But the nights, my friend. The nights are long and lusty." He raised his glass and clinked crystal with Stone.

"Well, I certainly won't be enjoying the same entertainments as you, but I did manage to bring my own delight along." Stone hesitated a moment, and for the first time in his life heartily hoped his best friend would keep away from his wife. The idea of sharing her again was not something he could deal with and, by her own admission, not something she wished to do again, either.

Cooper pulled him off to the side, away from prying ears. "Have no fear, Stone. I can see the worry in your eyes. Your wife is lovely and amazing with her mouth. But I am here to find my own lusty fun, not to intrude upon yours. I accommodated a friend's request because I knew what it must have cost him to make it."

Chagrined at how transparent his thoughts must have been, Stone sighed. "You are a good man, Cooper. For once, I hesitated to set the boundary for fear of offending you. Clearly, it was an unnecessary sentiment." Stone tossed the finger of scotch back and set the empty glass on a nearby table right as the dinner chimes rang, drawing them from the billiards room to meet their female counterparts. The ladies giggled and fawned as they were paired with a dinner partner. Stone had the luck to be paired with Theo's sister, Lizzy, but Theo was escorted by the Marquess of Wiggington, a known womanizer. It seemed Lady Hawksbury did not know his wife very well.

As dinner progressed, he watched his wife's face shift from surprise to annoyance, and at one point, he was certain she would stab her partner with a dinner fork. Nevertheless, she managed to restrain herself, and dinner proved to be a bloodless affair. After the meal, the men once again decamped, leaving the ladies to chatter for a bit as they smoked cigars. As he entered, Lord Wiggington and Hugh Denton approached him, the latter with a smile and his hand extended. "Stonemere, I had no idea you would be attending the Hawksburys' entertainment."

Stone took the offered hand of his cousin. Unable to outright ignore the marquess without causing a scene, he tried to find the semblance of a smile before answering. "Theo was keen to get out of London for a few days."

"Too bad you couldn't arrive sooner. It's been quite the gathering the last few days...and nights." Hugh grinned and offered a lascivious wink.

Stone didn't particularly wish to discuss such pursuits with his cousin, let alone the marquess, so he merely grunted.

"At any rate, I take it travel does not sit well with your wife?" Hugh swirled a brandy in his snifter and then took a sip.

Stone couldn't help flashing to the memory of his wife riding his cock in utter abandon as they jounced along the road to Hawksbury. "Theo travels quite well. As far as I know, she thoroughly enjoyed the trip." He worked hard at not emphasizing the word "thoroughly" so as not to besmirch his wife's reputation. This man was unworthy of any confidences he might share with one he trusted.

"Strange, Wiggington said she seemed rather out of sorts at dinner. Blamed the rough ride here." Hugh raised a brow.

It was all he could do not to laugh at the unintended double entendre, but he managed to control his unruly thoughts. "Perhaps something about the meal put her in bad humor. If you will excuse me, I could use a brandy for the digestion myself." And with that, Stone left Hugh and the Marquess of Wiggington.

After an hour of conversation and the opportunity to relieve themselves, the men rejoined the ladies just in time to step outside for a lakeside surprise courtesy of their host and hostess. He dearly hoped it would not be yet another reenactment of the Battle of Trafalgar. It had happened sixty odd years earlier, and no one deserved to be bored to death in such a manner.

Theo took her husband's arm, happy to be shed of the company of the Marquess of Wiggington. The man had been alternately crude and insulting throughout their meal. At one point, she quietly took her fork and jabbed him in the leg. Then she leaned in and warned him to behave himself lest the fork accidentally slide deeper the next time. The prevailing silence after her warning added to watching him limp into the billiards room had been worth the risk. The man was unbearable.

Of course, to be fair, not one man she'd ever met compared to Stone. He embodied what a man should be: fierce, protective, kind, and gentle, with an integrity and moral compass that pointed true. A soldier to his core, he was capable of defending what was his. Certainly, he had vulnerabilities as any human would. His nightmares occasionally woke her up, but since he still had not brought them up, she too stayed silent. Besides, they had improved over time, or so it seemed to her, and she slept beside him every night.

Stone had also proven to be overly dedicated to his work, to the point she often had to drag him from his desk. That tendency made their time at the Hawksburys' all the more special, since he eschewed bringing any work along. As the guests spilled out onto the back lawn of the Grange, Theo and Stone slowed their walk to steal a private moment.

"How was your dinner, wife?" He covered her hand with his own where it rested in the crook of his arm.

"Tolerable once the pests were taken care of." She blinked at him and tried to look as innocent as possible.

He chuckled. "I feared for a moment there would be bloodshed before the evening was through."

She couldn't keep the heat from simmering in her cheeks. Her husband knew her too well. "I fear a small amount may have been spilt."

"I see, so you did stab him with your fork? I thought perhaps he had escaped your wrath," Stone said with an easy contentment that said he was not upset by her revelation.

"I merely poked him a bit. The insufferable man kept blathering on about how his wife will one day remain locked away in their house while he tends to whatever it was he seemed to think would be his business. I had to stop listening while I decided if drawing blood was worth the risk both to my dress and my social standing. As you can see, my dress is unstained." She smiled and held her skirts out to one side to better display their pristine condition.

"You are a minx, my lady." The group had neared the rim of the lake, but they remained a little apart so they could continue to chat. "Did you notice Lady Atherton?"

Theo chewed her lip. She suspected the woman was half-drunk, but then she frequently seemed so. "I did notice she was a bit in her cups."

"Yes, well, I fear her husband is unaware, although how that might be is a bit of a stumper." Stone lifted a brow as Theo drew a breath to speak.

"If she is, it truly is none of our affair. One can only imagine what might drive her to drink." She patted his arm, enjoying the play of muscles beneath the fine cloth of his evening attire. "Stone, do you supp—oh!" Her words cut off as a loud whining hiss ripped through the air, announcing the first firework as it sparkled to life in the night sky.

As the second explosive launched, Theo found herself hauled behind the nearest bushes and shoved beneath a heavy body.

Chapter Twenty-Five

S tone peeked around the foliage as the blasts sounded overhead. How had they found him? His heart raced and his limbs trembled with the flood of vitality pumping through his veins. Christ, he had to get away. Had to find a way to get help and circle back to save the women. A woman's cry pierced the noise, followed by a child's wail. Too late! He was too late, again.

Despair had him hanging his head, though the tears made it hard to see anyway. No point in watching the horrors beyond. But then something soft and feminine wiggled beneath him. A woman. He had saved one! Relief pierced his sadness and gave him a renewed sense of purpose.

"Stone?" The fear in the woman's voice upset him.

"Do not fear. I shall protect you with my dying breath. I swear it. You will survive this night." And he knew she would, because he refused to let it be otherwise.

"Stone, what are you going on about?" She pushed against his chest as though she wanted to dislodge him from his protective stance.

The hiss and whine followed by a loud boom of each mortar stopped, and darkness fell. A smattering of applause and cheers sounded in the distance. He assumed the sepoys were celebrating their victory. A perfect opportunity to slip past. He rose up to crouching and helped the lady up as well as she rearranged her hoops and skirts. He couldn't understand why women insisted on such ridiculous clothing in such a hot dry place as India. But nonetheless, she was in full regalia, and so would move more slowly than him.

He would have to tow her along or possibly carry her if she couldn't keep up.

"Stone." The woman's voice sounded vaguely familiar, though somewhat scared and annoyed. "Stop this nonsense this instant."

"Silence, before you get us both killed." Women could be more trouble than they were worth, which was why he liked finding professionals or experienced widows to take the edge off.

"Achilles Denton, Earl of Stonemere, you will listen to me this instant."

She was getting more demanding, and how in the hell did she know his name? Or part of it, at any rate. She seemed to think he was his father. "Nice try, sweetheart, but I ain't the earl, nor will I ever be. I suggest you squash whatever dreams of a title you harbor and focus on surviving."

She grew very still and stared at him. In the moonlight, he could see her lovely face full of confusion, and something tugged at his memories. Had he bedded her before? Then the woman did the strangest thing. She stepped into him and cupped his face in her small hands. He hadn't noticed before, but she was quite tall for a woman, which made her the perfect height to kiss. And he suddenly wanted very much to kiss her. "Stone, I need you to look at me."

Her blue eyes seemed bottomless as she held his head steady and forced him to meet her gaze.

"It's me, Theo. Your wayward pet. Master, you must look at me. *See* me." Tears filled her bold sapphire eyes and spilled down her cheeks. The urge to hold her and comfort her grew strong. And stronger yet, with each tear that fell down her creamy face.

"I-I. Do I know you?" His confusion rankled, but somehow he knew he could trust this woman.

"Stone, it's me. Your wife. You aren't in India any longer. You're here, at Hawksbury Grange, with me. In England." She leaned up against him and pressed her lips to his as she did the same with her trembling frame. Her kiss was sweet and salty, but beyond that, her taste was familiar. Warm, welcoming, and not part of his past, but part of his present and his future.

She stepped back from him and stared for a long, tense moment.

"Zeus." She said the word firmly and clearly.

He blinked and stared at her again, and then, as if a fog had drifted offshore, he could suddenly see everything clearly. His wife stood before him, her heart in her eyes as she stared at him with tears streaming down her face, having just said her word to bring all things to a stop. "Theo? Darling, what's wrong? What have I done to you?"

She let out a breath and a whispered "Thank the heavens." And then she promptly wept.

Confusion reigned as he tried to sort out the last quarter hour in his head while he took his wife in his arms and attempted to comfort her. He remembered walking on the back lawn after dinner and having a conversation with Theo. But then nothing coherent. Little wisps of details, like the brush obscuring his view and fussing with her hoop skirt.

A hallucination. Dear God, he'd had a hallucination. It was a lucky thing he hadn't hurt anyone. Particularly his wife. If he had not already hauled her into his arms, he would have done so at that moment to ensure she was yet unharmed. And so he could hide his own embarrassing tears. The unfortunate truth was he didn't know if they were tears of joy that he hadn't hurt anyone, or tears of despair that he didn't know how to hide the truth from his wife any longer. He was, in fact, not a whole man in the mental sense.

Tears subsiding, she stepped back from his embrace and locked gazes with him. As though she bore a hole straight through his soul, she looked, assessed, and then nodded. "May we go inside now?"

"Of course. I believe I've had enough socializing for the evening." His head still felt fuzzy, as though the past continued to attempt to intrude on the present, but the comforting feel of his wife's hand in his helped him keep the waking nightmare at bay.

Once they reached their chamber, without a word she stepped away from him and reached behind her to find the laces to her dress. With a few strategic tugs, she managed to pull her gown off, and then her remaining petticoats followed. Next, she removed what was left of her stockings, which left her dressed in her chemise, corset, and bloomers. Still silent, she sank to her knees before him and finally spoke. "I am yours to command, Master."

Thrilled by her open display of submission to him and terrified that he might hurt her in yet another hallucination, he took her hand and helped her stand. "You are an angel of mercy. And while I would like nothing better than to sink into your welcoming heat and ignore what has happened tonight, we need to sit down and discuss events. Mayhap after I understand what happened, we can revisit your lovely display."

He hoped his delay wouldn't hurt her, but just as when she had a bad experience or reaction to their play and they needed to discuss what happened, he needed to do the same. Determined to assess what had occurred, he took her over to the bed, where he helped her out of her corset and then took off his own coat, shoes, and necktie. The rest he left in place in order to temper his ever-present desire for his wife.

Once they were settled on the bed with her in his arms, he asked her to fill in the blanks from their conversation on the back lawn. She told him what had happened, and he knew immediately what the cause was. The damnable flashiness of such a display annoyed him, but Hawksbury clearly did not realize it might set him off. Nor could he have predicted it before it happened.

As Theo told him everything that occurred, he winced and absorbed the memory of not saving the women and children. Of not being able to retrieve help fast enough to stop the massacre. It was like having it happen all over again. He reached up and wiped the sweat beading on his brow with a trembling hand. Taking a deep breath, he tried to settle in and come to terms with both the reality of his flashback occurring in such a public way and the fact that his mental state was a battle not yet won.

"Stone, how have you been coping with the hallucinations until now?" Theo's question prodded him.

"I sleep in small stretches, a few hours at a time, to avoid the nightmares. Sometimes I drink until I pass out to ensure I do not dream, or at the very least I do not remember." He drew a deep breath. Here was the part he had neglected to tell her. "And I went to The Market to dominate women. It helps me remember the sense of control that I lost. Somehow, it has helped keep the demons at bay."

"Until I came along and kept you away." His wife sounded so dejected and sad.

"Not true." He hugged her close. "You have helped me keep the demons at bay, and with you in my bed every night, I have far fewer nightmares. You have been a steadying presence in my life, which is why I am all the more disappointed by what occurred tonight."

"I imagine the sounds of the fireworks and the bright lights in the sky touched a bit too close to those of battle, which one could expect would give most former soldiers issues. But add to the mix whatever horror you experienced in India, and it stands to reason that you would have a nasty reaction." She held him tighter and refused to let him leave, even when he tugged a bit.

"I should tell you what occurred in India. It will help you understand and cope should something like this happen again." He drew a breath and dug deep for the fortitude to tell her what had happened. "You know of the Sepoy Mutiny a few years ago?"

"Of course, we all heard of the atrocities that occurred." Her matter-of-fact statement made it a little easier for him to continue.

"Well, I was located at Cawnpore with my cantonment. When the mutiny arose, things went badly very quickly. The East India Company was not prepared to deal with the kind of insurrection they faced. In some locations, we were simply too small in number to face off against what had once been our own troops. At Cawnpore, when the garrison was under siege, things were bad, but General Wheeler believed a peaceful departure could be arranged through a surrender."

Theo shuddered but made an encouraging noise, so he continued his tale.

"Things were going along. We were moving everyone out and to the Ganges river bank to be loaded on boats and taken to Allahabad. But something went wrong. A few boats were set ablaze, and then someone began firing. I was in the general's boat already, toward the middle of the river, when shots were fired. We could neither help nor escape. We floated and watched all our men be cut down." He drew a deep breath and absorbed the warmth and solace from his wife in his arms.

His shirt had grown damp where his wife pressed against him. Her quiet sharing of his pain eased his own burden a bit, and made it possible for him to continue. "As we floated, all I could hear were the screams of the women and the cries of the children as their men were cut down before their eyes. Later, some of the men and I fought off various rebel attacks on the boat and eventually got separated. We ran from the rebels after that and even swam for hours along the river until we were attacked one last time. In the end, only five of us were found by the Rajput matchlock men."

Theo rose and then knelt before him. "My God, Stone. No wonder you have nightmares. It must have been awful."

"It was. And for a while, I wondered why I survived. But then the letter came recalling me home, and it seemed I had been spared in order to ensure our family's succession." *And to find you.*

She took his face between her palms. "I am certain there is more in store for you than merely standing stud."

"You are always so optimistic." He offered her a wry smile.

"Do not dismiss me, Stone. You were lucky to survive. All that you must consider is how best to spend this extra time granted you."

Bitterness welled within him and burst forth on a half laugh. "Yes, well, since I've spent much of it debauching women and now have tainted a woman such as yourself with my—"

"Stop it this instant, Stone. You are a victim, but you are so much more than that. You merely have to see yourself as others do." She hesitated, and then pressed on. "As I do."

He set her aside and rose from the bed to stride across the room. He pressed his hands to either side of one window, letting the wood bite into his palms. He couldn't understand, now that she knew the truth, why she hadn't pushed him away. "How, after tonight, can you see me as anything other than a broken man?"

"How can one strong enough to tame me, to make me wish to be a better woman, be considered broken?" She clambered from the bed and darted across the room to press herself against his back. "How could half a man have survived all that you have and lived to tell of his experience? How could he find a way to continue to contribute to society, to gather other strong men of excellent character, and give them an example to live by?"

Stone groaned and turned around to embrace her once again, reveling in the feel of her curves against his own harder form. "I do not know what I did to deserve a woman such as you."

"Well, I do have my own drawbacks, but I like to believe it all balances out, more so now with your steadying influence."

Stone looked down, and their gazes met while her lips trembled as she attempted to smile.

"Take me to bed, Master."

"Not tonight, Theo. Perhaps I can simply hold you?" Exhaustion, mental and physical, pulled at him.

"Whatever you need. I am here to support you."

And with her last declaration, hope blossomed in his heart. Because if any woman could look past his deficiencies, it would be this one.

Chapter Twenty-Six

Refreshed after a good night's sleep with his wife in his arms, Stone had breakfast and then requested a buggy and carriage be brought around so he could go for a morning drive. As he waited, he decided to invite his wife to accompany him. Most of the houseguests were still abed, and no entertainments were scheduled until the afternoon.

One foot on the stairs, he heard an all too familiar voice call his name. When he turned and found Lady MacGregor, a Scottish widow with whom he had spent a great deal of time just before he left for India, his heart lodged in his throat.

"Stonemere." She waved him over to the salon doorway she partially occupied. "I thought that was you, my lord."

He wanted to sigh and pinch the bridge of his nose. This was a disaster of epic proportions. His former lover and his wife under the same roof? And the lover was the aggressive, territorial sort. *Not* a good situation. "Lady MacGregor, I am surprised to see you."

"Yes, well. I had a bit of a megrim last night, so Lady Hawksbury had her chit fill in for me at dinner. She claimed it would be good practice for the lass."

Stone wanted to laugh at the absurdity of her obvious avoidance of him until she could get him alone. Clearly, she intended to see if there was any possibility of picking up where they had left off before he'd left for India, a lowly lieutenant in the army. "Well, I am glad to see you feeling better. Unless, of course, you are still feeling poorly and are planning to leave early?"

Her green MacGregor eyes sparkled with laughter. "Not with such enticements as yourself and Lord Brougham still in residence." She leaned into him, plastering her breasts against his chest as she snaked her arms around his neck. Then she planted her lips on his as she tried to tease him into a deeper kiss.

Cursing himself a fool for not expecting such a move by her, he pulled his lips from hers. "Let me be very clear, Mary. I am not available for your games. My wife is with me, and even were she not, I honor my vows to her as seriously as I honored my commission in the army and the good name of my family."

He reached up and untangled her arms from his neck, just as a swish of skirts alerted him they were not alone. Damn and blast. He turned and caught a glimpse of his wife's blonde hair and dark blue riding habit as she turned the corner to the side of the house where the stables were located. "Your little ruse changes nothing. I am not interested in your wares." He ground the words past clenched teeth as his anger seethed beneath his calm exterior.

Lady Mary MacGregor gasped at his blatant insult, hauled her arm back, and attempted to slap him. But, he caught her arm before she could land the blow.

"Do not presume that because you are a woman, I shall take no action. You just insulted my wife with your unwanted advances as well as upset her beyond bearing. I suggest you make yourself scarce, if not entirely absent, and I shall consider overlooking this mark on our otherwise previously congenial acquaintance." Fury licked at his soul like flames from the deepest pits of hell. He was as angry at her for being presumptuous, as he was at himself for not being more cautious when she appeared so suddenly.

Determined to chase down his wife and set things straight, he darted down the hall where she had only recently been. Outside the house, he saw her tearing down the driveway in the buggy he had requested only a short while ago. Frustrated at the delay, he stormed over to the stable and demanded a horse. He consoled himself with the knowledge that he would have the advantage of speed on horseback.

Theo raced away from the intimate scene between her husband and the red-haired hussy of a woman she had never seen before. Shocked at what she had come downstairs to find, she'd stood there and watched them speak, though she could not hear a single word. But there was little she needed to hear after watching the woman press against her husband, arms comfortably twined around his neck, while she kissed him as though she'd known him intimately.

Devastated after their intense night together, Theo was certain a gaping hole could be found where her heart once resided. Tears blurring her vision, she gave the horse his head and hoped the wind would carry her tears and pain on the breeze and off to sea, or somewhere equally distant.

She'd barely crossed the Hawksbury property line when she heard the thunder of hooves behind her. To her surprise, her husband had managed to pull himself from the wanton woman and come after her. Well, she would not make this an easy conquest, because she knew as surely as he would catch her that it was too late for her heart to escape unscathed. To her horror, she realized she loved the very man who had carelessly claimed her heart and then tossed it away like so much refuse.

Flying over the bumpy road, one could only go so fast without risking both the horse's neck and her own. But she pushed the limits, her anger superseding her better judgment. Anger, hurt, and doubt all swirled in her gut like bad champagne. She waffled between wanting to vomit and wanting to turn back around and horsewhip her husband into a bloody pulp. How could she have allowed him to fool her? To gain her trust? Another glance back over her shoulder showed Stone gaining on her. When she turned back to her front, she spied the large pit in the road at the last moment.

Tears forgotten , she got the horse safely around the hole through sheer luck and determination, but she couldn't get one of the buggy wheels past it. As the wheel caught, she heard a loud snapping sound, like a tree limb breaking in a storm. Then the buggy listed as the horse broke free from the traces, leaving her to try to scramble from the wreckage before it went over. To her horror, her skirts twisted around her ankles, caught on something in the damaged conveyance. Stone drew closer as she looked over to him, and she felt one last stab of pain to her heart. Then he was gone from her vision as she tumbled into the road and everything went black.

Stone watched in horror as Theo's buggy wheel caught in the pothole. For a moment, he thought she might make it, but then he heard the loud snapping and knew her axle must have given way. With a curse, he spurred his horse for more speed, and once again found himself staring as a woman under his care suffered. The feeling of helplessness rankled as deeply now as the first time in Cawnpore, and he cursed loudly. With his heart tumbled beneath the heap of carriage that sat in the road, he grew crazed to reach her.

A moment later, he flew off his mount at a run and knelt in the dirt beside his precious wife. The woman he loved. Dear God, he was such a fool. Why could he not have told her before this moment? Now she lay unmoving, a gash in her forehead bleeding and her breathing shallow while he came to terms with his blasted feelings.

Her horse was long gone as he scooped her up and carried her to his mount. There he scrambled up and headed back to the Grange. Torn between a full gallop to arrive more quickly and a sedate trot to arrive more safely, he settled somewhere between. Each time he looked down at her still features, fear ripped through his guts and twisted them into knots. What if he missed the chance to tell her he loved her?

As he hit the main part of the grounds, he spotted a gardener with a horse and cart. Stopping, he called the man over. "Sir, I need to take your horse and cart. My wife has had an accident up the road."

"Yes, my lord. I saw her tear out of here earlier. I was worried then at her speed." The gardener helped him lay her on the bed of weeds, which, while not ideal, was better than him carrying her on horseback.

"Take my mount and ride ahead to warn the house and have someone call a doctor. I shall bring her up to the house in the cart." Stone took command as he always did, clear and decisive in his thinking despite the emotional trauma pushing at the edges of his calm.

"You can't drive a cart, my lord. It's unseemly." The weathered gardener looked surprised, but Stone had no time for it.

"It is not the first time I've driven a cart. Now go. My wife needs the doctor more than I need not to be seen in a cart." Stone couldn't have cared less that he had to drive a cart and mule to get her up to the house safely. Whatever it took to make things right with her, he was willing to do. Anything, if he just had the chance.

The gardener nodded, and despite his seemingly advanced age, swung up into the saddle and took off toward the house as fast as the horse would fly. Stone, meanwhile, set off after him at a much slower pace with his wife safely ensconced in the wagon. By the time he pulled up to the front of the house, the entire house party had gathered, with Lady Hawksbury heading up her house staff. Before he'd even dismounted, the formidable woman had Theo loaded onto a stretcher and on her way upstairs. He made to follow his wife, but the firm hand of his hostess pressed against his chest. "Forgive me, my lord, but you've done what you can. This is women's work until the physician arrives. Let us care for your lady wife and get her settled. Then we will call for you to visit her."

Unable to speak past the lump in his throat, he simply nodded. And then all the women were gone, leaving the men to mill about aimlessly. Cooper stepped up beside him. "She's made of stern stuff, 'Chilles." The comfort of his best friend falling into his old nickname told him both how unnerving the situation was, and how much his friend cared not only for him, but for his wife.

"Indeed, she is, Coop. Indeed, she is." He refused to think back on the scene he'd witnessed. It was too much to bear as he waited.

"Gentlemen, perhaps we should retire to the library to wait with Lord Stonemere for word of his wife?" Cooper offered the suggestion, and the group happily grasped on to the notion.

"I shall see that the horse is found and the buggy collected." Lord Hawksbury turned to head to his stable.

"You'd best take a wagon to collect the buggy. You will find it beyond repair, I fear. Of course, I shall be happy to replace the equipage," Stone offered as Cooper urged him toward the house.

"Never mind the buggy. Your wife's continued good health is far more important, Stonemere. Besides, after your earlier assistance, I certainly owe you a good turn." The man trotted off to his stable as the rest of the men filed into the house.

Stone entered the library and looked at each available seat. He found the idea of sitting violated every one of his natural inclinations to take action. To do something. So he settled for pacing before the fireplace and jamming his fingers through his hair as he waited for word of his wife. Time stretched and slowed, passing like molasses through a strainer. Each man looked at him, pity in their eyes, or shared worry and understanding of the difficulty he endured.

Guilt gnawed at his gut. If only he had walked away from Lady MacGregor as soon as he'd spied the woman. Or if he'd been quicker to chase his wife, perhaps he could have caught her and explained before she hied off. But then he also knew either of those options had little chance of changing the outcome. So he was left to pace, worry, and regret while he waited for word of his wife.

Much as with childbirth, it was the woman's job to shoulder the care and see things through. It was the man's burden to sit and wait, helpless to affect change or do anything useful. Patience at an end, he was turning to go upstairs and demand news when the doctor came charging through the house and rushed past without even the common courtesies.

Stone tried to take succor from the knowledge that a medical professional was tending to her now, but it was cold comfort. Needing a distraction—anything—he headed outside to see if Hawksbury had returned with the buggy. He found the pile on a wagon in the courtyard near the stable with a number of men looking it over. The stable master glanced at where the axle snapped and was pointing as he spoke to his employer.

Stone walked over and caught the last part of his words. "...I'd say 'tis no accident, my lord."

"What's this?" Stone jumped into the conversation, alarm bells ringing in his head. "Did you say this was no accident?"

"Indeed, my lord. See here?" The stable master pointed to the spot where the axle had sheared in half. "Right there on one side of the break, you can see clean saw marks and then splintered wood. It looks like someone partially cut through the axle so that any serious jostling could have caused it to break, let alone hitting a pit in the road like the one we found the buggy in."

"Bloody hell!" Stone cursed and tore back into the house. This was all his fault. He'd been ignoring the multitude of accidents of late, certain they were merely a series of coincidences. A spate of bad luck. Not someone trying to kill him! And now because of his own obtuseness, his wife was injured at best—he refused to consider the worst-case scenario. Once inside, he called for Cooper, the only man he trusted at the moment. His friend ran into the main hall in answer to his bellowing summons. "Cooper, this was no accident. The stable master found a partially severed axle."

Surprise colored every feature of his friend's face. "Who would want to kill Theo?"

"I was meant to take that buggy for a morning drive." Stone still found it hard to believe, but the evidence was more than clear. "She suffered an accident intended for me. I need to account for the whereabouts of everyone attending the house party since last night. Could you quietly ask about while I stand guard over my wife? On the off chance I am wrong and we are both the target, I do not wish to leave her alone until this bastard is uncovered."

"Agreed. I shall report back as soon as I have a complete list."

As Stone headed upstairs, fear for his wife's safety ate at him in a way he had never before experienced. How could he survive if anything happened to her?

Chapter Twenty-Seven

U nsure why she hurt all over, Theo tried cracking her lids a bit more. The bright light from the windows seared into her eyes and pierced her head. She could hear movement around her but refused to open her eyes further to determine who hovered nearby.

"Doctor, she's waking." A familiar female voice. Her mother?

"Lady Stonemere, can you hear me?" a man asked.

"My eyes are closed. I am not deaf." Theo couldn't control her grumpiness. Never a morning person, this one seemed especially hard. But what was a strange man doing in her room?

"Is she normally so dyspeptic upon stirring?" The irritating man continued to provoke her, and she still didn't know why he was there.

Could she be dreaming? In that case, she could make him leave. "You, sir, are dismissed." And then she rolled over, which caused more pain to spark to life all along her body. She couldn't contain the groan.

"If you will close the drapery, she will be considerably less cross." Mary's typically crisp tones, a thankfully familiar voice, cut through the concerned chatter. While her maid looked sweet with her dusting of freckles on her milky skin, the woman could take command of a house like a battle-tried field marshal. "Her ladyship is not at her best just after waking."

Well, that was quite diplomatic of her. She was a downright shrew and she knew it, but try as she might, she could never contain the grumpiness of rising.

There was a momentary rustling of sound, and then the room seemed to grow cooler and darker. Theo decided to try opening her eyes in her dream so she could better see what was happening. As she cracked her lids again, she could make out multiple forms hovering over her like specters from a gothic horror novel. She let out a small scream of fright and dove back under the covers.

A moment later, a loud thump like wood banging against a solid surface rang through the room, and then Stone was there. The reassuring warmth of his body wrapped around hers calmed her racing heart and banished the ghosts. It might also have helped that someone lit a lamp, casting a soft glow over the room. All around her were her mother, Stone's mother, Mary, and a man she did not recognize.

As she took in everyone, the morning's anguish came rushing back in like a tidal wave. Stone, his treachery, her mad dash from the Grange. And then nothing. A big black hole where her memory should be. And why was she back in bed when she clearly remembered rising and dressing hours ago? "Stone, you will remove yourself from my person this instant."

He stiffened and then slowly retreated, though he refused to leave her side. Regardless, she was still angry with him, and whatever had occurred did not forgive his transgression.

"My lady, you've had an accident, and you bumped your head rather viciously when you were tossed from the buggy." The man hovered over her and Stone as though he wanted to shoo the latter out of his way. "I am Dr. Thompson, the local physician."

"Well, that explains why you are in my room and I am back in bed. I assure you, Doctor, other than a rather horrid headache, I am otherwise unharmed." Theo really wanted everyone out of her room so she could be alone with her shattered heart.

"If your rather protective husband will step aside, I shall do a complete examination and fully assess your condition now that you are awake." The doctor looked pointedly at Stone, who had yet to budge.

"Stonemere, if you could leave, I would appreciate the privacy to get this examination over with. Please take our mothers with you on your way out. Mary may chaperone the doctor while we get this bit of silliness over with. I can see from the stubborn set of his jaw the doctor will not leave without a fight, and I do not have the reserves to address him just now." Theo waved her hand listlessly as she urged them all from the room.

After much shuffling and grumbling, Mary managed to usher the three disgruntled peers out of her bedroom so she could deal with the doctor.

"Excellent, my lady. If you would please sit up, I can begin my examination." The doctor turned toward his bag, rooted about, and pulled out some instrument that he then shoved in his ears. A portion of it dangled down his front and looked remarkably similar to her Great Aunt Matilda's ear trumpet.

As he came toward her with the trumpet part in one hand, Theo had had enough. "Stop right there, sir."

The man cringed and ripped the ear parts from his head. "My lady, you could make a man deaf yelling while he has a stethoscope on. Please, madam. I would like to conduct my examination and be gone."

Despite the fact all she wanted was to be alone, her head ached, and again she was feeling nauseated, so she realized allowing the doctor to continue might be in her best interest. She had become increasingly grumpy these past few weeks, as waking up with a headache and weak stomach every morning was wont to do to a body. "Very well, Doctor. Please do be brief. I am not feeling just the thing at the moment." Not to mention she couldn't lick her wounds in peace until she was alone.

After what could easily have been an eon later, with far too many questions to count, the white-haired old man stuffed all his instruments back in his case and nodded at her. "That was a nasty bump on your head. And considering you are with child, I would think you'd be taking better care of yourself. I should have a word with your husband—"

"With child?" Surprise had her head spinning again. "Doctor, did you just say I am pregnant?"

"I take it you were unaware, though how that could be with the stomach sickness and headaches you complained of, I do not understand. But yes, my lady, you are in fact bearing a child. As a result, I am going to strongly urge you to refrain from high-speed buggy races and horseback riding, among other more strenuous pursuits. Though a nice walk in the afternoon and leaving your corset off should allow for a healthier baby. Rest for the next few days, until you are feeling better. And, of course, send for me if anything out of the ordinary occurs—particularly if you have any cramping or bleeding. You and your baby are not out of the woods yet, but a few days' rest and more care with your person is wise."

"Thank you, sir." Despair nearly pulled her under a wave of exhaustion, but she managed to hang on a bit longer. "Sir, my husband does not know. I'd like to tell him myself."

The doctor nodded. "Of course, my lady."

"Thank you. Mary, please see him out, and I do not wish to be disturbed for a while." Theo lay back on the mattress to contemplate what to do, and to sleep. In whichever order inspiration struck.

"Your maid should not leave you alone, my lady. She needs to wake you every hour or so for the next twelve hours. After such a period, if all is normal, then you should be fine. If at any time you feel worse, you must send for me immediately." He stood by the door and waited for assent before finally departing.

Alone, Theo lay there and pondered what she should do. Her husband seemed devoted by all accounts, except for that kiss she'd intruded upon. Had he truly given up his profligate ways? What she needed was a little time to sort things out, but if he found out about the baby, she would have no chance to be certain he loved her, and her alone. And while she knew she would never divorce him, her heart ached with the kernel of doubt that had wedged itself within.

Stone stood outside of what had become his wife's chamber at Hawksbury. It had been theirs at the start, and it would be again, just as soon as he had a word with his little hellion. He'd allowed her to claim illness for two miserable days. He'd paced the hallway outside her door waiting to be let in to see her until the rug was worn through to the wood planks. And still she refused him entrance. He was quite done asking her permission.

A fortifying breath to steel his nerves, and then he swung open the door with nary a knock. "Theo, you will see me this very moment. I do not care what you are doing, how you feel, or if you are stark naked. We must speak."

He stopped in the middle of the room to find his wife taking tea by the window in a dressing gown. She looked terribly fetching in her morning dishabille. She grew a bit pale at his entrance, but typical of his headstrong wife, she neither flinched nor backed down at his blustering entrance. "Indeed, we do, Stonemere." She pointed to the empty seat across the tea service. "Sit."

The pit in his stomach hardened. She had taken to calling him Stone, reserving Stonemere for more formal occasions or in company. He had yet to have a chance to fully inform her of the moment she had walked in on, but he fully intended to correct that deficiency. He took the seat she indicated, sitting on the front edge with both feet firmly planted on the floor. There was little point in pretending indifference. He had easily sorted through his jumbled emotions as he'd paced her hallway, and had come to a rather inconvenient truth.

He loved his wife.

The problem now lay in convincing her of that fact. "Theo, I know what you think—"

"Stonemere, I know what I saw. That trollop, someone you once cavorted with, I presume, was wrapped around you like a left-handed wife." The animated, passionate woman he once knew had been replaced by an automaton, her words cold and lifeless.

"Theo, at least give me a chance to explain. I had just told her that whatever there had once been between us would not be renewed. I am married and content with that arrangement. I have no need of a piece on the side." He sighed and hoped for a flicker of life. Anything to indicate his words had gotten through. "She must have known you walked in, and took the opportunity to cause trouble. By the time I peeled her off my person and came after you, you were hieing off in the buggy."

"A convenient story. How am I to believe such a tale? To tru—" Her voice cracked, the first sign of emotion since he'd walked in. "Trust you?"

"Stop and consider, Theo. When have I ever lied to you? Even when you have not cared for the truth, I have been honest with you. I admitted when I visited your solicitor. I revealed myself to you at The Market, revealed a part of myself I believed would remain hidden from my wife. And only the other night, I shared with you the horrors of my military service. I have laid myself bare to you, and yet you doubt me on this?" The pit in his stomach had morphed yet again, now resembling more of a gut-shot wound—a gaping, seeping mortal wound.

He waited for one heartbeat, then another. She had yet to move, to acknowledge his words, and it seemed the battle was lost. Despite all he had shared with her, it wouldn't be enough. Numb all over, he stood on legs that resembled aspic more than flesh and bone and strode toward the door. With one hand on the knob, he couldn't look back for fear the pain in his chest might leak from his eyes. "If you'll let me know when you are ready to return to London, I shall have the carriages made ready."

"Stone!" His name, short and sweet, rang out across the room, followed by the rustle of her dressing gown.

He turned, and then she was in his arms, back where she belonged. Tears rolled down her face as she hugged him tight. "I was so devastated. I couldn't understand why you might choose her over me. I didn't trust in us. Please forgive me."

"Pet, you must stop. I am the one who needs forgiving. I should never have let her close enough that there would ever be a kernel of doubt in your mind." He wasn't sure if he could let her go again. Perhaps they should delay their departure another day?

"I am yours, Master. Yours to do with as you wish," she offered so prettily.

"Very well, how soon can you be ready, pet?" He stepped back from her and produced his handkerchief for her to dry her eyes. Somehow he would find the strength to assemble their party and return home without touching her. She was emotionally overwrought after a grievous physical injury.

Only on very rare occasions had he seen his wife cry, and other than her tears for him a few nights earlier, most of them had come when she truly felt remorse for some wayward thing she had done. While he would argue that one's feelings could never be wayward, his wife's strong emotions had led her into a precarious situation, and she remained unaware.

He'd prefer her to stay ignorant of what had happened until he could see it taken care of, but at the moment, he had no notion who might be behind his accidents. Despite his lack of information, he believed he'd have a better chance of sorting it all out in London. "I shall see to the rest of our things. Do not rush yourself. If you are feeling at all unwell, we will wait or find an inn along the way."

Damn, he'd hoped they might reconcile completely before the long trek home. Should he have demanded her submission? Demanded she give herself to him? Could he have misread the moment?

Chapter Twenty-Eight

"**M**aster?" Confusion swirled around her as Stone removed himself from her proximity. Determined to set things right between them before she took one step more, she shed her dressing gown, revealing her womanly curves to his gaze, and sank to her knees before him. "Please, Master. Remind me who I belong to. Help me to never forget again." She had doubted him, and in her mind, it might be the greatest transgression of her entire trouble-pocked existence.

As she knelt at his feet, naked and exposed, she realized exactly how strong her feelings for her husband ran. Fear of his rejection warred with her desire to feel his hands on her body. To be reminded that he was the one person she could rely upon no matter how awful things seemed.

"I fear I misunderstood your previous request, pet." He knelt down in front of her, tipped her chin up so their gazes met. "Exactly how should I best remind you who you belong to?"

Theo trembled with excitement and need. He was not lost to her. Together, they would forge ahead anew. "Twenty spanks. Please, Master."

"And then, pet?" He raised one brow in punctuation.

Dismayed at his question, she thought about what should come after her discipline. "Whatever pleases you, Master."

He hesitated and then nodded. "If that is what you wish, pet."

"Thank you, Master." She returned her gaze to the floor as he rose to loom over her.

"Then we shall begin with your discipline. I want you to be clear that this is discipline at your request to remind you who you belong to. This is not punishment, for you have done nothing wrong. Are we clear, pet?"

"Yes, Master." She waited, desperate to feel his palm warming her bottom, reminding her that she was his, and in truth he was hers. Perhaps that was more of what she had forgotten in her despair—that as much as he was her master and she his pet, he was also her husband. Her lover. Simply hers.

"Come with me." He motioned for her to rise with the curl of his finger, and she answered his call. He led her toward the bed she had lain in for the last few days. "Bend over the edge of the bed, like a good girl." He helped her assume the position. "If we were home, I would strap you to our bench and use a flogger to remind you of our bond. Instead, I have but my hand to help you remember to whom you belong, and that I belong to you as well."

Theo bent over the mattress, her feet on the floor as she waited for him to commence the spanking. His hand smoothed over her bare bottom, rubbing and warming the cool skin. Then his touch disappeared, only to return with a sudden crack of sound.

"One, Master." She counted the way he'd taught her. Thought about all they had shared and explored and knew herself to be a fool for having believed what that woman had wanted her to see.

His hand landed on the other cheek. "Two, Master."

Then they started coming in quick succession. Before she realized it, she was at ten. Her bum stung with a reassuring warmth that had her thighs pressed together, and an ache building in her pussy that only Stone could relieve.

He paused the spankings and wedged his hand between the very thighs she'd just been thinking about. "I see my pet's pussy is quite wet." Using his finger, he traced her soaked slit, teasing her sensitive flesh.

"Yes, Master." She forced the words past her teeth as she resisted the urge to push back against his touch.

"Soon, pet. First, we must finish this business between us."
And then his palm landed again, this time aiming more
toward the cuff of her backside and in toward her quim.

She continued to count with each blow until her backside
was inflamed from his reminder. Her core dripped with
need as her bare skin rubbed against the starchy fabric of
the bedspread. A simple reminder of who was in control.
"Twenty, Master."

Her frame shook with relief that the spankings were over,
but the need for release overtook her. The pulsing between
her legs had grown almost unbearable as she waited for
whatever he decided would come next.

"Stand, pet." He helped her follow his direction. "Show me
your bottom. I wish to see my handiwork."

She turned so that he could see what she assumed was her
beet-red bottom. It certainly felt like it must be such a color.

He ran his hand over the tender skin, stirring the flames
again. "Tell me, pet, to whom do you belong?"

"You, Master." She felt the truth of the words all the way to
her toes and back again.

He continued to stroke the heated flesh. "Very good, pet.
Now, this one may be harder. To whom do I belong?"

A new and different warmth ignited in her belly, right
where she imagined the babe hovered. "Me, Master. You
belong to me." She could not hide her smile as she said the
words aloud and relished them.

He chuckled behind her. "I should have known you'd be a
quick study. Indeed, you belong to me, and I belong to you,
pet. What we share here in the bedroom, and even beyond
in the public areas of the house, will not survive if you do
not believe the truth of that. Do you understand, pet?" He
turned her around so they were face-to-face.

"I do now, Master." Her heart skipped a beat as she looked
into his gaze. She could have sworn that she saw something
there that she had not seen before. Could he love her?
Despite all their challenges, could he love her as much as
she had come to love him? Just as she was on the verge of
blurting out the words, he interrupted her declaration and

took her mouth in a plundering, soul-stealing kiss that left her clinging to him as though he were the only thing keeping her anchored to the ground.

And then she was no longer anchored, but floated in his arms as he carried her to the head of the bed they had shared their first night at Hawksbury. There, he gently laid her out and stepped back. His coat came off first, then his vest. Next came his necktie, and Theo watched in disappointment as he tossed it aside. She did enjoy having him bind her hands as he did what he would with her body. But it seemed he had other ideas for their unplanned morning of reconciliation. In short order, he hauled his boots off using the jack by the bed, then dropped his trousers and shirt on the floor and crawled naked into bed.

Equally naked, they came together and kissed. She drove her tongue past his teeth and stroked the inner walls of his mouth in a brazen exploration that had her pulse racing again as easily as a feather catching the breeze. His hands roamed over her, exploring her dips and curves and even tracing over the small, firm mound that was yet her own secret. One she fully intended to share in time—but not yet.

Stone couldn't believe he'd almost misunderstood her earlier demand. Contrition had addled his wits and made him miss her clear cues. His poor pet had been driven to strip naked and kneel before him to make her point. And what a glorious sight she made kneeling in the morning sunshine, her golden hair aglow like a nimbus as she waited for his command. His cock bobbed between his legs as need speared through him once again. Spanking her had taken all his restraint. He'd wanted to strip naked and plunge into her hot pussy by the tenth blow. By twenty, he was damn near ready to explode in his pants.

But now the field was wide open, and they could do as they pleased. And he had a personal favorite in mind to help repair the rift in their dynamic. He broke their kiss and rolled onto his back. "Come, pet. Straddle my face and let me feast on you while you suck my cock."

Her blue eyes darkened and her nipples pebbled into small berries. With a nod, she scrambled over to him, swung a leg over his head, and lowered her glistening core to his lips. He slid his tongue out to trace the trail of moisture and moaned at the sweetness of her desire. Hungry for more of his wife, he wrapped his hands around her thighs and pulled her lower until he could see nothing but the red expanse of her arse as he sank his tongue into her.

"Oh, Master." She gasped, and then her weight shifted forward and her warm, wet mouth engulfed his cock—or as much of it as she could manage. As he drove into her quim, she worked up and down his length to where her fist gripped him at the root. But then, as he swore she'd reached her hand, she swallowed deeply, moved her fist, and took more of him into the tightness of her throat. Unable to control his need, he bucked his hips, shoving deeper. Theo choked a bit, pulled back, and then repeated the effort.

With each swallow and suck, he filled her in a way he'd never done before, and his inner beast surged to the fore, demanding to claim her once more. To plant his seed in her belly and make a child as the ultimate show of his manhood, of his claim on his woman.

And with that notion buzzing in his head, he flicked her clit a few times before shifting her off his face. He sat up as she did, his mouth wet from her juices. He laid her back on the bed, tossed her legs over his shoulders, and plowed into her tight channel with a driving need to fill her. Pelvis to pelvis, he ground against her, wishing he could find a way to be one with her, to fill her completely.

"Master?"

He groaned as she wriggled her hips. "Yes, pet?"

"Is that..." She licked her cock-swollen lips. "Is that me on your mouth?"

Fuck, is she trying to kill me? "Yes, pet." He ran his tongue over his lower lip and tasted her sweetness once more. "I still have your juices on my lips."

Then she reached and traced his upper lip, scooping up whatever moisture remained, and carried her finger to her own lips. As she sucked her finger into her mouth, he lost all control.

"Bloody hell, woman." He pounded into her, shuttling his cock in and out of her soaked pussy as she pinched and played with her own nipples.

And then her pussy clamped down on him hard, and she cried out, "Master!"

The tight clutching rhythm of her cunny pushed him over the edge and had him shooting his seed deep into womb. He continued shoving deep inside her, letting the zinging pleasure of release rip from his balls to his cock and out through his extremities as he found a level of release he'd never before experienced. Pleasure born of love and the unhindered sharing of two souls.

It had turned him into a bloody poet.

Spent, he slumped forward onto his wife's breast and lay there, helpless as a newborn babe. But the pillar of strength beneath him held him and stroked his hair as though she never wanted him to leave. And he sincerely hoped that was the case, because she would be stuck with him forever. He needed to sort out how to tell her, how to give her the property next to her orphanage and make her understand. Because a simple declaration of love would not suffice to express the magnitude of what he felt for this woman. He would sort it all out when he got back to London, right after he stopped whoever was after him. For the moment, sleep was required, so he closed his eyes as he lay there still joined with his wife and napped.

Chapter Twenty-Nine

T he next afternoon, their party arrived home after leaving exceptionally early. Despite a night filled with making love to his wife, he was eager to return home to put certain wheels in motion. As he escorted Theo upstairs, Parsons followed him up. "My lord, there is a gentleman at the door who wishes a word with you."

"Please tell him now is not a good time. My wife and I have just returned from a long journey and do not wish to be disturbed." Stone turned from his longtime employee expecting his directions to be followed without question.

Parsons cleared his throat. "My apologies, my lord. But I believe the man is your dead brother."

He and Theo both stopped and turned to stare at their servant. "Pardon me?" Theo paled and pressed her hand to her heart.

"The man currently in the front salon claims to be and looks remarkably similar to my lord's dead brother," Parsons calmly reiterated.

"I see. Well then, I suppose I shall be down in just a moment." Stone nodded at Parsons and then turned to hustle his wife to their rooms.

"Stone, I wish to go with you. There is no reason for us to go to our rooms." Theo tried to stop walking, but he refused to even consider such a thing.

"Absolutely not. I have no idea who that is sitting downstairs. I shall not have you put at risk unnecessarily. Once I know what the man is about, I shall call for you to come down, but until then, you will do as I ask and remain in our rooms." He moved her forward, brooking no further resistance, and to his great relief, his wife complied with his wishes. And then a cold wash of fear swept through him. If it was his brother, what of Theo? Would he want her back? Would *she* want *him* back?

"Do be careful, dear." She pressed a kiss to his cheek and slipped into their rooms, leaving him once again stunned.

Her easy affection always seemed to surprise him, and in the moment of uncertainty, it comforted him. Perhaps one day he would become accustomed to such intimate displays. But for the moment, he had other issues to sort out, starting with who was sitting downstairs in his parlor. If it was his brother, what did it mean? Considering he had no suspects, merely a string of events that had ceased to be accidents in his mind, could his brother's surprise return be his first big clue? A rather large pit opened up in his gut at the thought. They had been so close growing up, and never in all those years had Stone coveted the earldom. The notion it might be Odey behind the many attempts saddened him. One never wanted to think a family member—let alone a brother—might want one dead.

Drawing a deep, steadying breath, he determined to be on about finding out the truth and not wallowing in murky possibilities. The first step required him to see exactly who was downstairs. With a sense of great purpose behind him, Stone strode downstairs and into his front parlor. There a man stood with his back to the door, staring out the window.

He approached the right height for Odey, but he appeared a bit wider across the shoulders than Stone remembered. Granted, it had been nearly eight years since Stone had bought his commission and headed off to India, and three years since his brother had died. A man could change in all that time. Stone certainly had.

"Well, don't just stand there and stare, 'Chilles. Mother would certainly not approve." The man turned from the window, but his features were still cast in shadows by the late-afternoon sun.

"I'm afraid you have me at a disadvantage." Stone stepped closer, but sought to maintain enough of a distance between the man and himself should he need to take action.

"It's only been seven or eight years, brother. Have I already faded from your memory?" The man stepped even closer and shifted out of the shadows to reveal his face.

Stone stopped cold as a ghost rose before him in the form of his dead brother. Certainly, the man was older than he remembered, his face sunbaked from long hours outside, little lines fanning out from the creases of his eyes. Either laugh lines or markers of hard living; only the stories behind them would tell. All the blood rushed from his head to his feet as the last three years rushed at him, reminding him of all he had lost and gained. How could one feel both fear and joy in the same moment? "Dear God, it is you." The words escaped past his frozen lips, a mere whisper.

Odey grinned, and then the men were hugging and slapping each other on the back as they greeted each other. After long seconds of merely absorbing the moment, they parted, and Stone dragged his brother to sit down, but they both came up short as Theo swept into the room.

His wife, not unlike himself, had turned rather pale when she saw who had arrived. She stood in the doorway, her hands trembling as she took in the moment. "I-I see it is truly Odey who has returned, and not some imposter." She glanced uncertainly from him to his once-dead brother and back again. Then she took a small step toward them and stopped. Again, she looked from one to the other before taking another step, and another until she had slowly crossed to them and embraced his brother in an awkward welcome.

Stone cleared his throat. "I do recall having requested that you remain upstairs until I called for you."

"And I did try to stay, but you took entirely too long, Stone." She all but ignored the fact he'd been trying to keep her safe. For heaven's sake, it could have been some derelict trying to rob them at gunpoint and she would have walked in and possibly gotten herself killed. "Besides, it is, in fact, Odey, so no harm done."

"This time, pet," Stone ground out between his teeth.

Theo stiffened further, which was hard to imagine, and turned an alarming shade of red. "Stone, do not take that *tone* with me."

Odey glanced awkwardly back and forth between them. But Stone had little compunction about his proclivities in front of his brother, who not only shared them but had been with him as they discovered their preferences. "Odey is well aware of my proclivities, and even shared in many of them, once upon a time. So no need to hide anything before him, pet. And since you will be punished later, I doubt he will be unaware of them by morning." He slashed a grin at his wife, who scowled at him.

She then proceeded to ignore their conversation, and went on as though none of it had occurred. "Sit, Odey. I must say, while I am shocked, it is good—" She hesitated, seeming to trip over her words. "Well, what I mean to say is...I am sure Stone is pleased you aren't dead."

Stone sat and joined his brother and his wife, but not before he picked her up and sat her on his lap. Unwilling to examine the need to stake his claim on Theo before his brother, he naturally accepted the impulse and moved on. It could stem from any number of things, such as their recent reconciliation, the fact his brother was once her betrothed, or even that she was so recently hurt and he was still feeling rather overprotective of her person. "Yes, brother. How is it you aren't dead? And why am I just learning this? I am certain you have a story to tell."

Odey nodded. "Indeed, there is a story." He glanced at Theo and then back to Stone, letting yet another awkward moment stretch out. "I understand that you are, in fact, Stonemere now."

"I am." Stone hesitated as he waited for his brother's response. Did he want the title back? Stone considered the idea, however briefly, but rejected it out of hand. The title might have been forced upon him—even unwelcome at the time—but he had found the adjustment far easier since marrying Theo. His gut churned with all the sudden uncertainty.

Odey let out a huge sigh that sounded awfully relieved. "Thank goodness. I stayed away so long to give Parliament the time needed to sort it all out. I have yet to hear of a lord being recalled once a writ is issued. But these are modern times, and one can never be sure."

"Do you mean you did not wish to be earl?" Theo sounded as surprised as Stone felt at that revelation.

"I did not. Not for many years. I had tried to tell Father on one occasion, but he merely assumed it was youth and fear of responsibility driving my lack of interest." Odey shrugged. "And then you went and bought a commission, 'Chilles. I was alone with the full burden of the earldom's future bearing down on me like a locomotive. I decided to do something drastic, so I signed up to sail as a crewman to the Far East. I left Mother and Father a note so they wouldn't worry, but stated clearly that I had no intention of taking the title when the time came."

Stone's heart ached at the notion that his brother felt so deserted and desperate that he signed up to be a crewman on a silk run. Such a long and dangerous journey should not have been his only other option. "Obviously, something went wrong along the way."

"It did. But at first, it was wonderful. Certainly, it was hard work. Hard work like I had never experienced. But at the end of the day, I felt as though I had accomplished something useful."

"That I understand." Stone missed that feeling from his army life, at least before Cawnpore. He reached around his wife and held her closer, needing her scent and feel to ground him in the moment, and not in his horror-filled memories.

"Then one morning, a terrible storm rolled in, and amidst the struggle to keep the ship upright, I was knocked overboard." He paused and looked down at his hands wrapped tightly around each other. "I heard later that the ship went down and all aboard were lost."

"That was when we believed you were killed." Stone heard his wife's little sigh as he squeezed her gently.

Odey looked up and smiled ruefully. "Yes, well, that was also when I decided that my being dead might be easier for everyone. At least until I heard Father had died."

Stone saw the guilt flash over his brother's face. "It wasn't your fault. The doctor had advised him to relax more, maybe even retreat to Stonemere Abbey and get away from the city. But apparently, Father, as usual, ignored the advice."

A small measure of relief seemed to flit through Odey's gaze, but he certainly carried a fair amount of guilt. "Nevertheless, by the time I had received word of his passing, it was far too late to return. And then there was the hope the title would pass to you uncontested and all would be as it should."

Stone shook his head. "You should have written to me. I would have resigned my commission and come home. I could have done something to help you sort this out with Father."

"I tried talking to him. Many times. He was ridiculously insistent that I had to be the next earl and that the title would not pass to you. He was such a traditionalist. I don't think he could accept anything but me as heir." Odey shrugged as a sense of defeat dragged his shoulders down.

"But where did you end up after going overboard?" Theo jumped into the conversation, her curiosity an ever-ravening beast.

"Sardinia. We were near the Mediterranean Sea, and so I floated for two days clinging to a splinter of driftwood I found. And eventually I washed ashore. A local winemaker found me, cared for me, and then gave me work. I've worked for him for the last three years. He pays well and gives me food and shelter, so I have no expenses to speak of."

"And you like the work?" Stone prodded him.

"I do. It's good, honest labor, and the owner has mentioned making me a partner in the business as he has no sons to pass the vineyard on to."

Theo yawned. "Oh, forgive me, we have just returned home from a house party. I fear I am a bit worn out."

"Perhaps now that your curiosity has been quenched, you can retire until dinner?" Stone helped her stand.

"I believe I shall." She turned to his brother. "Odey, it is wonderful to have you returned to us safely."

Odey rose and kissed her hand. "It is good to be home. Rest well, my lady."

She swatted his arm. "Theo, please. We are family."

"Theo." He smiled.

Then she turned to Stone and placed a kiss on his cheek again. "I shall see you in a bit?"

"Of course, pet." He gave her a meaningful look, which she interpreted correctly.

"Yes, M- M-..." She cast an uncomfortable glance at Odey. "My lord." And then she all but ran from the room.

"You shouldn't do that to her, 'Chilles. She's always been a sweet, gentle soul," Odey chided him as they sat back down.

"Do not imagine you know my wife better than I do." Stone couldn't control the edge of annoyance in his voice, but he tried to remind himself she was his, and Odey clearly had no interest in taking the title back—if his words were to be trusted. "She is a hellion, and she utterly disobeyed my orders to keep her safe. But perhaps I was beyond the pale to call her 'pet' in your company. I take it you have not continued your interest in taking the reins in the bedroom." Stone was curious how much his brother had changed. He also had noticed Odey never really mentioned what spurred his return, which niggled at Stone's thoughts in relation to the accidents he'd had of late.

"Sweet Theodora? I cannot imagine such a thing." Odey sounded appalled by Stone's characterization of his wife.

"Imagine my wife racing my cabriolet through Hyde Park against Hugh Denton. And then you can imagine my sweet wife visiting The Market for lessons on how to please me."

Odey's eyebrows shot to his hairline. "Never!"

"Quite so. So please do not imagine my wife to be anything but what she is. A headstrong free thinker who makes me immeasurably happy." He turned to face his brother. "You have all but said you did not return for the title. Why have you come back?"

Odey stared at him for a moment. "Not for Theo, if that is what you are thinking. She was a kind girl and would have made a suitable wife, but we were never a love match, as you should well know."

Utter relief swept through Stone, damn near making him weak in the knees. "I had not suspected there was any great romance between you two, but you have yet to say why you have returned. If it was not for the title or the woman, then what?"

Odey stood. "I do have more to discuss with you now that we are alone. Perhaps we should retire to the library for a drink?" They headed into the more masculine environment, which retained a whiff of tobacco laced with leather and dust. "You are correct. I did not come home purely to tell you I am alive. It seems that someone may wish to truly see me dead."

A low, agonized moan ripped Theo from a fitful sleep. She had been tossing and turning all night with odd dreams where her husband would morph into his brother, usually at the most awkward of moments. Next to her, Stone muttered in his sleep and groaned.

Her gut twisted, because she knew he must be in the grip of another nightmare. She unwound the sheets from his legs, careful of any sudden thrashing movements, and then sat next to him on the edge of the bed. As she lay a hand on his forehead and carefully pushed the flop of hair from his face, he seemed to ease a bit.

This was the first nightmare he'd had since the episode at Hawksbury Grange, though if she were able to judge based on past nights, she'd say this was a less intense dream. She hoped that as he opened up to her, he might find more peaceful dreams in his sleep.

He rolled away from her and thrashed about as he cried out in distress. "Not the women…"

Determined to end his nightmare, she crawled across the mattress to where he'd moved and stroked his face again. "Stone, you must wake up. Come back to me." She said the litany over and over until a single tear slipped down her cheek and dropped onto his face. Eyes closed, she muttered the words and hoped she could cut through the pain to bring him back.

The first sign of his return was the strong grasp of his hand around one of her wrists, and then the warm press of his lips against her palm. "I'm here, Theo."

A sigh of relief escaped her as she opened her eyes to meet the coherent yet agonized gaze of her husband. "You've come back."

"I shall always return to you." The raspiness of his voice made her heart ache with the need to soothe such a fine man.

"I am glad to hear such promises." She hesitated and decided to press on. "Would you like to talk about the nightmare?"

He shook his head, but pulled her into the circle of his arms. "There is little new to share. It is simply the feeling of helplessness that torments me. The grief of hearing events unfold, and being unable to stop them."

Theo couldn't imagine such frustration and despair as he must experience each time he had the dream. "I wish I could make it all disappear."

Stone glanced at her, and seemed to weigh sharing something. "I think you may be aiding me in some way. The dream seemed less…intense this time. Normally, the images are so vivid and real, but as soon as you spoke to me, I began drifting away from the horror and surfacing from the dream."

Theo held on to the notion and let it give her comfort. "I am glad if it offers you some respite." She yawned terribly as the heat from his torso seeped through her thin nightgown.

Stone kissed the top of her head. "Sleep, wife. You need your rest, and I shall watch over you for a bit."

Unable to argue, she slipped back into slumber and pressed against her husband. Perhaps things were finally turning about and going their way. All she had ever wanted was a small measure of happiness, no grand love or epic romance. Truly, she was a simple woman at heart.

Chapter Thirty

T heo awoke with her usual queasy stomach and headache, a reminder that she had yet to tell Stone of her delicate condition. But now with Odey's unexpected return, and all the inherent uncertainty thrust upon their tenuous reconciliation, she needed more time to be certain. After a bit of tea and dry toast, she was back in the pink and decided to keep her scheduled visit with Mr. Harrington. She had hoped to have some word of the mystery buyer by the time she returned from the house party. Perhaps she could explain her story to the new owner and convince them to sell it to her?

Hopeful for good news, she had the carriage brought around and headed off. Once she was settled in her man of affairs's office, she tried to be patient as he went through his usual accounting of her portfolio. As she had long ago come to expect, everything was right and tight, not to mention a few investments that were performing above expectations. Pleased but still anxious for the news she truly came for, she waited.

"As to our last order of business, the property adjacent to your orphanage was indeed sold." The man looked up, and for once was reluctant to tell her anything.

"Yes, I am aware of that fact, Mr. Harrington. To whom was the property sold?" She didn't mean to be so crisp with the loyal man, but her patience had shredded with every moment that had passed.

He ruffled a few pages held in his hand and waved the dust motes from the beam of sunlight shining down on them. "Well, my lady. As to that..."

He huffed and puffed and fussed until she lost all patience. Leaning forward in a fit of unforgivable rudeness, she snatched the pages from his hand and read the words printed there. It was a copy of a bill of sale. Ah-ha! At last! She scanned down the page past much of the legal language that would put a corpse to sleep and found the pertinent section. As she read the words, her heart skipped a beat and then plummeted to the floor to lie at her feet.

The purchaser of the land was listed as Achilles Denton, the Earl of Stonemere.

Under no circumstances would she allow her upset to show in public. So she dug deep, kept her British composure, and handed the pages back to Mr. Harrington. "Thank you for getting to the bottom of this issue for me. I hope it wasn't terribly challenging."

"Not at all. I merely enquired of Lord Stonemere's man of affairs, as I had some notion of who had purchased it," Mr. Harrington tossed off, as though the connection were obvious.

"And how would you have known how to find his man of affairs?" Suspicion burned in her gut as she eyed her employee.

"Well, I had the address where I send updates on your holdings and from which I receive an additional retainer fee." As though he had only just become aware of what he revealed, his eyes flew wide until the very orbs in his head seemed to pop forward.

"I see. Thank you, Mr. Harrington." Fury thrummed through her veins as Theo rose and departed the small office. The poor little man trailed after her, mumbling excuses and apologies for which she had no time. The audacity of her husband to meddle in her affairs, and then his utter betrayal, buying the land she had wanted right out from under her! It was outside of enough.

On the street in front of the office, she found her carriage waiting, but the coachman and groom were having a hard time controlling the cattle. One of the front mounts was attempting to rear up. In desperate need to be in the coach and in private, Theo wasted no time in charging over to the horse, wrapping her shawl around his head, and taking a firm grip on the bridle. "Please check the tack and ensure everything is as it should be. The horse is behaving very oddly."

"Yes, my lady." The groom adjusted the saddle of the harness to check it was secure and still attached to the shafts. As he moved it, the animal attempted to rear again. Once it had resettled, the groom pointed out, "My lady, the animal is bleeding from beneath the saddle. 'Tis no wonder he's agitated."

Theo looked closer and wanted to horsewhip whoever would do such a thing to an animal. "You will remove the harness immediately. I shall hail a hack and send a stable boy back with a fresh harness and mount. Do see that everything arrives home safely." And with that decision made, she turned and went in search of a cab to carry her home.

One of Mr. Harrington's runners helped her hail a vehicle, and she was ensconced alone for her journey home. As she rode, she considered all she knew of her husband. Only a few days ago, she had failed to trust him, and as a result, nearly damaged their relationship beyond repair. She needed to give him an opportunity to explain why he bought the land and why he was paying her man of affairs to report to him.

Half an hour later, she strode into the study and found him talking with Odey as they looked over a stack of papers. She barreled ahead, needing to address both issues immediately. "Stone, I have just come from Mr. Harrington's office. I had to take a cab home because someone appears to have tampered with the carriage harnesses, which left one of the poor beasts agitated and bleeding. I have already set the stable master to deal with it, but you should be aware that something is not right. Our staff is not normally so careless.

You should address it posthaste." Even to her own ears, she sounded like a field marshal, but she was at a loss for how to manage the storm of emotions raging inside.

Stone cast an odd glance at Odey before addressing her. "Is that all, Theo?"

"No, I also need a word with you in private." She stood with her feet spread, ready to do battle. She imagined he could see the fury wafting off her like smoke from a fire.

"I shall go follow up with the stable master and see if I may be of assistance." Odey rose and quickly departed the room, closing the door gently behind his retreating form.

"Well, now that you have unceremoniously booted my brother from my study, what may I do for you, Theo?" Stone sat behind his desk and steepled his fingers beneath his chin as he looked at her with what she had come to call "the look of displeasure."

However, she was beyond worrying about possible punishments. Righteous fury fueled her once again as she launched into her tale. "Do you remember the piece of land I mentioned just before the Hawksburys' party?"

"Vaguely." Stone raised one brow.

"Yes, well, I'm surprised you do not have a better recollection of it since it appears you are, in fact, the mysterious buyer." She folded her arms over her breasts and waited.

"Obviously not mysterious enough to evade your detection." He pushed back from his desk and stood. "It seems you have found me out."

"Indeed, it does seem that way. Today has been very educational, you know. I also learned that you also pay my man of affairs a monthly stipend to keep informed of my investments." Her heart pounded as she waited for him to deny it. Hoped he would tell her it was all some silly mistake.

Instead, he cleared his throat, leaned against the front of his desk, and crossed the ankles of his boots. "Yes, about that. I daresay I have been doing just that."

The storm broke loose within and found various cracks in her shell to escape. And there were so many cracks. "We discussed this after I found out you saw him, and yet you failed to mention this arrangement? Failed to be honest with me? Used your supposed honesty only days ago to convince me I was mistaken about you and that hussy at the house party? You, sir, are a cad and a lout."

Beyond reason, she stepped forward, slapped him across the face with a resounding crack of her bare palm, and then fled the masculine confines of the study. Hurt and so very angry, she kept running straight out of the house. Three blocks along, she found herself on the dowager countess's doorstep, tears streaming down her face.

Chapter Thirty-One

S tone cursed himself for a fool. He'd utterly forgotten about the payments and reports his solicitor was receiving from Mr. Harrington. He'd meant to cancel the arrangement, but with all the accidents and falling in love with his wife, it had slipped his mind.

The purchase of her land would be easily explained away, but the reports and fees were by far a harder thing to address. Add to the mess the injured animal and yet another accident meant for him, and he struggled with the overwhelming desire to beat someone bloody. Of course, he was the prime candidate, but that wasn't likely to happen, so he gathered his wits and went in search of his wife instead.

In the foyer, he headed upstairs but was stopped about halfway there when Parsons cleared his throat. "Excuse me, my lord." The poor man looked stupendously uncomfortable. "If you are looking for Lady Stonemere, she left through the front door and made a left on the street, my lord."

"I see. Thank you, Parsons." Stone nodded and then stepped outside, but his wife was long gone in either direction. He sighed and pinched the bridge of his nose. *Fool.* He returned inside and found Parsons waiting for directions. "Please send runners to both the dowager countess's and Lady Carlisle's homes and request word of my wife's whereabouts."

"Yes, my lord." Parsons bowed and quickly disappeared into the bowels of the house.

Stone headed back to his library to both lament his oversight and consider how best to keep his wife safe until he discovered who was trying to kill him and Odey.

Less than an hour later, Stone knew where his wife had hied off to. Under normal circumstances he would have stormed over to his mother's and collected his wayward wife, but since he still had a target on his back, he grudgingly had to admit she might be safest where she was. And while he was grateful to have her out of harm's way for the present, he worried about the new rift between them. How would he repair the damage he'd done?

A knock on the door interrupted his musings and drew his attention back to the issues at hand. Odey walked in, accompanied by Cooper.

"'Chilles, we've got news." Cooper took a seat at the desk across from him.

"Good. Odey, we have another issue developing as well. Let me start with the most urgent item: Theo is currently holed up at Mother's house." Stone hoped Cooper wouldn't ask too many questions.

"Having a row so soon, 'Chilles? I thought you a more dedicated husband than that." Cooper looked at him pointedly.

"There was a misunderstanding which I plan to sort out, but the issue is that she is at Mother's house, which means Mother now likely knows Odey is both alive and home." Stone stabbed his fingers through his hair, frustrated by the whole situation.

"All is not lost. You should visit Mother immediately, check on your wife, and then enlist Mother's support in staying quiet about my return. I fear she will be less surprised than you might expect to learn I am alive."

"How's that?" Stone knew what his brother would say next, but it didn't hurt any less.

"She has known for nearly two years that I am not dead. After Father died, I didn't have the heart to lie to her." Odey wouldn't look him in the eye.

"But you felt no compunction about lying to me?" Stone demanded.

"It was in your best interest. If I hadn't lied, you never would have taken the title, and the whole purpose of the deceit would have been for naught." Odey locked gazes with him and pleaded with his eyes the way he once had as a boy.

And damn it all to hell, Stone couldn't ignore that look any more now than he could when he was young. "You're probably right. But it still smarts that you left me in the dark." He drew a steadying breath. "What news do you two bring?"

"Not so much news as a plan." Cooper leaned forward and explained everything. "So, you need to visit your wife and let her know you will be away for a few days while we lure the culprit out into the open."

"I've not told Theo about the accidents or the would-be killer. I'd prefer to leave her ignorant until all is resolved, for fear she will rush in and try to help. I'd kill the bastard, whoever he is, if he harmed my wife." Stone tried to tamp down the ferocity rumbling beneath the surface, but his emotions rode high with all that had happened. He was a far cry from the man who had married Lady Theodora Lawton a few months earlier. The woman had wormed her way past all his defenses and burrowed into his heart. As a result, he felt things now he'd once had buried deep within, but it was more than acceptable in exchange for feeling her love as well.

Odey shrugged. "Then ask Mother to keep her there for a few days. You can have someone pack her a few things and send them over."

"Fine. I suppose it's the only way to keep her safe. I should head over to Mother's town house and ensure her cooperation. If you two will gather the others, we can head out at first light." Stone stood and nodded to both before heading off to tackle two of the most formidable women he knew.

Stone entered his mother's sitting room and was almost relieved to find her alone. He needed to speak with her privately, but he was desperate to see his wife as well. "Mother."

"Achilles. You really shot into the brown on this one." His mother shook her head.

"I am well aware of the situation, and I am here to see my wife as soon as I have a word with you." He watched her stiffen up as though she might fight him on seeing Theo.

"Your wife does not wish to see you at the moment. The poor child showed up on my doorstep a mess, and barely coherent. I don't know exactly what you've done, but you hurt that child to the core. I was so worried, I sent for Doctor Sullivan to look her over."

Stone wanted to kick himself all over again. "I know I've made a mess of things. And I shall make things right with her, but I need you to keep her here for a few days."

"Theo is welcome here for as long as she deems necessary. Once you have made things right with her, I am sure she will return home. But in the meantime, you should have Mary come over with whatever she needs."

"I've already made the arrangements, and if she is sleeping, I shall check in on her before I go. But first, you will need to explain how it is my brother is, in fact, alive and well. Perhaps you'd like to elaborate on why you've lied to me for two years?" He quirked a brow, as his mother was fond of doing, to drive his point home.

She had the grace to look abashed at being caught out. "I see. Is your brother finally come home?"

"Mother, do not think to avoid the question. Why the lies?" Stone wanted to throttle her, but he also knew the urge would pass, as it often did.

"I'm sure he told you why we thought you should be left in the dark," she huffed, as though he asked a silly question.

"He did explain, but *you* bloody well owe me an explanation." He had been working to control his fury since Odey had told him the truth, but now he was close to boiling over. The struggle continued even as his mother rose and calmly walked over to the secretary.

There, she sat down, bent to the last drawer on the left, and unlocked it. "Odey never wanted to be earl, but your father wouldn't listen. Not until the only son he still had at home had run off. The real trouble was that your father was determined to make your brother the earl, when he should have requested a special remainder. Stubborn old goat."

"Why?" Stone knew something big was coming, and he had a niggling of fear at what he might learn.

"You see, if he had insisted on making Odey the earl, it was very likely the truth of his birth would come out. His illegitimate birth." She handed a stack of papers over to Stone.

"A bastard, you say?" Shock had him by the short hairs as he opened the top document. He read through it and realized it was Odey's birth certificate, making him born just over a year before his parents' marriage.

His mother looked off into nothing as she smiled. "Odey was my love child, my secret shame, until your father rescued both of us. And you, Achilles, you were the confirmation of my love story. I met your father at a house party not unlike the Hawksburys' and fell in love instantly. And then into his bed right after. I was desperate and in love. My parents were going to make me marry a parson's son who was so cold and pinch-faced. I cringed when he called, let alone if he touched me. As I expected, I managed to avoid an unwanted marriage. But instead of winning the man I wanted, I was banished to a convent in France for unwed girls."

Stone dropped into the nearest seat, shocked to his very core by his parents' unknown love story even as most of his fury drained away.

"It took your father almost two years to discover where my parents had hidden me. But once he found me, he rode up to the convent, rescued me from its walls, and whisked me off to Gretna Green, where we were married. We retreated to the abbey for a number of years, where fewer questions were asked. By the time we reentered Society, we had both of you boys and most people didn't bother to do the arithmetic."

Stone still couldn't believe it. He looked at the next sheet he held and found it to be a special remainder that was signed shortly before his father had died.

"Once Odey left, your father knew he had to let go of the need to make things right for his firstborn. He still felt guilty it took him so long to find us. The problem was, by the time he had the special remainder signed and passed through Lords, we got word of the massacre at Cawnpore. The first missives through stated no survivors. He couldn't bear the stress of failing his sons in his mind."

"Damn it all to hell, it's my fault he died. Why let me stay in India? Why didn't you call me back from service?" Stone looked at the document that officially made him Earl of Stonemere, regardless of Odey's existence.

His mother fidgeted with the rings on her fingers. "He wanted to, but I begged him not to. I convinced him to let you have a little adventure before you had to come home and settle into the staid life of a peer. It was my fault you were still in service when the massacre happened. My fault your father is dead." Tears pooled in her hazel eyes as she groped for her handkerchief.

Stone rose and pulled his mother into his embrace. "It was fate that I was there. You cannot blame yourself for that, nor for Father's death."

She held him close and cried all over his coat and vest. "You are a good son, Achilles." She sniffled a few times and pulled herself together. "I daresay we should have a proper welcome home for Odey. I would like to see my other son."

Stone's necktie suddenly felt overtight. "I need to request that you hold off on any fêtes for Odey. There is some strangeness afoot, and his relative nonexistence here in

London works in our favor as we try to sort the business out. If you could give us a few days, I promise you will have ample time to show him off and celebrate."

His mother looked mutinous.

"Our very lives could depend on it." He'd not wanted to make it sound so dire, but she had a mulish expression, which meant she would insist on having her way.

She paled considerably. "What in heaven's name?"

"As I said, odd things are afoot, and I need you to remain silent with regard to Odey's return for the moment."

"Of course, I would never intentionally put my sons in harm's way. I shall remain silent. But you will explain why you believe your lives depend upon it."

"There has been a series of what I thought were accidents. As it turns out, they are not." Stone continued on to explain some of his mishaps, as well as the one that had hurt Theo.

"I hope you have a plan to catch this dastardly man." His mother looked fierce enough that he worried for a moment she might adopt his wife's methods and charge into the breach.

"All will be well. My friends and I have a plan, and we will sort this mess out soon." He kissed his mother on the cheek. "Now, is my wife sleeping in the blue room over the garden?"

"She is, but I beg you, Achilles, leave her be." His mother grabbed his arm and looked at him with earnest concern.

He let a bit of his guard down so his mother would know how important a mere glimpse of his wife was to him. "Just a moment, Mother. I must see she is well before I head off to deal with whoever is hunting me."

"Very well. Go, my son, but do not wake her." His mother shooed him off, and he went eagerly.

Years ago, as a young man, when he'd first seen a woman submit sexually to a man, he'd had no idea the power that could come with the submission of the right woman. His wife showed him the depth of that power, the heights of ecstasy, and the lows of despair that came with such control.

He found the door he sought and opened it with nary a squeak thanks to well-oiled hinges. There on the bed, curled on her side as though protecting something she held against her belly, his wife slept. Her hair, loose and spread over the pillows, drew him. Made him want to touch her to feel its silken skeins slide through his fingers as he sank into her once more.

But for now, he would content himself with seeing that she was cared for in his absence while he carried memories of making love to her with him into the fray that awaited him. But unlike his time in the army, he had too many reasons to live, and all of them lived within the woman lying on the bed. All his hopes and dreams, his love, and his future were contained in her. And he fully intended to come back and lay claim to all of it. Right after he ended the threat looming on the horizon.

Chapter Thirty-Two

T heo sat up in the twilight-soaked room and peered into the dusky shadows. Momentary disorientation gnawed at her until a familiar voice whispered past the heavy oak door.

"I am quite capable of carrying a dinner tray to my daughter-in-law, Mary. There is no need for you to dart about me like a bee."

The dowager countess's strident but muffled tones relieved her moment of panic while raising her curiosity. Why was Mary here? Feet firmly planted on the floor, Theo rose from the bed and stood as the door swung open.

"What in the devil do you think you are doing, child?"

"Standing." Theo stated the obvious in lieu of wading into battle outright.

"The doctor ordered rest for you, at least for a day or two." Lady Stonemere cut to the chase as she set her burden down on a nearby table.

"I feel quite recovered. There is no reason to act as though I have been stricken with some disease." Theo huffed and determinedly moved farther away from the bed.

"Well, here is beef tea and some bread crusts for you. It should be a nice restorative after your episode. If you won't lie down, then at least sit down while you partake." Her mother-in-law ushered her over to the table and sat her down as though she were a young girl and not a countess.

"What time is it?" Theo ignored the pang in her heart at the notion that night was falling and yet her husband had not appeared to at least attempt to convince her to return home.

"It is half past seven. Dinner was served an hour ago, since I prefer to eat early."

"I see." Theo's stomach dropped, and had she not already heaved up its entire contents earlier, she would have done so. She stared at her dinner and blinked rapidly in hopes of holding back the tears that seemed determined to make an appearance.

"Yes, well, you have been asleep for a few hours. I'm surprised you slept right through your husband's rather boisterous arrival earlier as he demanded word of his missing wife."

Theo's gaze snapped up to the dowager's knowing smile. "He came?"

"Of course he did, my girl. The man is so besotted with you, I couldn't have kept him away had I tried. He insisted on seeing that you were resting comfortably before he would leave."

Hope bloomed warm and bright in her chest. "And where has he gone?"

"He is off dealing with some pressing matters associated with Odey's return. Once those are settled, he will return to sort out whatever it is that stands between you two, and he has requested you stay with me until then. He even sent Mary over with some of your things, though I daresay his request has nothing to do with the child you carry." She looked pointedly at Theo's stomach.

Firmly ignoring her mother-in-law's probing for the moment, she eyed her beef tea and crusty bread with listless interest. What could be more important to Stone than addressing their marriage? She couldn't begin to consider the ramifications on their relationship if they could not resolve his high-handed behavior.

And what of their child?

Her hand flattened over the barest hint of a bump in an instinctively protective move. A fierce need to defend the life nestled within her swelled at the notion of anyone or anything threatening her babe. No, regardless of what might come, she would protect her child with her last breath. Even from her husband's overbearing ways.

On that note, she resolutely lifted her spoon and filled the bowl with broth. She would eat for her child and ensure they had every advantage she could provide. But as her husband was surely well aware, her patience would last only so long.

She let the silence stretch a bit longer before replying. "He does not yet know about the child, and I do not wish to keep that knowledge from him. But I shall not tell him until we resolve this issue between us, which means I shall only allow him so much time to attend to his business before I expect him to address my grievance."

The dowager sighed. "I beg of you, do not be rash."

"I shall take care of myself and my child. But as my husband has learned, I shall not be ignored." Determination welled up within her as she shored up her spirit. "A day, two at the most, and then I shall see him."

"Very well, my dear." The dowager countess nodded and turned to leave, but stopped midway. "But I caution you not to allow either your head or your heart to rule absolutely. A balance of both is required in a successful marriage."

And then she disappeared through the door, leaving Theo alone to consider her words and what the next few days might bring. She considered it more than odd that Stone would ask that she remain with his mother, but at the moment, she was far more concerned about her evening meal and then her sleep. It had been a horrible day, and she firmly hoped that with Mary's assistance, in the morning she would feel well enough to tackle the future of her marriage.

By the next afternoon, Stone, Odey, and Cooper were ensconced in Cooper's hunting box just across the county from Stonemere Abbey in Southampton. The rest of the

Lustful Lords—Linc, Flint, and Wolf—camped around them to keep watch for the would-be killer. Exhausted after spending the evening planning their trap. They had set the lure by carousing at their various clubs and putting the word out of their imminent departure, and the absolute last thing Stone wanted to do now was tramp about the countryside looking for stags. But if the trap were to work, then the bait must be dangled, so the three of them headed out for an afternoon foray.

"I do hope this little ruse works," Stone grumbled as he stalked through a trickling stream.

"Well, it certainly won't if you continue to discuss it, 'Chilles." Odey sounded as exasperated as Stone felt, but likely for different reasons.

"Yes, well, you don't have an unhappy wife at home. I have made such a mess of things with Theo, I fear I shall never hear the end of it once she learns the truth of it all." Stone ducked to avoid a low-hanging oak branch.

Odey grunted. "Brother, do not think that because I am unmarried, I do not have my own trials of the feminine form. The fair daughter of the winemaker Seignior Tedesco, the beautiful Mariella, still leads me a merry chase." Odey sighed and stepped up on a small boulder. "But I declare here and now, I shall return to Sardinia and lay claim to my woman."

Cooper and Stone chuckled. Odey had declared many things in just such a manner growing up. Most of them never came to pass and were quickly forgotten.

Cooper winked at Stone and Odey. "Lads, what you need is a woman like my Sarah. Soft in all the right places, sweet of disposition, and a widow with no desire to marry. She's always happy to see me, but never at my doorstep. It's the perfect arrangement."

"With the exception that if you fail to marry, then you will fail to produce an heir. Which means that wastrel brother of yours will replace you when you die and leave the family fortunes on the Faro tables in some gambling hell. But please, do go on about dearest Sarah." Stone cast a gimlet eye at his friend. How Cooper could still be in denial of his responsibilities boggled Stone's mind.

Cooper sighed. "I'm still looking for a way around it, but should I remain stuck, I shall simply marry some chit who has been conditioned to look the other way once the heir and a spare have been produced."

Stone and Odey both laughed. "Times are changing, my friend," Stone pointed out. "Girls are holding out for love, and even if they aren't, I should stand as your cautionary tale. I married for the requisite heir and have found myself unequivocally, irretrievably, ridiculously in love. I promise you I had no intention of doing such a thing, and if I had, I would have imagined it a far simpler affair. The truth is, love is messy."

Odey and Cooper grimaced.

"Messy, painful, and hard to manage, but absolutely one of the most wonderful experiences of my life," Stone continued. "I wouldn't undo it if I could."

"Dear Gawd, he's lost to us!" Cooper cried out, dropping his forehead on Odey's shoulder in a dramatic fashion.

"Do be serious. We are meant to be bait here, not participating in a stage drama," Stone groused as he laid his shotgun across his arm and walked away from his brother and his best friend. He'd at least spoken from the heart. Those two fools were still lost when it came to women. Maybe one day they'd each find their way. "Gents, the sun will be retiring soon. I think we should do the same. We shall try again tomorrow."

"Very well," Odey and Cooper agreed as they turned to follow Stone back to the hunting box.

The next day went much the same as the first. The three friends walked about the countryside, occasionally taking shots at deer or other wild game they came across. But no attacks were made. That night, they called the other three into the cabin to discuss their options.

"'Chilles, you can't give up yet." Odey lounged on the couch with a drink in his hand, the picture of the country gentleman.

Stone felt more like a landed fish still hooked on the line. He wasn't sleeping, he was tired from all the faux hunting they'd done, and he missed the devil out of his wife. "It seems the plan isn't working. Flint and the others have seen nothing but the three of us gadding about like motley fools waxing poetic about whatever crosses our minds. If the killer hasn't followed us, then this is all for naught."

"Have a little faith, Stone." Linc, always the jokester, offered a pat on the back. "Perhaps the man had some other business besides killing you he needed to tend to."

"He could appear at any moment. We cannot afford to let our guards down." Wolf, ever the somber one among the group, seemed more dour than usual.

"Wolf's right. Besides, I wouldn't mind a crack at this mysterious person." Flint slammed a fist into the palm of his hand.

"I agree, 'Chilles. It's only been a day and a half. Give it at least one more day. Then you can run home to Theo and plead your case." Cooper raised his scotch as though toasting the idea.

They were right, of course. He was restless and merely wanted to see his pet again. He itched to have her on her knees for him, willing to do anything he requested. He might even spank her bottom to remind her running away from him would never be the answer to their problems. "You take the egg. Another day, but if he fails to appear, I shall not tarry longer."

They all nodded in agreement, and then Flint, Linc, and Wolf stepped back outside into the brisk night air and resumed their posts. Stone, Odey, and Cooper remained inside and drowned the aches from such excessive exercise in scotch and companionship.

Chapter Thirty-Three

T heo stood dressed, ready to go despite her usual morning symptoms. How she'd managed it was a testament to Mary's patience and her own fortitude. But manage it she did, and all so she could storm her husband's castle and engage in battle. She'd given him a day, which was twenty-four more hours than she'd wanted to give. And to her frustration, she still had seen neither hide nor hair of him.

That was a state that would be remedied in a very short while. She merely had to make it three blocks, and then she could demand he set aside whatever business he had put before their marriage. It was outside of enough, and she planned to let him know.

Marshaling her reserves to carry her downstairs, she took her coat from the dowager's butler and headed down the street. On foot. There wasn't a book, bauble, or investment that could have enticed her into the confines of a carriage at the moment. Not even for a three-block jaunt.

With each step, she reinforced her resolve. She reminded herself of the fact this was Stone's second such transgression, and he'd had the nerve to use the resolution of the first incident against her at the house party! She had trusted him, surrendered her heart and soul to him, and he had trampled both without a care. If he did not come forward with sufficient reparations, she would have to sever the intimacy of the relationship. They would revert to the cold Society marriage she had dreaded all along. And while it might kill her to do so, she would find a way to make it work so that her child did not want for anything.

But then there was no further time to ruminate. She arrived home, and before she could place her hand upon the doorknob, Parsons greeted her as though she often entered the house via the front door before nine o'clock in the morning. "Good morning, Lady Stonemere."

"Parsons." She handed him her coat. "Is my husband at breakfast?"

"I'm afraid Lord Stonemere isn't in residence this morning." Parsons stood holding her coat, his face ever impassive and uninformative.

Theo paused and considered this bit of information. Her husband had been known to forgo breakfast on occasion. "Has he gone to the railway office?" She reached for her coat, assuming she would simply hunt him down.

"No, my lady. He is gone to Southampton with his brother and Lord Brougham. I believe they are hunting." Parsons intoned the news as though he had just announced breakfast was served.

"And did he say when he would return?" She bit her lip, trying to curb her freshly ignited fury.

"He did not, my lady," Parsons replied.

"I see." But truly, she did not see. His mother had stated he was addressing some business related to his brother. And yet Parsons said he was off hunting. Without a foreseeable return date. Though she had not subscribed to too many of her mother's edicts growing up, she did not believe in causing a scene—even in one's own home—if it was avoidable. "Parsons, I shall need my coat back. Also, if you would please send word immediately upon my husband's return, I would greatly appreciate it."

"Very good, my lady." Parsons assisted her with her coat. "May I call the carriage around for you?"

"No, thank you. I shall walk." It was both good for the digestion—regardless that she had not had more than a toasted crust of bread—and it would be good for the excess energy she'd acquired along with the news of her husband's whereabouts. In fact, three blocks might not be sufficient to calm her fury before she spoke to the dowager countess.

With clear intent, she returned from whence she came. Once in the dowager's home, she sought her out. As usual, the dowager countess sat in her sun-filled sitting room at the back of the house. "Mother Stonemere, there you are." Theo swept into the room and plopped onto the settee closest to her mother-in-law.

She peered very closely at her embroidery hoop and then jabbed the needle into the material before looking up. "Good morning, Theo. You are up betimes and looking in the pink."

"Thank you, my lady. I am feeling much better, though I must say I had the strangest conversation with Parsons this morning." Theo had calmed a bit, but was still distressed over her husband's apparent abandonment.

"Wherever did you see Parsons at this hour of the morning?" She stabbed the material once more and pulled the thread through.

"Why, at my home, of course. I decided I was ready to see Stone and discuss our differences. But to my surprise, Parsons informed me that my husband is off hunting with his brother and best friend." Theo watched the dowager's expression for any evidence that she might know more than she had previously revealed.

Her quarry paled a bit. "Hunting, is he?"

"Quite so. And here I thought he was addressing a pressing issue related to his brother's return." Theo raised a brow as she waited for a response.

The dowager stabbed at the needlepoint again and went right through the material and into her finger. "Oh dear!"

Theo leaned forward, partly concerned that her mother-in-law had pricked herself and partly aware that she had the woman dead to rights. She certainly knew something. "I don't think you bled on your needlework. Perhaps you should set it down while you tell me what is afoot with my husband. I daresay something is going on here that I have been specifically left out of."

The dowager looked abashed at being caught out in a fib. "Fine. He preferred you not to know, but he didn't forbid my telling you, and besides, it's too late at this point." She set her needlepoint aside and faced Theo. "Achilles has set off to draw out the man who has been trying to kill him. I assume they are pursuing this issue at Lord Brougham's hunting lodge."

Theo gasped, and her heart fluttered. "Whatever do you mean?"

As the dowager explained what little she knew, Theo grew angrier and more afraid for her husband. By the time the dowager was through, Theo could barely sit still to wait for word of his return. And yet, under the circumstances, she had no choice but to be patient and wait.

Morning came far too early for some members of their party. Stone and Odey left Cooper behind, nursing an aching head from an excess of drink. The two of them, trailed by Wolf, Linc, and Flint, wandered off in a more easterly direction than they had previously followed. They tracked a stag into a clearing, and unmindful of their purpose, became caught up in the hunt. Halfway across the open field, Odey stopped.

Stone noticed his pause but kept his eyes focused on where he had last spotted the deer. "Don't stop now, we've nearly got him."

"'Chilles, look at us. We're sitting ducks here."

Odey's comment had Stone turning to face him.

"Bloody hell. How could I have forgotten?" He glanced once more in the direction he last saw the stag. With a sigh of resignation, in part because he was sure this was all a waste of time, he stepped toward Odey. "If we dash over that way"—he waved toward the tree line a hundred paces to their right—"we can get some cover in a jiffy."

As a single unit, they turned and started in that direction, when suddenly the tree bark ahead exploded, followed by the report of a rifle. A stinging in his arm flared as he and Odey dropped to their stomachs, and then a second shot rang out. Still down despite having rolled over, they saw Flint tussling with someone across the meadow. They rose and bolted toward the two men struggling for control of the rifle. Behind them, Wolf and Linc were charging in, clearly having wound up on their side of the clearing.

As they neared the two men, the gunman slammed a fist into Flint's face, which had the man laughing. "You'll need to make a better effort than that, old man."

"Bloody toffer!" Stone recognized the voice even from a distance and under the strain of the fight.

The gunman was Hugh Denton, his cousin.

With a curse, he lunged toward the two, but had to pull up short as Hugh swung the butt of his gun wildly. He managed to clip Flint in the head and break free. Twenty paces back inside the tree line, a horse stood waiting for him. In a matter of seconds, Hugh bounded onto the horse and took off through the forest.

Stone lifted his hunting rifle and sighted the man's torso as he made his escape, but at the last moment, honor refused to let him shoot a man in the back, and certainly not a family member. Though, clearly, his cousin had no such compunction. Odey also carried a weapon, but his marksmanship lacked compared to Stone's military-honed skills. With a curse, they made chase, but were nowhere near as fast as a horse, even in the denseness of the forest. After ten minutes, he and Odey gave up and went back to check on Flint and the others.

They found the three of them walking, Flint with his head bandaged by a length of what appeared to have once been his shirt. Stone hated that anyone was hurt, though they'd all known the risk when they'd agreed to help. "Is everyone well?"

"We are," Linc said, and then nodded at him. "But you seem to have been winged."

Stone looked down at his arm in surprise. His fawn-colored hunting coat bore an unexpected red stripe. "Blast it, this was a favorite jacket."

"Here, we should bandage you up and head back to the box. Did you see who it was?" Wolf asked as he tore his own shirt to provide a bandage.

"I'm rather unhappy to say I did," Stone said as his friend wound the strip of cloth around the wound and tied it off.

"Whoever it was, he was a puny thing, and I'd appreciate another go at him without the rifle to hand." Flint's hands fisted, his simmering violence a palpable thing.

"I suspect that can be arranged, unless our cousin skips town before we can catch up with him." Odey took Stone's weapon. "Let's head back and collect Cooper. I'd say if we hurry, we can at the very least match his return to London, if not beat him."

Chapter Thirty-Four

After a short trek to the hunting box, they collected their things—including Cooper—and made a mad dash back to London. Fresh off the train, the six of them headed straight to Hugh's rooms.

"Flint, take the rear alley. Ensure there is no back door for him to slip through. Linc and Wolf, if you two will take the sides of the building and the front corners. That leaves Cooper to watch the front entrance. Odey and I shall head upstairs to see if he might be in residence." Stone nodded, and they each took off to their respective positions.

He and Odey headed inside and up the stairs to Hugh's rooms. At the top of the third floor, Stone looked down the hall and could see his cousin's door was cracked open. "Double damn."

They approached the opening and pushed the wood panel wider. Inside, the apartment was a mess, items tossed everywhere. "Either he returned home and was in a hurry to get out again, or someone else is looking for Hugh as well."

Odey stepped inside and went into the adjacent sleeping quarters. "Tossed in here as well. Whoever it was—most likely his creditors—did a thorough job of it. Even sliced the mattress up. The proprietor will not be pleased about this."

Stone sighed, tired, filthy, and frustrated that his cousin had got away. "I'll send round some blunt to offset the damage. It's not their fault my family member turned out to be a downy cove."

"You're a right brick, 'Chilles. Always have been. Let's for home, then." Odey smacked his shoulder, and they headed downstairs to collect the men.

They all met in front of the building again. Stone looked at each man and could see they were as tired as he was. "I appreciate everyone's assistance. It looks as though Hugh has fled London, or simply never returned. Either way, I think home and a wash is in order before we go any further. If you all are still prepared to assist, come by Curzon Street at eight tonight. Perhaps a tour of London's underbelly will provide some information on his whereabouts."

They all nodded in agreement, and then split off to head to their respective homes.

Twenty minutes later, he and his brother strode into the town house. As they dropped everything, Parsons organized the staff and saw their things were taken away. "My lord, you have a visitor in the library."

Surprised, Stone glanced at Odey, who lifted a shoulder in bewilderment. "Who the devil is in my library?"

"I did explain you were away hunting, but your cousin insisted you would be home shortly. As he was family, it seemed more prudent to let him wait for a while rather than tossing him on his ear." Parsons delivered this news with his usual aplomb.

Curious what his cousin was up to, he looked at Odey and nodded. "Parsons, do have the stable master and a few of the sturdier staff available should there be trouble."

"Very good, my lord. I also took the liberty of informing your wife you have returned. She was by this morning and insisted I alert her the moment you were home."

"Well, damn. Send another runner if you can't stop the first. Tell her I've gone back out, but I will be by to see her later." He looked at his brother. "The last thing we need is her arrival in the midst of whatever this is."

"No doubt, 'Chilles. But will she heed your notes?" Odey raised a good point.

"Doubtful, so we had best get this interview over with." Stone turned and marched into the library, where Hugh sat before the fireplace with a scotch in one hand and a pistol in the other.

"So very good of you two to return. I was beginning to wonder at the delay." Hugh waved the weapon. "Do come in, and close the door behind you. No need to involve the staff in this tête-à-tête."

Stone agreed for the moment, so he did as directed, but Odey attempted a subtle shift out of Hugh's peripheral vision.

"Ah. Ah. Ah. Please, do stay right where I can see you, Odysseus. You are absolutely part of this conversation." Hugh set his drink down and rose. "You see, the two of you are currently the only obstacles to my side of the family taking over the earldom. And frankly, it should have been ours—by three minutes. My father was born first, but when that stupid cow of a nursemaid presented the babies, she gave your father over first. The wrong child."

Stone couldn't stop his snort of derision. "Such idiocy. The birth was carefully documented to ensure the correct child was identified as the heir. The former earl was a bastard, but a careful one."

Hugh waved the pistol a bit. "It's time to set right what went awry long ago. Regardless, your father made a horrible earl, right from the start."

"Only a fool who knows nothing of the responsibilities of an earl would make such claims." Stone couldn't help but steal a glance at the clock on the wall.

Hugh gripped the pistol more tightly and poked the air in Stone's direction. "Do not push me, Achilles. I could simply shoot you here and then make it look as though Odysseus killed you for the title, thereby eliminating all possible obstacles."

Odey seemed altogether calmer than Stone felt, but then he wasn't anticipating the imminent arrival of his wife to the party. Stone needed to wrestle back control of the situation, if not the pistol itself. "What exactly is your plan here? Even if you killed both of us, your father would still stand between you and the title."

Hugh laughed, but there was a razor-sharp edge to it that had pins and needles prickling along Stone's spine.

"Father is not long for this world. If either of you deigned to attend family gatherings more often, you might have heard that my father, like his brother, also has a weak heart. It seems possible the entire family is inherently flawed. I imagine he shall drop soon enough. One way or another." The words came out flecked with spittle and a snarled mess, but were still understandable. Hugh drew a calming breath. "As for my plan, it is in fact time to go. The resurrected son and current earl are due for a tragic accident."

Stone absorbed the news that fate was not being kind to his family. Hopefully she hadn't deserted them altogether. But then the door burst open, and his wife sailed into the room.

Theo swept in, ready to do battle with her idiotic husband. Who tried to catch a man who'd attempted to kill you without the aid of Scotland Yard? Or the Metropolitan Police? Even a private inquiry service? Her husband stood near his desk, with Odey not far from him. The two men looked particularly stressed, what with the clear frowns upon their faces and the ridges between their eyes. They looked strikingly similar in that moment, but for Odey's leaner visage. Distracted by her ruminations, she drew up short when she realized there was a third man in the room. His movement caught her by surprise, almost as much as when she realized he was tucking a pistol against his leg.

She turned to see Hugh Denton, Stone's provoking cousin. His mere presence made her stomach sour. The wild dismay on Hugh's face paired with the twitchy way he glanced from her to Stone alerted her that something wasn't right. As if in a scene from a gothic horror novel, she could feel the tension in the room as the three men waited to see what she would do.

The dark wood of the library suddenly felt claustrophobic as panic swept through her limbs to choke the breath from her body. The snap of the fire sounded loud in the stilted silence, adding a cheery background as a counterpoint to the moment.

Drawing a deep breath, she turned toward her husband first. "Stone, I do not appreciate you disappearing to the country to go stag hunting with no warning. I was forced to attend the Cabots' soiree alone, and you know I detest musicales after the Swinton affair." She swept dramatically over to the fireplace and laid a hand on the mantel.

"My apologies, Theo. It was poor form of me to leave you in the lurch." Stone edged toward her and closer to Hugh. The thick Aubusson carpet muted his footsteps, but she could feel his presence, his nearness.

The weapon wobbled in Hugh's hand down by his leg, and she feared he would do something rash before she could intervene. It seemed logical that if Stone had been hunting his would-be killer and his cousin currently had a weapon concealed in the drapes of his coat, Hugh must be the man Stone sought. The question was, what had she walked in on? An apology? A confrontation?

She sniffled and tucked her face against her forearm while leaning on the mantel and cried out, "It was simply horrid, Stone." Meanwhile, she wrapped her other hand around the handle of the fire poker and drew it against her skirts. The weight of the iron weapon had her listing gently to one side, but she righted herself, keeping it hidden from the unsavory man not far from where she stood. Then she looked up at her husband, who was an arm's length away from her. "They made me sing." Her declaration came out as an agonized whisper. A thought too awful to truly say aloud—and it would have been, had it been true.

Then she whirled toward Hugh and lurched in his direction. "Have you ever been made to *sing* in public?" She emphasized the word as though there was nothing she wanted to do less in public.

Hugh darted a glance at the two other men in the room, then looked back to her. His expression hardened, annoyance at her interruption as clear as the necktie around his neck. "What are you on about, woman?"

Stone growled behind her, but she needed him to stay put a moment more. "Singing. *In public!*"

Hugh stared at her as though she had grown a third eye or a second head. "Lady Stonemere, you interrupted a rather pressing matter I have with your husband. Would you mind leaving us?"

"Well, that was very rude of you, sir. This is my home, not some gentleman's club." She dug deep for all the haughty disdain she could muster as she glared at the impertinent man. "I shall not be spoken to in such a manner."

"Achilles, your wife is going to get herself added to the guest list should she remain."

The threat—and Theo knew it for what it was—had Stone stepping closer to the two of them, which caused Hugh to dispense with any pretense and raise the gun.

Fear raced through Theo, spiking her body with adrenaline that seemed to bring everything into sharper focus. The grain of wood seemed so pronounced, the musty smell of the books grew earthier, and the fire snapped louder, more fiercely than before.

She saw her chance, and so she took it, without hesitation. Her child would not be born without a father. With a speed that surprised even herself, she raised the poker from her skirts and raked it in a downward arc that knocked the weapon from the villain's hand.

From there, Theo scooted to her right and away from the men, because Stone and Odey were both leaping forward and tackling the injured Hugh. Despite being essentially one-handed, he still fought them both for a moment or two. Then, to her relief, they subdued him just as Parsons and the stable master barged into the study with a group of men besides. She was pleased to note there were at least two uniformed police officers among them.

In short order, Hugh Denton was detained and taken away as Stone and Odey both sat down. Her husband seemed to be cradling his arm, and it was then she noticed the bloodstained cloth wrapped around his upper limb. He'd been shot. Theo's knees turned gelatinous and her stomach attempted to depart her body through her throat as she imagined her life without Stone. Fortunately, that all subsided when everything turned black.

Chapter Thirty-Five

S tone's heart had dropped right along with his wife's body. With no women to gainsay him, he installed his wife in their bed and sent for the doctor. He alone tended to her as she lay unconscious. Shallow but even breathing on her part and the repetitive action of dampening her brow with a wet rag helped him stay calm. After a few moments alone, her lashes fluttered, and then she looked up into his eyes with her deep-blue gaze.

"Thank God, you're awake." Relief rushed through his veins, a heady cocktail that had his head spinning. His heart tumbled as his breath snagged. Hands shaking with the need to touch her, yet fearful of her rejection, he forced his words past numb lips. "I need you to know that I bought the land next to your orphanage—*for you*. I was having the land cleared and a playground installed. I wanted to show that I understand you. That you matter to me in a way no one else ever has or ever will. I love you, Theodora Denton, Countess of Stonemere."

His heart thumped in a terrifying rhythm, but her only response was to capture his mouth with hers. He sank into her welcoming vibrant heat and relished her response. The softness of her tongue as she explored his mouth had ripples of pleasure running through him all the way to his toes. The heady scent of woman and lilies filled his nose as the sweetness of her taste collided with his desire. After a moment of the passionate exchange, he drew back and grinned at his headstrong wife.

"I love you, Achilles Denton, Earl of Stonemere. You are my rock and my heart."

He leaned in to kiss her again, her taste the sweetest ambrosia he'd ever known. Their tongues tangled as he pressed her back into the mattress. A sharp knock was all the warning they were given before the door opened and the doctor and Stone's mother walked in on their steamy kiss. "Well, I'd say our patient is feeling better," the doctor commented as he rounded the bed to where Stone sat with his wife in his arms.

"Doctor Sullivan, thank you for coming so quickly. She fainted earlier after a rather large upset, and I was worried, as she tends to have an unusually robust constitution." Stone let go of her and moved back to allow the doctor access.

"Stone, you did not tell me you called Doctor Sullivan." Theo looked balefully at him as she crossed her arms. "Doctor, I am quite well. I merely fainted when I realized my husband had been shot, which, I might argue, is not an unreasonable thing for a wife to do in such a case."

The doctor looked back at Stone, brows raised.

"My wife waited to faint until after she had accosted an armed assailant with a fire poker, so you may understand my trepidation at such feminine hysterics. She has a fortitude unlike most women." Exasperation with both the doctor and his wife—whom he loved to the very depths of his soul—had him ready to simply demand they all do as he wished. Of course, he was coming to understand that approach was not a winning proposition when it came to his wife.

Theo looked at the doctor and motioned him closer with her finger. They had a short whispered conversation, and then the doctor straightened, picked up his bag, and started out the way he had come. He paused by the dowager and said something to her, and then they both left the room. Stone looked from the closed door to his wife in surprise. "What in the world was that all about?"

"Stone, sit." Theo patted the mattress beside her.

"Theo, you are terrifying me." He knew fear. He'd lived through it in India, the worst being at Cawnpore. Sitting in the marsh by the river, floating downstream to avoid the mutinous native army, and then discovering he was, in fact, the Earl of Stonemere. But none of those events compared to the soul-crushing fear he felt right in that moment. The terror was prompted by the possibility that the woman he loved, the woman he couldn't take his next breath without, might be about to tell him she was sick or dying.

"Stone, do sit down. I am not dying."

Her annoyance snapped him out of the paralysis that had gripped him like a vise. He sank to the bed and cupped her face. "I can't possibly lose you when I just found you."

The tensile strength of her slim hands wrapped around his wrists reminded him that she was both alive and resilient. Whatever was happening, they would survive together. He never had to tackle any endeavor alone again. His intrepid wife would be at his side.

"Stone, I'm carrying our child." She smiled at him.

The softly spoken words sounded muddled in his chaotic mind. *Child.* The single word stood out and grabbed his attention as no other word could have. "Pregnant?"

She nodded as tears welled in her eyes.

"We're having a baby?" He blinked rapidly. Something seemed to be clouding his vision, and he couldn't see his beautiful wife clearly. "I'm going to be a father?"

She nodded again, or he thought she did. His vision was off. And then something tickled his cheek. He reached up to brush it away, but his fingertips came up wet. He looked down and realized he couldn't see his wife through his tears. Tears of pure unadulterated joy. The woman he loved was gifting him with a child. Their child. "I must be the luckiest man in the world."

She laughed. "And me, I'm the luckiest woman. However did a runner-up earl and a hand-me-down countess get so lucky?"

"It was fate, my love. Fate and the love of a headstrong woman." Then he scooped her up and hauled her into his lap before he slammed his lips down on hers. No kiss could ever express all the emotion raging through him, but he decided it was certainly a good place to start.

The End

Start reading His Hellion Countess...

Chapter One - June 1861

Robert Cooper, the Earl of Brougham, twined his cravat around the redhead's wrists at the small of her back and smacked her ass. The woman cooed her approval as she lay bent over the edge of the bed.

"Do keep the racket down, love."

He opened his trousers and pulled out his cock. He liked an enthusiastic lover, just not a noisy one. And having her restrained made his balls throb and his cock stiffen. Though, if he were forthright, not as much as it once had.

"Let the girl be, Cooper." Marion Thomas, Baron Lincolnshire, was balls-deep in a brunette's mouth as he made his suggestion. "Some of us enjoy the sounds of passion."

A low moan of pleasure interrupted them as Grayson Powell, Viscount Wolfington, smacked the backside of the woman he currently had strapped to the spanking bench. The raven-haired beauty he was treating to a stout spanking sounded as excited as Wolf seemed to be, if his rather impressive cockstand was any indication.

Cooper ignored his friend and refocused on the woman he was about to fuck. Reaching down, he slid two fingers into her wet slit and pumped in and out. She moaned softly when he added a third finger. While not the tallest or the stoutest man amongst his set, his cock had proven intimidating to a woman on more than one occasion, so he worked his fingers in and out to ensure the sexy redhead would enjoy taking him.

Once her hips bucked against his hand, he slipped free and notched his cock at her opening. As he slid inside her pussy, the door of their room opened, and Flint—Matthew Derby, Marquess of Flintshire—entered. His face was bloody and bruised, but he tossed everyone a grin.

"Anyone mind if I jump in?" he asked as he opened the front flap of his trousers.

Wolf waved him over. "I think Millie has a hankering for a lobcock."

Flint grabbed his shaft by the base and slapped it against his other hand, making a thick smacking sound. "Nothing soft here." He moved over to Millie and nudged her lips with his erection. "Open up, sweetheart."

The woman stared at Flint's cock for a moment and then eagerly swallowed him whole.

Cooper shook his head at his friends, though watching the eager girl sucking his friend's rather impressive cock helped bring his excitement up another notch. Then he returned once more to riding his way to ecstasy. He laid one hand on the redhead's hip and grabbed her bound wrists with the other as he pounded into her generous curves. He'd come to enjoy the carnal delights of a well-endowed woman, and at the moment, he planned to avail himself of hers. What was her name? Mary? He didn't remember precisely, not that it mattered.

All around him, the sensual sounds of sex filled the room. The slap of flesh, the slurping noise of a well-sucked cock, and the low groans of the participants climbing toward their climaxes. Sliding his hand from her hip to reach under her, he sought out his partner's small nub. As he stroked her clit, she wailed and heaved against him, increasing their tempo. He kept up the bruising pace even as his balls tightened. The redhead crashed over the edge of bliss, crying out her pleasure as he continued to stroke into her. Then, with one last thrust, he exploded inside her with a groan of fulfilment.

All around him, his friends were reaching their satisfying ends. But he needed to tend to the woman beneath him. He rose from the bed and withdrew from her body. Immediately, he released her wrists. "Stay still, love." Then he fastened up his trousers and inspected her wrists to ensure her skin was not overly abused.

"Thank you, my lord," she said as she sat up.

"Think nothing of it. I appreciate your eagerness. Now off with you."

He smacked her on the bum once more, eliciting a giggle from her as she departed. The other girls were either following suit or just finishing up with his friends. Was that a strange feeling of disappointment? Longing? No, it was envy that welled within him and had him feeling just the smallest bit jealous of what Stone had found with Theo.

Pushing aside the wayward thought, Cooper settled down in a nearby chair and waited for the rest of his friends to join him.

Flint sat down first, his trousers still hanging open a bit. "Hell of a night."

"It would seem so." Cooper took in his friend's blood-spattered shirt, split lip, and black eye. "I hope the other fellow looks worse."

"Never doubt it." Flint winked and poured himself a brandy from the decanter that sat nearby.

Wolf joined them then, his clothing set to rights. "Has anyone heard from Stone?"

Cooper laughed. "I believe he is still madly in love with his wife, however unfashionable that may be."

Linc finally joined them, sitting on the bed with his legs up. "I'm beginning to think he has the right of it."

Cooper looked at his friend, curious. "How do you see that?"

Granted, he had seen Stone and Theo's relationship up close in a way none of the others had. He understood the bond between them, even if he didn't wish to emulate it for himself.

"Why not? We all have titles to continue. Why not find a willing woman to do that with? Why strive for a typical *ton* marriage? Lifeless. Practical. Cold. When I must marry, I hope to follow his lead." Linc shrugged.

"Not I," Cooper averred. "I'm pressing on with the original plan. I'll find a suitable wife, one who is scandal-free, an heiress in her own right, and content to settle down to a regular *ton* marriage. We'll do our duty to the title and go our own ways most of the time."

He could picture quiet evenings at home sitting by the fireplace, a drink in his hand, and his favorite dog, Sally, asleep at his feet. His wife would be appropriately occupied tending to his household.

Flint snorted. "Cooper, have you gone soft in the head? No woman will let you have your dog in the house."

The others chuckled, but Cooper knew better. He'd already identified his prospective bride, and it would be a solid arrangement once he was certain there were no deep, dark family secrets lurking in the proverbial closet. His man of affairs had assured him that the investigation he was conducting would be wrapped up in a matter of days. Then he could approach her brother and make a formal agreement, as soon as he was ready.

Lady Emmaline Winterburn would be both docile and accommodating of his demands. Fortunately for her, he was of a mind to pluck her from the obscurity of spinsterhood and set her up as his countess. He fully expected her to all but fall at his feet in gratitude.

About the Author

Sorcha Mowbray is a mild mannered office worker by day...okay, so she is actually a mouthy, opinionated, take charge kind of gal who bosses everyone around; but she definitely works in an office. At night she writes romance so hot she sets the sheets on fire! Just ask her slightly singed husband.

She is a longtime lover of historical romance, having grown up reading Johanna Lindsey and Judith McNaught. Then she discovered Thea Devine and Susan Johnson. Holy cow! Heroes and heroines could do THAT? From there, things devolved into trying her hand at writing a little smexy. Needless to say, she liked it and she hopes you do too!

Find all of Sorcha's social media links at
link.sorchamowbray.com/bio
~
or scan the QR Code

Read the Whole Series

His Wanton Marchioness
A Lustful Lords Novella

She waited her entire life to be married, and she refuses to let anyone interfere with her happiness...not even her new husband.

Elizabeth Grafton, the Marchioness of Carlisle just married the man of her dreams. Or he was. Now, he barely spends time with her. But most disturbing, he comes to her bed under the cloak of darkness—the man won't even light a candle!—and insists she keep her nightgown on until he leaves.

Alexander Grafton, the Marquess of Carlisle is deeply, madly in love with his wife. But, he wants to do things to her that a man could only do to his mistress. He's struggling to keep his baser instincts in check, and that was before his wife decided to seduce him. If she knew what he really wanted...she'd run away.

Armed with "professional" advice, Elizabeth sets out to thwart all of her husband's best intentions and show him just how shameless she can be. Can her wanton nature tempt her husband, or will he win their battle of wills?

His Hand-Me-Down Countess
Lustful Lords, Book 1

His brother's untimely death leaves him with an Earldom and a fiancée. Too bad he wants neither of them...

Theodora Lawton has no need of a husband. As an independent woman, she wants to own property, make investments and be the master of her destiny. Unfortunately, her father signed her life away in a marriage contract to the future Earl of Stonemere. But then the cad upped and died, leaving her fate in the hands of his brother, one of the renowned Lustful Lords.

Achilles Denton, the Earl of Stonemere, is far more prepared to be a soldier than a peer. Deeply scarred by his last tour of duty, he knows he will never be a proper, upstanding pillar of the empire. Balanced on the edge of madness, he finds respite by keeping a tight rein on his life, both in and out of the bedroom. His brother's death has left him with responsibilities he never wanted and isn't prepared to handle in the respectable manner expected of a peer.

Further complicating his new life is an unwanted fiancée who comes with his equally unwanted title. Saddled with a hand-me-down countess, he soon discovers the woman is a force unto herself. As he grapples with the burden of his new responsibilities, he discovers someone wants him dead. The question is, can he stay alive long enough to figure out who's trying to kill him while he tries to tame his headstrong wife?

His Hellion Countess
Lustful Lords, Book 2

A duty bound earl and a jewel thief might find forever if he can steal her heart...

Robert Cooper, the Earl of Brougham must marry in order to fulfill his duty to the title. He's decided on a rather mild mannered, biddable woman who most considered firmly on the shelf. But, her family is on solid financial ground and has no scandals attached to their name.

Lady Emily Winterburn, sister of the Earl of Dunmere, is not what she seems. With a heart as big as her wild streak she finds herself prepared to protect her brother from his bad choices, even if it means committing highway robbery. But marrying their way out of trouble is simply out of the question. What woman in her right mind would shackle herself to a man, let alone one of the notorious Lustful Lords?

Cooper's carefully laid plans are ruined once he must decide between courting his unwilling bride-to-be and taming the wild woman who tried to rob him—until he discovers they are one and the same. And when love sinks its relentless talons into his heart? He'll do anything to possess the wanton who fires his blood and touches his soul.

His Scandalous Viscountess
Lustful Lords, Book 3

Once upon a time, a boy and a girl fell in love...but prestige, power, and a shameful secret drove them apart.

Julia fled abroad after the death of her husband, Lord Wallthorpe. She has finally returned to England, but little has changed.

Except for her.

As a dowager marchioness, Julia lives and loves where she pleases. And the obnoxious son of her dead husband does not please. But what can an independent woman do? Why, create a scandal, of course!

Viscount Wolfington is no stranger to the wagging tongues of the ton. Between being a Lustful Lord and the scandal of his birth, he learned long ago that society had little use for him. So when he walks into The Market and finds the woman who once stole his heart being auctioned for a night of debauchery, he jumps at another chance to hold her—even for just a single night.

As Julia and Wolf unravel their pasts, will villainy win again, or will love finally conquer all?

His Not-So-Sweet Marchioness
Lustful Lords, Book 4

He's shrouded in shame, fighting with his demons in the shadows. Until she sets her sights on him...

Mrs. Rosalind Smith once followed her heart and love to the battlefield and left a widow. Spending the remainder of her life alone is enough... until she meets a man who's need for pain sparks an answering flame deep within her soul.

Matthew Derby, the Marquess of Flintshire is a fighter, it is all he's known since childhood. Throwing his fists is the only way to keep his need for pain at bay, and a certain gentle woman off his mind. She deserves a better man than him—Lord or not. Though when faced with the prospect of losing Ros, Flint realizes he has found something to fight for...something to live for.

To Ros' dismay, everyone around her believes her demeanor too sweet for someone like Flint. When his world begins to unravel and his dockside violence bleeds into the drawing room, a shocking family secret won't be the key to all the answers. Questions remain, can he solve the mystery, tame his dark needs, and still win Ros' heart?

His Reluctant Marchioness
Lustful Lords, Book 5

*A notorious woman must rely on the devil himself for help.
Too bad she learned long ago never to trust anyone...*

Frank Lucifer is having one hell of a week. His gambling hell is short staffed after firing his floor manager, and his half-brother has offered him a title—one he doesn't need or want. Then the woman he's obsessed with dismisses him from her bed, and the problem is he doesn't know who the hell she is.

Mistress Lash has her hands full. Her apprentice is missing under sinister circumstances, and Scotland Yard refuses to lift a finger. A liaison with Frank Lucifer—however attractive she finds him—is something she no longer has time for. Besides, someone should take the arrogant rake down a peg or two.

She sets out to find her apprentice on her own, but everywhere she turns, up pops Lucifer. He's following her, and she's growing suspicious about why that is. When he suggests they join forces, she reluctantly agrees. After all, one should keep their friends close and their enemies closer... she's just not sure which he is. Yet.

Working together to find her missing apprentice, she worries about her ability to protect both her heart and her own secrets from the perceptive man. And as events play out, she must decide if Lucifer is the villain she is searching for... or just the devil who haunts her scorching hot dreams?

Other Books by Sorcha

The Market Series
Discover the series that started it all...

In this sizzling series The Market becomes the setting for Londoners of all walks of life to discover pleasure, lust, and even love. But can they do what is required to claim the ones they've fallen for?

Love Revealed (The Market, Book 1)

Love Redeemed (The Market, Book 2)

Love Reclaimed (The Market, Book 3)

The Market Series Books 1-3 (Boxed Set)

Love Requited (The Market, A Short Story)

One Night With A Cowboy

The One Night With A Cowboy series is a set of short stories linked by cowboys and Soul Mates Dating Service, a dating service with an uncanny ability to match up soul mates. These sizzling little treats are perfect for a quick hot read.

Claiming His Cowgirl (Book 1)

Taking Her Chance (Book 2)

A Cowboy's Christmas Wish (Book 3)

Roping His Cowboy (Book 4)

One Night With A Cowboy Books 1-4 (Boxed Set)

Stealing His Cowgirl's Heart (Book 5)